Praise for Geoff Rickly's
SOMEONE WHO ISN'T ME

"A spiral staircase in a burning building."

—GERARD WAY, MY CHEMICAL ROMANCE

"*Someone Who Isn't Me* is a massive, blaring achievement—a seamless rendering of what it is to be dissected, to answer for the impulses, dreams, and wishes of your several past selves. This book is simultaneously generously populated and deeply intimate, a tight needle to thread, though it is done beautifully."

—HANIF ABDURRAQIB, AUTHOR OF *A Little Devil in America* AND *They Can't Kill Us Until They Kill Us*

"A front-row seat to a feedback drenched lifestyle. Rickly blows up every rock star cliche and creates something indelible from the ashes. Redefining what it means to be a human being under both the pressures and inspirations of performance. It conjures an intimate interior of challenges within the epic dream-come-true backdrop."

—DAVID GORDON GREEN, DIRECTOR

"*Someone Who Isn't Me* is a special kind of contraband. In this hallucinatory debut, Geoff Rickly explores the dazzling and tragic allure of hard drugs. Rickly takes us on a spikey journey through the human psyche of a man who knows the world intimately, but no longer recognises himself in it. An outstanding debut, thrilling, fierce and hallucinatory. A book to shake your soul out."

—COLUM MCCANN, AUTHOR OF *Apeirogon* AND *Let the Great World Spin*

"Sending currents of deep, humane wit through its vortices of imagination, *Someone Who Isn't Me* is a wild, hypnotic ride that makes a lasting music of the holy and the diabolical. An incandescent debut. I think it rewired my neural pathways."

—Hermione Hoby, author of *Virtue*

"This is the most compelling piece of writing I've read in a long time—bizarre, beautiful, mind-bending, and indelible. Every element in this book is wildly inventive and impactful, from its rollercoaster plot to the stripped-bare vulnerability. Rickly has written a new classic."

—Juliet Escoria, author of *Juliet the Maniac*

"The modern literary novel is often a vapid fantasy, the author's best guess as to what a lived life feels like. *Someone Who Isn't Me* is the opposite. This is honey spilled on sandpaper. The pages are blistered and stained and tactile and true, they reek, they weep, they vomit, they scream. This book is a gift and a warning, an effigy for the living: Rickly performed an autopsy on himself and these are the coroner's notes."

—Sam Tallent, author of *Running the Light*

"Raw nerve, live wire, blisteringly psychoactive. This novel will set your mind racing, kick your heart into highest gear."

—Bud Smith, author of *Teenager*

"A seasick, lyrical book. Take a ride with this gorgeous mind—there's no other like it, except your own. This work is a poetic and hard-won example of how we can grow up."

—Amy Rose Spiegel,
author of *Action: A Book About Sex*

Someone Who Isn't Me

Copyright © 2023 Geoff Rickly.

All rights reserved. No part of this publication may be reproduced, distributed, or transmitted in any form or by any means, including photocopying, recording, or other electronic or mechanical methods, without the prior permission of the publisher, except in the case of brief quotations embodied in critical reviews and certain other noncommercial uses permitted by copyright law.

ISBN: 979-8-9875818-2-7 (Paperback)
ISBN: 979-8-9875818-1-0 (Hardcover)

Library of Congress Control Number: 2023934963

This is a work of fiction. Names, characters, business, events and incidents are the products of the author's imagination. Any resemblance to actual persons, living or dead, or actual events is purely coincidental.

Cover image by Jesse Draxler.
Cover design by Jesse Reed.
Interior design by Adam Robinson.

Printed by Bookmobile in the United States of America. Third Printing.

Rose Books
Sedona, Arizona
www.rosebooks.co

Someone Who Isn't Me

Geoff Rickly

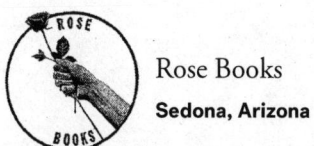

Rose Books
Sedona, Arizona

IBOGAINE

(IBOGAINE; Endabuse; 12-Methoxyibogamine; Ibogain; Tabernanthe iboga, C20H26N2O)

A naturally occurring psychoactive substance found in plants in the *Apocynaceae* family such as *Tabernanthe Iboga*, *Voacanga Africana*, and *Tabernaemontana Undulata*. When used as indicated, ibogaine is classified as a psychedelic with dissociative properties.

The psychoactivity of the root bark of iboga shrubs, from which ibogaine is extracted, was first discovered by the Pygmy tribe of Central Africa who passed the knowledge to the Bwiti tribe of Gabon.

Often ingested to facilitate psychological introspection and spiritual exploration. Preliminary research indicates that it may help with drug addiction; however, there is a lack of data in humans—largely due to its prohibition in the United States as a Schedule I Controlled Substance, and its association with serious side effects, including death.

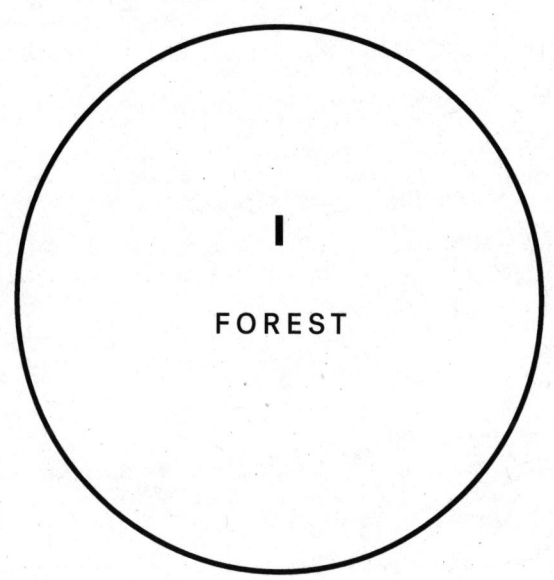

I

FOREST

No one ever hears music past the first time. Everything after is just a high-fidelity echo, fading already, even in the midst of our own incarnations. Then we're born and we walk around for a little while, humming, whistling, tapping our feet, trying to find the beat, the note, the sound. Anything to get us back to the source, just one more time, before we start the slow, certain process of dying to ourselves, life shrinking little by little, the echo growing fainter and further, until one day it falls silent. If only we could hear that song one more time.

I looked for music everywhere: in basements and VFW Halls, in roller rinks. I learned the guitar and fell down the stairs holding it in my hands. I sang in church choirs; I sat through funerals just to hear the organ play. I started a band and screamed into rusty microphones, jumping around the stage until my shoes filled with blood. But it wasn't enough.

Sure, sometimes I'd close my eyes and the band would play and I'd feel a pulse in my whole body and my mouth would drop open until I was the O in holy, but it only lasted for a moment. It was so big and memory is so small. I couldn't contain it.

I once saw a man get shot outside a club we had just played, somewhere in Arkansas. It sounded like God's own snare drum at the beginning of time. An orchestra tuned up in the scattering crowd. The incident's conductor raised his hands in the air. I was sure it was the start of something special. But the music never came.

I tried everything. I turned up the stereo and stuck my head inside the speaker's cone until my whole skull rang. I stuffed my ears with cotton and pressed my chest against the megaton subwoofers beneath the festival main stage until my body threatened to shake loose.

I fell back on the ways of science, the teachings of my chemist father, trying to isolate the most essential properties of song by process of elimination. First, I threw out any record with words. Being a singer myself, I knew how useless they were. After that, it was anything with guitars, then drums, and so on, until I only bought records that sounded like the faint hum of empty train tracks at midnight.

Things went on like this for the better part of three decades—my life spinning around me like a record on a turntable, the world getting smaller and faster as the needle moved closer to the center label—until every recognizable tone and timbre fell away and all that was left was the static and skip of the runout groove,

ca-chic-ca-chic-shhhhhh
ca-chic-ca-chic-shhhhhh
Over and over again.

After watching my band implode on the last tour of our career, I spent a couple of days wandering through San Francisco, drinking coffee. I had almost entirely given up on music. Still, I walked around, humming, whistling, tapping my feet out of habit more than anything else. It was in such a state that I lost myself in an upper room at City Lights, flipping through the writers of my youth: Burroughs, Corso, Ferlinghetti. Those old junkies sure knew how to make a point, even though they were probably full of shit, too.

I picked up a copy of *Howl* that must have been printed earlier that morning—the tang of ink was fresh like bitter grapefruit. It had echoes between its covers. Earlier voices, earlier thoughts. There must have been a time when its ideas were new and pure, but this was just a reprint. Already, I could feel it breaking down in my hands. I walked to the window and turned the book's pages until I saw a phrase that produced an immediate physical reaction in me: *listening to the crack of doom on the hydrogen jukebox*. I wanted to believe in the existence of that sound so desperately that it felt like being stabbed. For a moment, I held the phrase in my mind, letting the discomfort build, then I closed the book and threw it out the window.

Unfortunately, the staff saw me do it. After I paid for the book, I tried to explain myself. I had thrown the book out the window as the result of an aesthetic decision. Staying in San Francisco, rather than going home, had been an aesthetic decision as well. Increasingly, these were the kinds of choices I felt capable of making. The store's manager struck me as an incredibly kind, patient man. As he escorted me outside, he softly confided that he understood just what I meant.

Howl was waiting for me against the curb. It looked better having had the shit kicked out of it. All echoes should have a few bruises. That's just life: A thing happens once and it's pure, everything after is a facsimile, which degrades. But surely there must be a way to follow an echo backward into an original state of grace. At the intersection of unrelated things, couldn't there be a place where echoes might collide, briefly making something new?

My mind accelerated without a weight to pin me to the present moment.

Out loud, I said, "I am going to kill myself." But the aesthetic was wrong. I picked up *Howl*. Each line depressed me more than the line that came before it. In this very city, Ginsberg had found the original music. He had heard something. He had lived. But that was such a long time ago. I dropped the book and kicked it down the sidewalk. Wind blew through a pile of garbage sitting at the curb. A voice called out to me.

"You want to know the secret?"

The garbage sat up, kicked some newspapers from his body, and pointed to the book.

"I can show you."

I didn't have anywhere else to be, so I followed him.

I went looking for the sound at the bottom of a bag of heroin. We traveled from the bookstore to Kearny Street, then through the Tenderloin, and down the 6th Street corridor, where meth heads paced the corners, tapping worn-out sneakers on the pavement's loose keys. Here, clocks ran a little faster, sunlight burned a little brighter. But we were looking for something else. At the BART station on 16th and Mission, figures materialized in the shadows, stepping out of corners to see if we wanted a taste.

My companion held out his hand and said, "This is the guy."

I gave him all the money in my wallet. An exchange took place. Church bells were ringing. Somewhere in the station, people were drumming on plastic buckets. Down the block, a car horn blared. Trains were approaching. My mouth began to water.

"Do you hear that?" I asked him.

It got quiet as the dealer slipped something into his palm. He cupped both his hands around it and spoke softly. I leaned in close and listened. I never really got a good look at the guy's face, but when he opened his hands, he was beautiful.

This is what it's like: the shit comes on and you're running up that *ancient heavenly connection to the starry dynamo in the machinery of night.* The echo gets louder. More vivid. You can almost see the source through the upper atmosphere—it dances just ahead of you. Then, you're stuck in a cloud and nothing makes sense. Pretty soon, you're falling and the echo is fading until,

ca-chic-ca-chic-shhhhhh
ca-chic-ca-chic-shhhhhh
Over and over again.

New York pulled me back home. But it's all the same no matter where I go. Each time, that runout groove comes a little quicker, hits a little harder. Twenty minutes, followed by that stutter, skip, pop, repeating endlessly until I pick up the needle and start the process over again. Even still. Records are miraculous things. For such small circles, they have an amazing capacity for emptiness.

I stand on the corner. I walk around. I wait for my man to come and I give him money.

He says, "Be careful with that." He says, "Shit is strong." He says, "Fire."

I nod. I smile. I go to work and spend a lot of time in the bathroom.

I fall asleep at my desk.
I skip lunch.
I skip dinner.
I stand on the corner.
I turn thirty-four.
I turn thirty-five.
Thirty-six.
I turn thirty-seven, leaning on a wall, feeling like a tube of toothpaste with all the fresh squeezed out.

I'm shivering on the corner of Manhattan and Huron when my old roommate Don walks by, wearing a torn, striped T-shirt. Immune to the cold, he sports no jacket, carries no sweater. His platinum hair looks hacked off with a machete where it falls over his cloudy blue eyes.

He says, "Surprise, surprise."

He says, "I'd ask how you've been, but."

Snow is falling. I can't stop sweating.

He says, "Been meaning to talk to you anyway."

He says, "Since you stopped returning my calls."

He says, "Thought I might find you here."

My eyes are running. I can't stop sniffling.

He says, "Look at this."

He pulls a Polaroid out of his back pocket. The gesture contains all the sharp angles of his guitar playing. I sneeze into my sleeve, which leaves a spot of blood on the fabric. Don shows me the photo: a man with a microphone. Bright lights throw his shadow against the back wall of the stage.

Don says, "Look familiar?"

The street's quiet. I check my phone. "You got an extra twenty bucks?"

He holds the photo up, "Just look."

"Is that Sean?"

He says, "Sean's been dead a long time. That's you."

"Looks just like Sean."

He says, "Couldn't stop what happened to him."

He says, "I can't stop what's happening to you now."

He says, "But I hope you'll consider something. As a favor for me."

He pulls a printout from his front pocket: *Crossroads Mexico Ibogaine Clinic.*

He says, "Experimental treatment."

He says, "Famously unpleasant."

I look down the street. I check my messages.

He says, "Can you hear me?" He folds the printout and says, "Go to Mexico. Get help." He tucks the folded paper into the book I'm carrying: *The Architecture of Happiness*. I look over at the squat gas station on the corner and back at Don's blank face.

"Did you have that cash?" I ask.

Don opens his wallet, hands me two ten-dollar bills.

My phone rings and everything starts sparkling, but it's just my mom, so I hang up. Don takes the phone and types something into my contacts but then it rings for real and I run down the block without saying goodbye. I see my man and he takes my money and I go in the bathroom and then things finally sparkle for real.

Alain de Botton wrote that *political and ethical ideas can be written into window frames and door handles.*

Inside the Esso station's bathroom, there are no windows. Each wall is the same dark shade of purple as the floor. There's a single light fixture, painted black, above the sink. A brass doorknob hangs loosely from its splintered socket—I wonder what ethical ideas de Botton would read into that. If there really is an enduring connection between our identities and our locations, then who am I inside this room? I pour a line of heroin onto the open pages of *The Architecture of Happiness* and it lands in a grey strike across the black text:

If one room can alter how we feel, if our happiness can hang on the colour of the walls or the shape of a door, what will happen to us in most of the places we are forced to look at and inhabit? What will we experience in a house with prison-like windows, stained carpet tiles and plastic curtains? It is to prevent the possibility of permanent anguish that we can be led to shut our eyes to most of what is around us, for we are never far from damp stains and cracked ceilings, shattered cities and rusting dockyards.

Snorting the powder from the page, I momentarily shut my eyes. I can almost hear the city shattering around me: the brittle sounds of acrylic paint cracking on the ceiling, the iron docks rusting with a high-frequency sigh in the distance. I hold my breath to listen more carefully but blood is pounding in my ears. A sharp thwack, followed by the squeaky complaints of the door knob; I lift my head off the sink.

"Hold on. There's someone in here."

Back on the street, the knife edge of morning splits the sun open like a pomegranate into thousands of little seeds of light, each one glittering briefly before spilling into the cold winter air coming off the water.

"Don?" I ask, the puff of my breath disappearing. "Where did you go?"

I lean against a fire hydrant for a moment to watch the city dance around me in its sequined dress. As long as I'm here, I have everything I'll ever need.

Then, things get soft. The street takes on a palliative quality. A frozen city drifts down on top of this one, covering everything in a layer of virgin linen. The East River irons out, beyond the India Street Ferry dock. I can see it through my eyelids, which have softened too, lending the world an aura of gauzy radiance. Even the headlights of oncoming cars have their own little cotton-ball halos. I want to pull one from its bumper and pop it in my mouth. I can already taste it on my tongue, the snow crackling against my teeth in a thin shell of minty white chocolate.

Cold snaps at my skin as the wind picks up. Its breath fills the narrow, fluted streets of Greenpoint with a sound like a voice singing, pushing a lone cold note down the lengths of Kent, Java, and India. At the avenue, the wind joins the high keening sweep of the B62 bus. It's a painful sound with all the soft violence of great love songs.

But that's not the only thing that's singing. The whole city is. Even the snowflakes are! I hear them throwing their crystal bodies against the sidewalk all around me. I hear their sharp little deaths. I hear the bells of distant cathedrals.

I hold my breath and, for a moment, I swear I can still feel the old magic sparkling, deep inside. But only for a second, only while I'm high. A glimmer. Then the world returns to cement grey and trampled boxes, the sky a puff of smoke, trapped in a snow globe. And then it's all real and it's jackhammers and garbage trucks. People shouting down from scaffolding. And me with my teeth rattling and my spine shaking.

And no song. Just me and my hand, buried under a full inch of snow, where it sits on the newspaper stand for the *Brooklyn Eagle*. Just me and the *Brooklyn Eagle* and the tips of my fingers like crushed blueberries at the bottom of a slushy.

Just another day of standing in front of my office on West Street at 9:45 a.m. Another day of construction. A set of contractors hunched over some blueprints, disagreeing loudly about how best to bring down the whole goddamn wall. Three guys in black hoodies huddled in a doorway, whispering. One of them points his finger at me, cocks his thumb, and mouths the word, *bang*.

Just what I need. Another mystery. Another headache. Another sniff of dope before work and then I'm inside and I'm sideways, peeling my face off the cold aluminum surface of my desk, a thick strand of spit gluing my cheek to the computer's keyboard.

"Here he is," my coworker announces, waving our office phone's receiver in front of my slowly opening eyes. He silently mouths, *conference call,* he mouths, *new client,* he mouths something that looks like, *a school of dangerous fish have blossomed in the lobby—grab a fistful of violets and meet me in the next life.* I take the receiver and hold it to my ear. People are already having a conversation without me. But I can't stop thinking about what my coworker said as he handed me the phone: I can almost see the vibrant colors of the *dangerous fish* swimming in the lobby—what was it he said, *blossoming*—yes, I can see the fish unfolding, color after iridescent color, peeling off from a central school and swimming down the halls, over and around the desks and computers.

A voice on the phone is saying, "Not so much fascist sympathies as a preoccupation with certain iconic symbols of the second World War…" Suddenly, all the fish are swimming in regiments. I put my hand over the mouthpiece, "What the fuck?"

My coworker kicks my chair and shakes his head, mouths, *don't start.*

I hold the receiver away from my face and squint at it. What else had he said? *Grab a fistful of violets and meet me in the next life.* I open the top drawer of my desk, revealing an economy-size bag of Skittles. Green, Red…Purple.

"Violets," I tell my coworker, forgetting to shield the mouthpiece. The conference falls silent. No one speaks. My coworker raises a firm hand above my head, to demonstrate that I'm an animal and he's my trainer.

The phone crackles, "Who is this?"

The bag splits, raining candy out across our desks.

My coworker holds up a single finger in front of his lips—*Shhhhh.* I pick up a handful of Skittles and chew them down. The sugar hits immediately, reactivating the heroin in my bloodstream, sending a wave of euphoria out through the office. My grip on the conversation continues to loosen. The air cools down. A generous blue sky swells against the window. My body rises from the chair and floats to meet it.

The voice on the phone repeats, "Who is this?" The question seems suddenly philosophical, playful—*who is anyone, except who they're pretending to be?* I turn from the window and flash a big, benevolent smile down at my coworker, whose upturned face is playing an intense, cartoonish game. He's so expressive, I think, as his features crease with worry, eyelids drooping down, pouty lower lip pushing out, all wet with spit. What a delight! I clap warmly for his performance.

Out the window, I can see the *Pitchfork* offices on one side, *VICE* on the other. The Freedom Tower rises above the river so that we can just make out all the Condé Nast properties inside.

"We're speaking to you from the top of the world," I shout. "We've got the whole city before us. I can see the entire music industry from where I'm standing. They love us."

My coworker picks up the phone. I can hear him attempting to sound reasonable. He's speaking in numbers and deadlines. Achievable weekly goals. What's the point? Out the window, biplanes glide gently over the highway on warm currents of air, doing tricks, tracing loops above the FDR, before coming back down and landing on the East River.

My coworker joins me at the window, shaking his head in disbelief, "We got the job. They told me they *admired your confidence.*"

I place my hand against the glass, covering the sun. The light breaks into rays between my fingers. "People need to believe in something," I tell him, feeling the day collect in my palm. "It doesn't matter what."

In the packed elevator car after work, I notice three young guys in black hoodies nodding at me conspiratorially. When we reach the lobby, the bell dings and the crowd slowly files out into the street. Looking over my shoulder, I can see I'm being followed, so I pick up my pace, hoping to lose them in the shuffle. But by the time I reach the corner, they've managed to catch up.

Now I'm surrounded. The three men pass cigarettes around, taking their time to light them. They're younger than I am. Each of their faces has the quality of a loaf of bread taken out of the oven too early: doughy, half-baked. The one on my right keeps on ashing his cigarette, checking his watch, looking around the corner.

"Funny how the world keeps bringing us together," the one in the center tells me.

The third man is standing just behind my left shoulder. I can hear him exhaling heavily into his fist.

"I'm sorry, guys," I raise my hands in defense.

The one in the center puts the cigarette in his mouth, "For what, exactly?"

I hear a laugh behind me. The guy on the right won't stop looking at his watch.

"I think maybe I owe you some money."

The one in the center takes a long drag. His brow creases as he leans away from me. He knocks his head back and barks, "HA." A *HA*-shaped puff of smoke escapes from between his lips. The other two begin chuckling.

"If anything, it's us who owe you money," he shouts.

I reach into my pocket for my keys, grab the sharpest one. I take a step back, only to knock into the man standing behind me. He comes around to stand with the others and stammers, "Excuse me, sorry."

The man in the center lowers his voice, "We work at the metal label upstairs?" He searches my face for recognition. "We went head-to-head with your old outfit, Collect Records. Both of us bidding on the same album. Then Collect goes bust. We end up getting the record for free. Ringing any bells?"

"This is about *music*?"

"Supposed to be," he shrugs. "At any rate, I'm glad we're finally working together."

"We work together?" The heroin euphoria is wearing off.

"Sure," he says. "We hired you. PR. For our new signing? I was on the call earlier."

"There was a call earlier," I repeat, trying to mirror the angle of his posture.

"I liked your little speech about seeing the whole city from your window. Their manager really ate that up. Still. You're not wrong. It is a small world. Especially for you. Wasn't Collect just across the street?"

I look at the red-brick office building across the street. He's right. That is my old office. I might spend the rest of my life bouncing between jobs on this one run-down block in Greenpoint.

Now one of them steps forward into my personal space, "I'd hate myself if I didn't tell you I'm a huge fan of Thursday. Man, 'Understanding in a Car Crash' was my jam. My senior yearbook quote was, 'I don't want to feel this way forever.'" He places his hand on my shoulder and looks deeply into my eyes. He's just a boy really. I feel the sincerity burning off of him: *Chess Club, Basketball, "I don't want to feel this way forever."*

The other two nod their heads approvingly.

"Do you ever talk to those Thursday guys anymore? Steve and..." he looks around, timidly, "the other three that I can never tell apart."

"You mean Tim, Tom, and Tucker?" That touches off another round of laughter.

"Yeah," one of them snorts. "Exactly."

"Tom, guitarist: well over six feet. Tucker, drummer: shorter than me. Easy to identify, even to the most casual observer."

One of them lifts his cigarette to his lips, raises an eyebrow, "Wasn't there a third one?"

"There were a bunch of us. But in the band, our differences became trivial—we all shared an identity." I search the empty street for the right words, "Maybe we were interchangeable. Maybe we were all the same person."

"You were close," the kid in the center offers. "That's touching." Leading us away from the waterfront, he throws his cigarette into an open drain and asks, "Still talk to them since you broke up?" The streetlights finally come on, throwing perfect discs of light onto the cobblestones ahead of us.

"These days?" I ask.

I blink and, for a second, I'm back in the van. We're all coasting on some featureless stretch of desert highway, my band members are dreaming into the afternoon. Tucker yawns and turns over on the middle bench. Steve starts a movie on his laptop and settles in, crossing his arms over his chest. Tom presses his headphones down hard over both ears. Tim sits shotgun and chews on one of his fingers. Nothing else is happening, nothing else matters. We're together, with the road stretching out forever ahead of us.

"All the time," I say. "In fact, I'm with them right now."

Then I'm home, standing in the center of an empty apartment under the pale flower shadow of the woman I love. A note on the table tells me she has an event tonight and not to wait up. Three miniature rubber bands rest on the paper, with an arrow pointing to them:

> *I keep finding these all over the place. It scares me every time. You're still clean, right? Maybe you can scour the apartment, clear it all out? As a gift to me? We could use a fresh start. Spring is almost here...*
>
> *Love you,*
> *Liza*

I lean in above the note, breathing her in. But then she's gone and home is dull and empty, lit only by fading winter light. There's a bundle in my pocket, wrapped in the same red rubber bands as the ones that scare Liza. Dealers use them to tie single-dose glassine bags into bundles of ten, first folding each one into a rectangular envelope, stamped with a brand name.

I gather the rubber bands and drop them in the garbage before looking around the apartment for anything else I might've forgotten. There's a rolled-up dollar bill tucked behind the couch. Burnt tin foil under the sink. A cut plastic straw in a flower pot by the window. Some pill bottles stuffed in the back of the cabinet. Our home might be constructed entirely from drug paraphernalia.

The thought makes me claustrophobic, so I shed my coat, pull off my sneakers, and break open the bundle, spilling the colorless powder onto Liza's handwritten note. I pull a dollar out of my pocket, roll it, snort the dope off the paper, lick the spot above *Love you, Liza*, and pop the bag in my mouth like a stick of chewing gum. The whole series of motions blinks by in a second, reminding me of escalator rides up from the subway at 42nd Street: first a rush of noise, a blur of motion, then everything stops for a moment while your feet lift off the platform and your body ascends into a sea of lights. It feels effortless. It feels automatic: an efficient system designed for the upward conveyance of human forms.

I whisper, *this is it, this is life*. But it's better than that. Heroin is the opposite of life, the precondition of existence. It lights the world from within, coronating each individual object to its purpose, establishing value, asserting thusness. Life is the shadow on the cave's wall. Heroin is the fire.

And it's working.

A record spins on the turntable, producing a faint music that sings of another time in a purely spiritual place. The pictures on the walls of my apartment snap into focus with an elastic clarity, emitting soft pillowy light, as if they've been transported to an art gallery in Chelsea. Through the transubstantiation of chemical virtue, every memory can be golden, every emotion can become holy.

Here. Liza and I, sitting on the beach in Boracay, each with a half empty can of beer, drinking down the sweet salty flavor of rust, our bodies thin limbed and tangled under a canopy of fruit trees, bursting and fizzing.

And *here*. The two of us, riding the Brooklyn Ferry down the East River, so broke that our idea of a date was a six-dollar ride around the city.

And *here*. My band, sweating it out on the stage of the Roseland Ballroom on West 52nd, before the place shut down forever, before our band split up.

The photographic paper looks wet and sticky, covered in oil paints and expensive varnish. Each moment is illuminated in a high-contrast renaissance style. I can smell the ocean, feel the surf spraying on my face, the beach falling away, up and over, tumbling down.

Still Life with *Oysters and Lemon*. The title calls out to me from its cover, lying under the couch. A stolen artifact from the used bookstore at Grand Central Station, where I used to score dope after work, under the painted constellations. Inside, Mark Doty had written, *I live in a capital of light*. I wanted to visit that capital, to hold that light. I wanted to *come into being the way matter is said to do, from the collapsed bodies of dead stars, streaming out into the world*. So I slipped the volume in my waistband and left the station. But the more I read, the more I began to suspect that there was something dangerous hidden in those pages. *Now I think there is a space in me that is like the dark inside that hollow sphere, and things float up into view, images that are vessels of meaning, the flotsam and detail of any particular moment. Vanished things.* The passage came without warning. By the time I realized what was being said, it was too late. Already I could feel a hand reaching down inside me, turning the key in a hidden door. I dropped the book and slid it under the couch with the toe of my shoe.

One Sunday several months later, I was searching for it under the carpet, when I noticed a circular pattern in the floorboards where the planks had been cut from a different wood. Pulling up the carpeting, I saw that the marks extended in a full circle around me, slightly bigger than a manhole. I called our landlord and he told me that our apartment had originally been a duplex. There had been a spiral staircase in the middle of our living room, but it was covered over before we moved in. When I asked him what was down there, he told me it was a storage space. He said, "My mother claims it's all old junk but she likes to *wrap the truth in cotton*." I thought the translation of the phrase from Polish to English was so beautiful that I dropped the subject entirely. But now that I'm down here under the couch, brushing my fingers along the spine of the book, I can feel all that junk—all those vanished things underneath the floorboards—rising to the surface, licking the face of the dark with hot little tongues. So much heat, so much noise.

Silence. **A record** skipping on the turntable, its needle scratching against the center label—*ca-chic-ca-chic-shhhhhh, ca-chic-ca-chic-shhhhhh*—everything losing clarity, becoming increasingly opaque, windows closing on the eternal world, one by one...

Until I'm left staring up at the ceiling, with the carpet tickling the nape of my neck.

Gathering myself off the floor, I see the pictures smiling down at me from the walls. But they don't look real. They can't be. I would remember having been that happy. I would carry it with me for the rest of my life and never need drugs again.

I stretch my neck and touch one of the photos. Liza snapped it the day we met. In it, I'm smiling uncertainly at an orange rubber spatula—this is seven or eight years back. I was working the register at a friend's kitchen store, down on Bedford, picking up a few shifts between tours to make rent. Liza said she had no choice but to take the picture. I looked so out of place. To test me, she brought a few items to the counter to see what I could tell her about them. "This one's a Spiritualizer," I scanned the label. "It's for spiritualizing vegetables." My boss turned from the inventory list on her monitor, "That's a *SPIRAL*-izer, for making zucchini noodles. Decorative carrots, shit like that."

Liza took the box off the counter and put down a long silver tray in the shape of a salmon. "What about this?"

I picked up the platter, "This is a fish plate." My boss grunted and took off her reading glasses.

Liza smiled, "Can't you just put fish on a regular plate?" The world emptied itself of trivial things. Nothing existed except for that smile.

"Fish can only go on this particular plate," I mumbled, feeling myself go pale. "A steal at $129.99."

My boss coughed and added, "Goddamn right it is."

Liza removed the platter, "Maybe we should just keep things simple." She handed me a spatula and, when our fingers touched, something passed between us. The spatula fell to the counter. Suddenly, we were at dinner. Then, we were rolling around the naked floorboards of our first apartment. We were in a bathtub. Then, we were back standing under the fluorescent lights of the kitchen store, staring at one another.

I turn away from the wall. My hand cramps. Everything tightens. I look back at the orange spatula in the picture. Then the scene jumps forward and we're in an ambulance. We're at the hospital. We're talking to an addiction counselor. Liza is signing papers. When I look down at my hand, I've punched the wall, breaking the picture frame. There's no blood, no cuts, but glass pebbles dot the skin of my knuckles.

On the way to the bedroom, things get hazy. My breath won't come. For a second, I think I might fall down again but the bed is underneath me. My chest hurts. My heartbeat is slowing. Possible side effects of heroin use include respiratory distress, reduced cognition, death. I attempt to run a quick calculation for the concentration of heroin in my system, but it doesn't matter. I'll figure it out in the morning. I'm almost certain this isn't what dying feels like.

It's time to go. There's a man standing over my bed. His voice is soft and patient. He speaks in gently running pipes, refrigerator hum, the hushed emergency of traffic through walls, *Come now, it's time.* I can't quite see him, but there's something comforting about his presence, like an old blanket passed down for generations. He smells of fresh tobacco in a leather pouch.

"Where are we going?" I can taste soil in my mouth when I speak, rich and loamy.

I've opened the staircase, it's time to go.

"Does it hurt?"

Come along. It's okay.

The bedroom door opens.

Liza slips into bed, subtly rearranging the sheets around me. I feel her hand slide in under my arm, glide up the front of my shirt, and find its place curled around my shoulder. She moves her lips gently up my neck as she presses her hips to my side, exhaling when she reaches my jawline.

I could shake her. I could take her in my arms and ask her to help me. But I don't. I can't bear the thought of putting her through all that again. My pulse is slowing where it reaches for her lips, but she doesn't feel it. She's at peace. Her fingertips are already fluttering against my skin. Her feet are already kicking gently as they walk her through sleep's entryway. The vibrant outlines of her dreams shine out through her eyelids: she's on the beach behind her parents' house. Brightly colored birds run through the surf before diving skyward, where kites with long silk ribbons dance above the heads of everyone she loves. A banquet is laid out on a long wooden table, family and friends all eating together. Bonfires at dusk. Fireworks.

I am all alone.

Come with me. *It is time.*

I smell freshly picked tobacco, taste mineral-rich earth. Pipes gently run. The refrigerator hums. I walk to the bedroom door. A man is standing in the center of our living room. He's hard to see, blurred around the edges, but there's nothing threatening about his posture. He motions to me, patiently, and points to the hole in the floor. A stairway stretches down, out of sight.

The way is open. You are ready.

"Am I going to be okay?"

You have left one place. You will go to the next.

Everything hurts. I can barely lift my head off the pillow. My eyes are somehow both dry and sticky. When I manage to pry them open a sliver, I can see Liza in the mirror above her vanity. Slits of winter light slip through the blinds, striping her face. The predawn effect is futuristic and sexy, a scene from *Blade Runner*. She pulls down her sweater, shakes out her hair. In her smile, she's got love enough for everyone, including herself, and in her strong, steady eyes, a patience for all the pain involved in life on earth.

My legs hurt. My back is stiff. I whisper, "Good morning, sweets," but she doesn't seem to notice. I wonder if maybe I'm not dead. I think that probably I am. There's a battery acid taste of blood in my mouth, so my nose has been bleeding again. I rub my face with the soft sleeve of my shirt as Liza throws herself down on top of me.

"You're awake!"

I keep my eyes shut but she turns her searchlight look of love and human connection on me. Its warmth bathes my face and, for a moment, all aches and pains disappear from my limbs.

"I've got a shoot," she says, her mint breath washing over me. "Have to run."

"Ok," I grumble, pressing my eyelids closed with the pads of my fingers.

"Is that dried blood around your nose?" she asks. "Should I be concerned?"

I crack my eyes open. Liza purses her lips and makes worried little kissing motions.

"Humidifier's broken. You know how dry it gets."

Her features relax. She leans in and cups my face with her soft hands, "Last night was eye-opening. Aphrodite is a wonderful guide. I feel like I finally understand my purpose in this world."

"Guide?"

"5-MeO-DMT. The session. In Forest Hills. I texted you about it."

"You were smoking DMT? With a goddess in Queens?"

"Had some questions needed answering. You know how hard it's been for me. The ups and downs with your health issues."

I flinch at the words, *health issues.*

Her voice gets soft and dreamy, "But last night I saw you. In your truest form."

"Oh god, I hope not."

"You were so beautiful—a comet, all made of mirrors. But I recognized you. As if on some level I'd always seen it. Right then I knew. Part of my purpose in this life is to fight for you."

I peel my eyelids back to see the golden honey highlights of her bangs falling around her rich hazelnut eyes. I see the cinnamon sugar glitter of her skin, speckled with vanilla bean freckles. She looks like a benevolent, edible goddess. *Aphrodite. Aphrodonut.* My eyelids droop.

She shakes me, gently, "Understand? I've got your back."

I lower my voice, "We should probably talk."

"What?" Liza asks, rubbing her thumb across my cheek.

"Something happened last night."

She takes her hands off my face and cocks her head, "You're going to have to speak up."

"There was another overdose." I try to raise my voice but it barely registers. Even within the confines of my own body, I hardly make a sound. "I think I died this time. But everything is still the same."

"Seriously," she tells me, sticking a finger into her ear. "Can't hear you. I was lying on my back, crying so hard during the DMT—because my love for you is so big—both my ear canals filled up with tears." She closes her eyes and pounds the side of her head with the heel of her palm, trying to knock loose an ocean from the turn of a shell. "Think you said you ate *the chicken that I fried in thyme but it tasted like game*? What's that mean?" She flexes her jaw, twirls her finger around, first in her left ear, then her right. Her voice jumps in pitch and volume, "Did it taste like duck?" She's getting worked up, shaking her head in spastic little-kid circles, when I reach out to steady her.

"You're absolutely insane," I whisper, pulling her close, soaking up all the warm, comforting chemicals that radiate from her body. My nervous system thrums softly with oxytocin, dopamine, serotonin.

"What?" she yells. I don't answer. I'm busy pressing my face into the center of her chest, inhaling the scent of her skin, hoping to catch the last remnant molecules of DMT as they metabolize out through her pores. Matters of life and death can wait.

A small stream of saline spills out from her left ear. She shakes loose and jumps up from the bed, catching the liquid in her fist. "Got it!" She raises her arms triumphantly and marches out of the room, stopping briefly in the doorway. "Wait—now that I can hear you—what were you trying to tell me?"

In the absence of her body's warmth, all my hurts return. My nose runs. Tears of withdrawal stream out from the corners of my eyes. I decide to go with it, embrace it as a sudden rush of emotion. "I love you so much that I don't know what to do." My voice cracks, "I really don't know what to do."

She touches the doorframe and looks back at me, "We've been through so much." Her features cloud over for a minute but she brightens again. A laugh escapes as she wipes a tear from the corner of her eye, "It's good to know you're still such a little romantic. Come home early tonight, okay?" She pulls a scarf off its hook on the wall and twists it smartly around her neck. Her posture is so effortlessly upright. She narrows her eyes and looks toward the mirror. "I made soup. Don't eat what's in the paper bag, though, okay? That's for Lola."

She turns abruptly and walks away, kicking up a light breeze which momentarily lifts the papers off my desk. All the life in our apartment follows her out the front door. I slip out from under the sheets as the orange blossom trail of her perfume settles on our bedspread.

Blood runs out of my left nostril, landing in several heavy splats on the top of my foot. As far as death goes, this looks about right: a scene of minor violence in this world and you wake up in the next. But what would the new world be? So far, it seems like an exact replica of the last, just with the volume turned down. There's something depressing about the thought of each successive life emptying out into a less vivid copy of itself.

I look from the red spatter to the mirror, trying to see myself the way Liza does. Every therapist I've ever had has told me that we're all capable of deeply loving ourselves. But I'd never actually seen anyone who was, until I met Liza. When I look at my reflection, all I see is bad posture and dry skin, a sinister roommate who wears my clothes.

"You're a comet," I tell my pale twin in the glass. "You possess a beauty all your own."

When I was a child watching my mother ready herself for work in the medicine cabinet's glare, I saw only alternating expressions of unshakable determination and thoughtful despair. My father was up and out of the house too early for me to ever see his expression in the mirror. Mostly, I guess, he just looked tired from the long commutes. An hour and a half in each direction was unimaginable to a little kid. But it's nothing compared to the twenty minutes before Liza leaves the apartment every morning. That junkie eternity before the first bag.

My sheets are soaked through with sweat. A rancid smell wafts up from the mattress. I open a window and grab my hoodie from the armchair. As I'm sliding my hand between the left pocket's seams to find one of the last three bags of heroin, a stray cat streaks along the fence at the edge of our courtyard. I open the glass doors.

"Lola!"

The cat stops, rears back on her haunches, and looks at me, cautiously. Her fur bristles. I run back to the fridge to grab the paper bag Liza mentioned.

"Treats!"

I cross the room and step out barefoot into the freezing concrete courtyard. Lola jumps down off the fence. She can't take her eyes off the paper bag in my hands. All the hair stands up on my legs. Steam rises from my skin but the heroin in my pocket keeps me warm. Lola runs her tongue along her teeth with an audible smack when I open the paper bag.

"Chicken innards. Lucky you."

The cat is under my hand, chewing the heart before it hits the ground. Congealed blood hangs thickly from her whiskers. I break open the tape on my little packet of dope and look into the fold. It looks light. My man is stiffing me again, no doubt in my mind. I roll up a dollar bill and insert it down into the fold of the bag. Lola has finished eviscerating the chicken parts and sits, calmly cleaning herself, at my feet.

"Liza saved those for you. Thoughtful as ever." I look up at the icicles melting off the gutter above my door. Lola straightens her back. "I tried to talk to her, Lola, I swear I did. But she can't hear me."

The cat turns away, looking into Liza's herb garden. Between the scallions and thyme, there's a cluster of little green stalks with spearmint-shaped leaves: catnip. I grab a couple handfuls and sit down in front of the cat.

"I feel like I'm talking to the world through a closed door."

Lola extends a tentative paw.

"My volume's been turned down."

She sniffs the catnip and pounces forward.

"You can hear me though, right?" I stroke the top of the cat's head. "You can feel my hand." She stops chewing and cocks her ears back. Her tail slaps bitterly against the concrete.

"I know, I know. You don't like to be touched."

I pick up the bag of heroin and adjust the dollar until it sits above the little pile of powder in the corner. I give a quick sniff and the dope's gone. Lola settles down. Her eyes glaze over. I crumple up the bag and pop it in my mouth, slowly sitting back against our apartment's glass doors. The cold metal frame feels good against my skin. Lola rolls onto her back, stares up into the clouds.

"It's not easy being a street kitty."

Lola raises her front paws, batting at something only she can see.

"You have a good heart. You're kind. You listen. I wish there were more people like you."

Lola looks up at the sky. She presses her paws together and makes a quick pulling motion. She won't let go.

"I see it." A single golden piece of string hangs off the black rim of a large cobalt cloud. Lola has it in her claws.

"You've got it, Lola, don't let go."

I close my eyes to concentrate on the texture of the winter concrete beneath me: soft and warm. I'm not worried. I trust the cat. She'll pull down heaven for both of us.

Something buzzes in my sweatshirt pocket. I lift my head off the pavement. The cat's gone. There's a single text message on my phone.

/Work?

In the cab on the way to the office, Liza's face appears on the seatback video screen. She's interviewing a vegan donut maker, who's decked out in an ill-fitting, neon onesie and tactical paramilitary sunglasses. He's standing on a rickety stool, dribbling chocolate syrup on a donut from a great height. "You need maximum altitude on the glaze," he shouts down at her. She's laughing just off camera.

Despite her job as producer and on-air talent for a local New York City food series, Liza's never had the uptight features of a TV personality. Instead, her audience appeal comes from a sort of warm glow that lights up the screen and washes over the person she's talking to, making them briefly irresistible. She sees life in soft focus, with perfect angles. In her presence, the whole world shines.

The taxi stops short. My head knocks into the screen. Silver sparks pop all around me, accompanied by the ringing of glass bells. At the center of my field of vision, pixels begin to soften in a perfect ring around Liza's face, forming a kind of solar corona. The screen flickers and turns as black as the night sky. All its light concentrates and condenses into a small bright sphere that goes sailing out through the taxi's window, leaving a trail of crystalline orange blossoms in its wake.

The driver opens the partition, "Seven dollars."

"She's the comet," I tell him, grabbing some bills in my sweatshirt pocket. "Not me."

Stepping out onto the curb in front of my office, I reach into my sweatshirt pocket for one of the remaining packs of heroin. My fingertip passes through a split in the seam. I kneel down to search for anything I might've dropped. A few pigeons peck at a cigarette butt, some broken glass, half a tortilla. I check and recheck my pockets. There's nothing in them but empty space. Panic rises in me as the taxi pulls away. I can picture the wad of bills passing through the partition and into the cabby's hand. Did I hand him two bags of heroin with my cash?

"Have a nice life," I yell after the car.

There's another bundle tucked in the back of my bottom desk drawer. I head upstairs and fish it out. The workday tumbles down after me and then I'm back at home, no thoughts in my head. A used-up sun sets out the window, filling me with familiar emptiness. Life feels safely far away.

Things could go on like this forever.

"What are you doing sitting in the dark?" Liza calls to me from the doorway.

The lights snap on. It feels as if someone has peeled off my skin. All at once, the oven is on, her coat is in the closet, and she's next to me on the couch, peering into my eyes.

"Your pupils are very small," she says, pursing her lips.

"Nothing more than a healthy reaction to the new high-powered lights I installed," I say, pointing at the ceiling.

She narrows her eyes, "Did you really get new lights?"

"That's *gift giving* and now I've got some *quality time* for you."

Her eyes go wide, "Someone's learning my *love languages!*" When she leans back against the arm of the couch, she places her feet in my lap. I push the socks down over her ankles and slip them off, one at a time.

She perks up, "Did you read the whole book? Learn all five?"

I bring her right foot up to my mouth and press my teeth into her delicate arch.

She stretches her back and groans, "Your language must be *physical touch*."

"I speak," I tell her, dragging my lips up the length of her leg, "in *acts of service*."

In her dream, Liza is screaming, but it leaks out into the black of our bedroom as little more than a whimper. She's entirely still, except for a twitch in her pointer finger, which rests against my cheek. I shake her, gently, until she sits up with a start. She pulls away, moving to the far edge of the mattress.

"I was awake," she says, "but paralyzed. Saw the room through my eyelids. Everything so clear. Shadows collecting in the doorway. Physical shadows. They got thicker and harder until they were an entire man."

She points to our bedroom door, open a crack.

"He was standing still. But moving toward me. I was trapped. I couldn't move. The door was closed but he kept passing through. He came inside. Over and over again. Nothing could keep him out."

I grab her arm, "What did he say?" The air smells rich and dirty, as if all the floorboards underneath our bed are filled with moss and soil. I can't shake the feeling that there's someone standing incredibly still in the next room. "Did he show you the open staircase?"

She shakes off my hand, "Stop it. You're freaking me out."

I keep my eyes on the bedroom door, waiting for the blurry figure to appear. The radiator kicks on. Liza pulls up the covers, drifts back into sleep. I count to a thousand and I do it again, lining up all the seconds in a regiment around us. The room fills with sleepless time. I stay up all night, building an army. I do whatever it takes to place myself between Liza and the threat.

It's morning and I'm standing on the corner. I'm walking around. I'm waiting for my man to come, so I can give him money.

He's saying, *Watch out with that.* He's saying, *That's the pure.* He's saying, *Hospital shit.*

I'm nodding. I'm smiling. I'm going to work and spending a lot of time in the bathroom.

I'm falling asleep at my desk.
I'm skipping lunch.
I'm skipping dinner.
I'm standing on the corner.
Monday.
Tuesday.
Wednesday.

Thursday. Just another day of standing in front of my office on West Street at 9:45 a.m. Another day of construction. Another set of contractors huddled around some blueprints, disagreeing loudly about *underlying structural integrity or lack thereof.* Another headache. And today, my usual entrance is blocked off.

I try to find a way inside but end up walking in a complete circle, leading me right back to where I started. A construction worker waves me off, pointing toward an obscure back entrance where three young guys in black hooded sweatshirts huddle around a pair of glass doors, whispering. When I get close, they fall silent. Everything that's happened will repeat itself again today and tomorrow and forever. The same people, the same problems. I could be alive or I could be dead. What's the difference? It's depressing enough being anything at all.

The one in the center steps in front of me to block the doorway.

"Sorry, man," I give him the brush off. "No time."

"Make time," he says, throwing an arm around my shoulder. There's a deep scar on his chin, which pulls tight when he speaks. "Or you're going in the East River."

He's not one of the young men from the record label upstairs after all.

"I'm sorry. I thought you were someone else."

"I'm not," he shrugs. His muscles make noises like knuckles being cracked. He opens his mouth and runs his tongue over a row of yellow teeth. His presence makes it clear that violence is not a function of the body but something spiritual. He believes that he can hurt me and, when I look into his green eyes, I believe it too. One of his buddies says, "That's right." The other looks like he might shit himself. When I search their droopy, windswept faces, I recognize a few local dudes that floated me some dope a week ago when I couldn't get ahold of my man.

"All this over fifty bucks?" I ask the wiry one with his arm around me.

He licks his teeth, "I'd do it for free."

I feel my wallet being fished from my back pocket, hear the cash coming out.

Someone says, "We're good."

The wiry guy grabs me by the shirt and drags me to the glass doors, "Look at yourself."

It feels like someone punched me in the nose and there I am, sitting on the ground, staring at my reflection in a newly installed set of glass doors. The entire world briefly shines back at me in the glass.

My reflection looks agitated but I feel nothing. He rubs his nose and curses under his breath but I remain motionless. He says the word "depersonalized" and I think, yes, that's it, *depersonalized:*

a persistent feeling of observing oneself from outside one's own body. For the rest of the day, I watch everything my reflection does from a distance, as if he's someone else.

Hours pass. Bags of heroin disappear into bathroom stalls, into rolled-up dollar bills. Some album promos get mailed at the post office on Meserole. Then, out on the street, I catch my reflection, leaning against a bus stop, watching shadows crawl along the sidewalk. The long spire of St. Anthony's crosses Manhattan Avenue before slowly climbing up the side of a building.

My reflection makes a phone call, then walks into C-Town on Manhattan Avenue, where he wanders the aisles pretending to look at groceries. When he picks up a can of tomato soup, I think, *We don't even like tomatoes.* I'm unwilling to take responsibility for his actions, but I also refuse to think of him as a separate person with his own tastes, his own impulses. He's still mine.

My reflection looks down at the phone buzzing in his hand and runs to the front of the store, just in time to see my man walk in, wearing paint-covered sweatpants and heavy work boots. As always, when he sees me, the first words out of my man's lips are, "My man." My man does contractor work—bricks and concrete—when he's not selling hard drugs. When he speaks, it's as if he's laying steel beams for a future conversation:

"Three missed calls. Damn. Son must be desperate. But you know me. Old reliable."

My reflection says, "I seem to have misplaced a couple bags. In fact, I may have given them to a cab driver with the fare."

My man is unfazed, "Tip your driver. Tip your dealer."

I watch the two of them stalk the aisles, looking at Entenmann's cakes and crullers. My man says, "Raspberry Crumb. Love that one. Pops used to get it. When we was small. Addicted to that shit. And honey dip. From Peter Pan."

My reflection asks him, "You know Peter Pan Donuts?"

"Pfff—yeah, I know Peter Pan. You think I just sprang up out of the ground to deal dope one day?"

My reflection puts his hands up in surrender, *I didn't mean it like that, man.*

"This is my neighborhood. My gramps owned half this block. Before all the white people came. Started pushing us out. No offense to you." My man stops to blow a kiss at a young cashier with hoop earrings and straight, silky hair. She rolls her eyes but there's a smile on her lips.

"You know her?" My reflection asks.

"You listen to a word I say? This is my hood. These are my people."

My reflection listens carefully, worrying the corners of two folded-up hundred-dollar bills in his jacket pocket, as he enters the freezer section. When my man reaches the frozen pizzas, he looks at my reflection in the glass of the freezer doors, and I wonder if he sees what I see: the reflection of my reflection, the ghost of my ghost, floating in the cold phosphor glare of the market, hungry but unable to eat, thirsty but unable to drink. The store is overflowing with health and vitality but my reflection drifts through the aisles as if he's walking through the walls of an abandoned building.

My man hands him a bundle of paper towels. My reflection takes it, slips back two hundreds and asks, "So you gonna get that coffee cake then?"

My man looks over his shoulder, stifles a laugh, and calls out at the top of his lungs, *"My man."*

My reflection walks down the street, materializing in a series of shop windows on Greenpoint Avenue. But it's getting dark. He checks his phone: 5:30 p.m. Three missed calls from Liza and three new messages:

>|Hey, when you coming home?
>
>|On your way yet? I just tried you.

|Everything ok? I'm getting worried.

My reflection stops at our local gym and goes down to the lockers. The room is empty, so he pulls a plastic baggie from the wad of paper towels and dips a key in, passing it first under one nostril and then the other.

I think, *Cocaine? We don't even like cocaine.*

In between each bump, my reflection puts his face close to the mirror and peers directly into the image of his own eye. It's chilling. He stares me straight in the face without realizing I'm even there. I understand. It's a delicate operation. His concentration must be total. If opiates constrict the pupils and uppers cause them to dilate, then there must be an exact amount of coke he can snort to look sober. But he hasn't found it yet.

"C'mon," he says, "come on, c'mon." He checks his phone for the time, 5:55 p.m., then dumps the rest of the bag out on the edge of the sink, rolls up his last dollar, and draws as much of the pile up his nose as he can. "Fuck," he says. He sneezes into his sleeve, pausing momentarily to look at the white paste before snorting it back up from the damp fabric.

His pupils are still tiny. If he goes home like this, Liza will definitely know he's been using again. The phone rings, screen lighting up with her picture. My reflection slaps himself twice in the face. When he catches my eyes in the mirror, I can tell he's decided to do something drastic. He licks his fingertips and gathers up the remaining cocaine on the ends of his pointer and index fingers. With his other hand, he pulls down the bottom lid of each eye, takes a deep breath, and rubs the coke directly on his eyeballs.

The figure in the mirror doubles over, then straightens up, bracing himself on the edge of the sink. When his eyes open, they're shot through with blood. He holds his extended fingers up to the mirror in a backward peace sign. "Fuck," he says, to the mirror. "Fuck you." A pair of flies circles the lightbulb above his head, making sizzling sounds when they get too close.

He pockets the phone, takes the stairs two at a time. On the way home, taxis fill the streets, streaming by in an unbroken line. Could one of them be driving around with my heroin in their glove compartment? No, this is no time for negativity. Those bags must still be here, somewhere deep in my sweatshirt pockets.

My reflection ducks into RiteAid and slips a bottle of Visine into the waistband of his pants. Twenty minutes later, in the hallway to our apartment, the phone reads 6:25 p.m. There's a text from Liza saying we need to talk. The screen goes back to sleep but a pair of eyes hovers there, red, even in the phone's glossy black surface.

Two drops of Visine, two slaps on the cheeks. My reflection slides his hand down between the seams of his sweatshirt pocket, once, twice. No luck. Two bags still missing.

My reflection swings the door open. Liza's sitting there with her arms crossed over her chest, staring out the window at the back of our apartment. Her hair's pulled up in a severe ponytail, exposing her dark roots and the few strands near her scalp that have gone white.

"Hi, sweets," my reflection says, but Liza doesn't reply. Instead, she pushes off from our ugly beige couch and walks to the glass doors, in smooth, confident strides. I can't help but notice the sleek motions her muscles make beneath the flawless skin of her thighs, which are immaculately tan, even in the deep January gloom. My head fills with illicit pictures: my palms running up her legs, under the elastic of her shorts, my tongue pressing into the flesh at the back of her knee. But then she stops and clears her throat, her back to me. We watch each other silently through our reflections in the glass.

She asks, "Is there something you need to tell me? Just be honest."

The heat is on. I can't stop shivering.

She says, "I need to talk to you. Sit down."

I try to hug her, but she steps back, causing me to lose balance. The next thing I know, I'm sitting on the ground, watching my reflection wipe a drop of blood from his nose, unsure which side of the glass I'm on. Liza draws the curtain. Our apartment instantly seems so much smaller. She seems so much smaller without her twinned image in the glass.

"Found these in the courtyard. Lola was playing with them, like toys." In her open hand, the two missing bags of heroin. They must've fallen out of my pocket while I was hanging out with the cat, looking at clouds. She places them on the coffee table on top of a book with the title *Codependent No More*. My body is screaming at me to pick up the bags and run out the front door. The image of the two bags burns into my retina: bright white paper with a black lightning bolt stamped down the center. I can't look away.

"Lola could've died," Liza says. "If she'd eaten them? Then what? I'd be the one to find her. I'd be the one brokenhearted, lying to our neighbors so they wouldn't think you're some monster that poisoned their favorite cat and left me to deal with the consequences. It's careless. You don't care about anything anymore."

I try to look at Liza but can't see her clearly. Maybe my reflection is the one in the room with her and I'm the one in the glass.

"How long has this been going on?" she asks. "Why couldn't you just tell me?"

I can't seem to speak.

Liza whispers, "Honesty. I need honesty." For a moment, she drifts into a private reverie. "My friends thought you might be using again. For a while now. But I knew for sure when I got sleep paralysis last night. That shadowy figure in our room? He felt like some sort of messenger from my subconscious."

"I saw him too," I say. "He showed me what's under the floorboards."

"You didn't see him," Liza closes her eyes, inhales deeply, "Because he wasn't real." The refrigerator kicks on. Someone flushes a toilet in the apartment above us.

"He *was*," I say. "Realer than I am. I can still hear his voice."

She raises her hand like a stop sign between us, "What are you even talking about? A bad dream? Look around. This is real life. This chair. This book case. That lamp. All of it is real. Your bloodshot eyes. Real. The bags of heroin on the table? Those are real. And this body in front of me? This person? That I love?" She lets her hand drop. "You're just a memory that I can't let go of."

"You told me I was your purpose."

Liza stands absolutely still but I can see everything inside her, crumpling.

I've imagined this conversation so many times: there would be screaming, throwing things across the room. Never did I imagine a hush, a few whispered words, and this feeling. It's as if all the clocks in the world are winding down. I want to stop. I want to take her in my arms and protect her from whatever's hurting her. But I can't. I can't stop myself.

"The DMT must be wearing off," I say. "And with it, your love."

Her voice gets so small, "You know that's not how it works."

"When you do drugs, it's self-discovery. When I do drugs, I'm a bad guy."

"Heroin is killing the person that I love. I don't want to be an accomplice."

She turns and heads for our bedroom. After crossing the threshold, she faces me again. "You can't stay here. Not like this. Not this time. This has to be a boundary." She looks down at the carpet. Closing the door, she stops for a second and speaks to me through the slivered opening. "You need help. I hope you get it."

One of my lower molars begins throbbing, dully. I gather myself up off the floor and walk out of the apartment, all alone, the image of the two bags of heroin still burning in my eyes.

The messages start coming while I'm wandering around in the cold Brooklyn night.

Steve, my old bandmate, writes,

|Liza called. You ok?

My mom writes,

|I'm worried. Need Dad to come get you?

The drug counselor I've been lying to for the better part of a year writes,

|Gimme a call.

It's almost hard to believe that all the world's shame is out there, bouncing around from satellite to satellite. Or that we've invented such a sophisticated little device to collect it and put it in our pockets. But we have. And now everyone knows everything.

So, I do what I always do: I call my man.

He tells me to meet him at the KFC on McGuinness by the Key Foods. When I get there, he's sitting at a table with the oldest guy I've ever seen. He waves me over with a french fry. I order a Diet Coke just to maintain appearances.

"*My man*, this here is The Mayor of Greenpoint. Say hello."

I offer my hand to the old guy but he doesn't notice. He's doing a little dance with his feet under the table.

"Guess how old I am?" The old guy asks me. "Guess." I feel like I've just walked in on a kid's birthday party.

"Go ahead," my man says, "guess."

I have no idea what the correct answer is in this situation. Is it rude to tell him that he looks like he's been dead for about a thousand years?

"Seventy?"

The old guy claps his hands and starts nodding up and down at my man, who passes him a five-dollar bill and tells me to sit down.

"Ninety-one!" The old guy tells me. "Ninety-one years old and still going strong."

"Yeah, G," my man tells me, "you could learn a thing or two from The Mayor here. Like telling that girlfriend of yours to lose my number. For starters."

"She messaged you?"

"It was not a very nice note, G. She said I *prey on the pain of the innocent*."

"Hey—" I put up my hands but can't think of anything else to say.

The old guy waves the discussion away, "Too much trouble, I tell you. A young guy like you? Forget it. Why bother?"

"She loves me?"

"You been on the stuff, how long—five years?"

"How'd you figure that out?"

He taps a long arthritic finger on the side of his nose. "Heh, heh. What did I tell you, my friend? Stay on the dope long enough and it gives you all kinds of gifts. I get powerful indications and forethought. Plus, the incredible anti-aging properties I previously mentioned."

I take a pull on the straw of my Diet Coke, "It's given me over $20k in credit card debt. My band broke up. My lady kicked me out. It's freezing in here and I can't stop sweating."

"Stick with it, my boy," the old guy pets the back of my hand. "Stay in the game like I have and all your problems will drain down to the essentials: do I have my mind and do I have a fix? The rest is noise. Noise fades. Trust the process. Look at me!" The old guy breaks out in a fit of giggles, shuffling his feet around under the table.

"Yeah, G," my man tells me, "could be a lot worse. You've got the money for tonight's dope. You've got—what's that—looks like you've got a garbage bag of your essential belongings."

The two of them start up laughing. The old guy points to the bag and says, "The secret bag, ready to grab at a moment's notice. We've all got one. Let me guess, a change of underwear, some extra socks, books, and one granola bar."

"A junkie go bag," my man nods. "Classic."

I can't tell if the old guy is winking at me or having some kind of spasm.

"Now for the main event." My man begins to croon to his chicken sandwich in a surprisingly tender voice, *"Cash rules everything around me. CREAM. Get the money."*

I interrupt him, "About that—"

The singing stops. The old guy sags, visibly, "How unfortunate."

"G," my man puts down his sandwich, "tell me. You didn't. Call me. Out here. Without no money."

"I know sometimes you'll float a bundle or two on credit."

"Oh no," the old guy puts his hands up over his face and peers at us between the fingers.

"G, come with me," my man stands up.

"Please don't hurt him," the old guy says. "You know how your father felt about that."

"I'm not gonna hurt him."

"And we have to get to our NA meeting, remember," the old guy taps his wrist where a watch would be. "I hate to be late."

"Stop worrying," my man says. "This'll only take a minute."

"You guys actually go to Narcotics Anonymous meetings?"

"Yeah," my man laughs. "I got a few customers that need to see my face."

"Sounds depressing."

"Just business." My man runs the tips of his fingers over his freshly shaved scalp. "Thought I might find you there. When you was missing. Last summer."

"At a 12-step meeting? God, no," I tell him. "I was in New Jersey."

"New Jersey," my man repeats, phonetically, as if he's never before said the words. "They got NA there too. No doubt. Now follow me, G. This won't take a minute."

The old guy is doing his dance again, "Oh, I just love the stories! Those people have such imaginations! Where do they come up with it all?"

When the bathroom door closes behind us, I feel the cool relief of chilled glass on my face before the copper taste of the mirror registers in my mouth. My man is strong. No wonder he works construction by day. My neck feels like it's caught in a vice. When my vision clears, I can see my man pulling something out of his waistband in the reflection of the mirror I'm pressed up against.

"You think I'm out here, walking around with three different types a felonies in my waist, so I can give credit to some junky that just got kicked out of his house?" In the midst of his brutality, my man's words flow out of him in great winding streams. Perhaps his inherent genius is always lying dormant, waiting for moments like these. Perhaps he's a scholar of violence as well as a teacher. "This may come as a surprise, G, but investment in the well-being of New York's homeless population is not why I do this."

I can see a shadow in my man's hand. He's waving it around like it's important, like it's the whole point. Then he brings the shadow up close and pushes it in my face. I can see its texture. The words *carbon fiber* come to mind, the words *high caliber*. I smell ketchup on his fingers.

My man puts the shadow back in his waistband and lowers his voice, "No dope for you. Fucking timeout. Feel the consequences. Three Days. Not from my guys up here. Or down on South 2nd. Not from the assholes in Chinatown. Or those three low-rent tough guys outside your workplace."

He lets go of my neck and the blood rushes back to my head. My man is all I see. I stand there staring at him.

"What?" He says. "Didn't think I knew about that? *Pffft.* The Mayor's not the only one, you know. I got powerful inclinations and forethoughts too. Dope gives me power. *This* gives me power." He grabs something in his pants. "They won't be hassling you no more anyway. I took care of that. You're my problem. Mine. Now fuck outta here and let me take a shit."

I walk back to the table to grab my bag. Everything is wobbly. I can't feel my legs beneath me but the floor looks like it might rise up and smack me in the face. The old guy is holding a bony finger up to his lips, *shhhhh*. With his other hand, he waves me around to his side of the booth. I stumble over to him and sit on the table. In his palm, he hides three paper packets of heroin, about thirty dollars' worth. He slides them into my hand.

"Don't give up yet, kid," he tells me. "You're just getting started."

I go to the bathroom of the nearest coffee shop that's still open and lock the door. My phone falls out of my hands, into the sink, where it keeps buzzing.

Don writes,

> |What did I tell you? Go to Mexico, get help.

Don writes,

> |70% svccess rate for ibogaine vs. 20% svccess fr rehab. Don't be stvpid.

Don writes,

> |Why do you think it's illegal in the states? BECAVSE IT WORKS.

I pick up the phone and type,

> |You're not my roommate, anymore.
> |I'm not Sean. You don't need to save me.
> |Besides, 'I looked at that brochure.
> |$7,000??? Where the fuck am I even supposed to get that?

The white space of the phone's screen stretches inward between messages. It goes on and on. There might not be any limit to it. Seven thousand dollars means nothing in a place of boundless depth. If I could step through the glass into that unrestricted space, I could finally stretch out and let myself breathe. I could find the time to figure all this out on my own. Space is just compressed time, after all. I watch it falling in big fat snowflakes through the field of perfect white. Then, a black line of text appears on the screen, ruining everything.

Don writes,

> |Any amount of money
> |From any source or place is reasonable to remove this fvcking disease.

/Jvst my thought.

I put the phone to sleep and lay it down flat on the paper towel dispenser.

I take off my shirt and wring it out in the sink. In the mirror, my chest is glistening with sweat. My hair is slick with it. The cold coffee shop air feels like a thousand hot needles on my wet skin. I can hear the chorus of our most popular song repeating in my head:

I don't want to feel this way forever.

It suddenly sounds childish to me. A fist tightens in my stomach. I double over and throw up Diet Coke into the sink. It looks like milk, running down the drain. My blood pressure drops. I sit down on the toilet. My arms and legs are very heavy. Everything is getting mixed up in my head.

Go to Mexico, get help. I don't want to feel this way forever. Go to Mexico, get seven thousand dollars help. I don't want to feel this way. Go to Mexico, get any amount of money help. I don't want to feel.

Go to Mexico. *Get help.* The words continue ringing in my ears as the barista barges in on me in the bathroom. He asks me to leave, turns to his manager and says, "The epidemic of our time," as if time were the epidemic and we're all subject to its disastrous effects.

I get up off the bathroom floor, grab my shirt, and leave the coffee shop, deciding to ride the train all night. In the morning, I'll go to work, make a plan. But for now, the subway is the only warm place I know and it runs all night long. The cold outside isn't meant for survival, only preservation. I can already feel my body trying to place itself in the city's public record.

Every life is a mirror story, every timeline an alternate. Right now, Liza is walking around inside the cozy rooms of our apartment. In some other world's glassy surface, I'm walking around those same rooms—we're touching, we're laughing—maybe in that world I really did install new lights in the living room. I try to picture it but already the whole place has sunken into darkness. A drawer closes in me. I feel the key turn and now that other life is rattling around down there with all the other junk. It's so easy to accept these things but it shouldn't be. *There's always more stuff in a closed box than in an open one.* Didn't someone important once say that? Or was it that *an empty drawer is unimaginable. It can only be thought of.* I can't remember who said what but I can vividly imagine the drawer, so right now I must be absolutely bursting.

I cross Meeker, walking between the concrete legs of the Brooklyn–Queens Expressway, which snarls down at me like an enormous feral dog. Vagrants huddle beneath its belly for shelter. Descending the stairs at Nassau Avenue, I look down at the messages on my phone again. Their worried chorus makes me want to throw my phone in the river. But one of them is not like the others.

My chemist father writes,

> /One of my misgivings about Hawking radiation is that when a very short-lived pair of virtual particles winks into existence in the vacuum, if the pair is on the knife edge of the event horizon, one particle should disappear into the black hole and the other should radiate away. Since the black hole is losing particles, it must be losing mass—but what about the mass that is ADDED by the partner that disappears into the black hole? I have some questions...

My father knows so many things that I will never know. In deep space, there must be drawers that are both empty and unimaginable. But I'm stuck in the shallowest space, between my last fix and withdrawal. The stairway unfurls beneath my feet, a grey carpet rolling down and down and down.

Beneath the street, it's still daytime. The G moves in fits and starts. But the A train moves fluidly in its eternal routine, crawling through tunnels, briefly stopping at each station and opening its mouth before moving on to the next destination. At 175th Street, it swallows a handful of uniformed police officers and spits me out. So I pace the platform, waiting for the next train to Far Rockaway, a route with thirty-one stops and enough smooth track for an hour of sleep or more; an oasis of quiet before rush hour starts.

The messages keep coming. A solemn parade of *Are you okay*s and *Can I help*s. It's all so exhausting. I might just throw myself down on the soft bed of the tracks to make it stop. I picture the train smoothly gliding over my head in a whoosh of silk sheets.

Inside the subway's dream, desire is all there is. An intensely unshowered man slumps in the seat next to mine, staring at a Styrofoam container resting on the lap of an MTA worker across the aisle. The MTA worker lets the food go cold in her lap, watching a pair of club kids tear at each other's clothing in the center of our carriage. One of the kids keeps looking my way like she recognizes me but can't figure out why I'm on the train at 4:30 a.m., clutching a garbage bag to my chest. She doesn't know it yet, but she's like us—one of the city's unwanted thoughts, compartmentalized here, safely out of sight.

I close my eyes and concentrate on the cold metal body of the train, the soft ring of headlights and all those little windows sparkling through the darkness beneath the city. Maybe I'm finally approaching the beauty that Liza saw in me, that comet streak. My stomach tightens. I can feel her, closed up in that deep drawer, threatening to set fire to everything I've packed away.

Inside the drawer, little flames of sunlight catch on autumn leaves, streaking them orange and yellow. I remember this. A crisp day on the edge of the park. Fall spice in the air. Liza says one of the local shops is baking an apple pie. We're walking arm in arm, behind a dog walker. "I love the big fluffy ones," I tell her. "Sheep Dogs, St. Bernards, Golden Retrievers."

Liza smirks, "Of course you do." One of the dogs plants its feet in the middle of the sidewalk, raises its nose and starts sniffing around.

I stop short and ask, "What's that supposed to mean?"

The lid of the drawer rattles, a sound like a train engaging its brakes.

"You look like one of them," she runs her hand up my shoulder to scratch me behind the ear, "*Mr. Cuteface*. Always with a big dumb smile." Leaves stop falling. The air clears. Black lacquered walls rise in the distance. Stillness. Liza straightens her shoulders, "Come on. You're adorable. I puppy love you. Okay?" The dog walker yanks on the retriever's leash ahead of us and we start moving again.

"Now I feel really sexy."

Liza rolls her eyes. Coming in the other direction, a tall, handsome man with dark hair and a perfect five-o'clock shadow winks at her. She smiles back, that same world-stopping smile I fell in love with.

"What was that?"

One of the dogs ahead of us starts whining. The dog walker jerks its leash.

"Don't get jealous, *Mr. Cuteface*," Liza pats my back. "Be a good puppy."

Someone taps Liza on the shoulder and we turn around.

"I'm sorry, I just had to stop you." It's Mr. Five-O'clock, looking dashing. "You have the most beautiful smile I've ever seen."

I square my shoulders. "I'm standing right here." The drawer groans. A few leaves fall to the ground, red and black.

Liza nudges me, "Don't be rude."

Mr. Five-O'clock steps forward and hands her his number. He never even acknowledges my presence. Liza takes the number with both hands. Thanks him. He turns away, winking at her a second time. A dog barks in the distance. The sidewalk lurches. We keep walking, in silence.

"Jealousy is not an attractive trait," Liza tells me.

"All your talk of boundaries," I say. There's a rumbling beneath us. Metal on metal. The leaves are really coming down, now, bruised purple. "Do you remember our second date? You were late. Like significantly. Some guys catcalled you into a bar to buy you a drink. *And you went.*"

Liza scoffs, "They just wanted to show me the bathroom."

"I'm sure they did!" The retriever ahead of us won't stop barking.

"It's the oldest bathroom in the city. I thanked them and left. *To meet you.* Now cut it out."

"Can't you imagine how that makes me feel?"

I start laughing. A mean type of laughter. Bad laughter.

"Every guy in New York is praying for me to drop dead."

Staring straight ahead, Liza lowers her voice, "Then stop making it so easy on them."

I open my eyes and the homeless guy next to me is performing a magic trick, right there in his seat. His massive army surplus parka has retained the hardened outline of a sleeping man while the soft creature underneath has shimmied one arm out of its sleeve and tied it off with a small length of rubber hose. I watch him thread the needle into his vein with surgical precision. He takes the plunge, pulls out, and falls back into the shell of his coat.

A look of pure contentment washes over the man's face. New York City has been in a housing crisis for years, but he's discovered a loophole in the system: a bag of heroin that contains housing concentrate. And not just any house: Dream House, that perfected place that only ever exists in the idealized future. I watch the lamps coming on in his attic, dusting their light particles over a staircase that stretches down through his center, before dropping off into blindness above the locked cellar. No detail is overlooked. Each corner is snug. Every shadow has been nailed to its corresponding wall.

I was building my dream house with Liza and now it will stay perfect forever, in an impossible dream. Maybe it had always been impossible. Who can imagine any house at all in this city? Here the cellars are all full of subway tracks and the attics are full of other people. We hit a bend and the homeless man slides across his seat back and comes to rest against my shoulder. World peace sleeps in his features. He's in the tower now. Safe.

I will never find that peace again. I'm a man *whose tower has been destroyed*. That's a quote from a lobster. "Fuck," I yell at the top of my lungs. A cold hand slaps me across the face. Or possibly from a poet who kept a lobster as a pet. It's getting harder to hear myself. Every thought I have is like walking over a bridge that collapses when you cross it. The poet walked the lobster at the end of a blue silk ribbon. The wrong thought at the wrong moment can destroy a neural pathway forever. The lobster was said to have a very serious disposition, despite the ribbon. "I have to keep moving forward," I tell my homeless companion. "It's time to go to work."

An MTA worker calls after me as I exit the train, "I think you dropped this."

Through the closing doors, he hands me a water-damaged piece of paper. These are the only legible words on the page:

> *Our stories disclose in a general way what we used to be like, what happened, and what we are like now.*

> we beg of you to be fearless and thorough from the very start.   let go bsolutely.
> We st at the turning point. Here are the s we took, : We admitted

I've never seen the paper before. I hold it up to the glass and mouth, *this isn't mine*, but the man nods back at me, *yes, yes it is*, as the train slides away forever. I fold up the paper and put it in my pocket. With everything slipping away, I want to hang on to this stranger's advice, I want to learn to *let go bsolutely.*

Most of the workday disappears into a thick, dreamless sleep, until a trio of voices shouts out of the elevator: those three identical-looking young men who work in the record label upstairs. When they notice me laid out on the lobby's brown leather couch, they invite me out for a cigarette.

Outside, I bum a Marlboro though I don't smoke. I still can't tell the young men apart. One of them says, "We saw what's-his-name, your coworker, trying to wake you up earlier." One says, "He's a real character. Asked us if we should call an ambulance. We told him: 'that doesn't sound like very good PR for a PR firm.'"

One says, "He went home an hour ago, said you never even made it upstairs. Asked us to tell you he quit."

Another one pulls his sleeve up and points to the skin underneath, "I did it. I got it. Look." Tattooed up the length of his forearm, in my handwriting:

I don't want to feel this way forever.

The one standing to his left says, "Ain't that some shit."

"Shit, fuck," I yell, involuntarily. A dry palm smacks me across the cheekbone. Fuzzy stars fill my eyes, then the massive, red-brick building comes into focus across the street. One of the smokers catches me eyeing my old office, "You had a good run anyway."

The smoker to my right agrees, "That Touchè Amore record is a classic."

Another one takes this as encouragement, comes around the circle to my left, and says, "Man, I'm sorry, but I got to ask about the man, the myth, the Martin Shkreli."

His friend cuts him off, "That fucking guy. I remember running into you the morning he hiked up the cost of that AIDS drug. Your label hadn't been dragged into it yet but it was already quite the scandal. You told me there 'had to be some mistake.' That Shkreli was 'one of the good ones.'" All three of them start laughing. Someone snorts, "*One of the good ones.* Classic."

Holding the cigarette in the corner of my mouth, I try to explain, "When I met Martin, he was a quiet kid who had a giant pile of cash he wanted to put into my little DIY label."

"Sure. But by the time Shkreli was on TV, rolling his eyes at Congress and picking fights with members of the Wu-Tang Clan, even you must have seen it."

"He believed in me," my voice cracks and they get quiet.

"Could've happened to anyone," one of the kids says, trying to salvage the conversation. He swaps positions with his coworker. The two of them on the ends switch spots, again, and the one in the middle flicks out a small, burning projectile, cherry exploding against the building's facade. "Break time's over, losers."

The smoke cloud thins out as it moves down the block, carrying away the young men in their hooded sweatshirts. I take the Marlboro out of my mouth and examine it, a small piece of currency that I don't know how to spend. I can't figure out where to go, what to do, now that work's over. Are there any friends left who will take me in? Is there any way to get more money and, even if there is, how do I make these three heroin packs that the old guy slipped me last two more days? It's impossible to think with this song spinning around in my head. *I don't want to get to Mexico for help. I don't get to feel this way for Mexico. I go to Mexico forever.*

My teeth are chattering. I worry that I've got an infected tooth. The street empties around me. Buildings go dark. I lean back into the doorway and take out one of the heroin packets, using my phone's screen as a surface. I roll up a dollar, split open the envelope, pour out the dope. I whisper, *take me home*, and snort the whole pile but nothing happens. My teeth keep chattering. I stick my finger in my mouth to press on the tooth. Blinding pain. I'm stunned. Why would the old guy make a show of slipping me a bag of fake shit? I open the second bag and taste the powder. My tongue goes bitter, then numb. The dope is real, not lactose filler. I snort the entire second bag. Still nothing, so I say *fuck it* and do the last bag, but I don't feel anything. No music, no lift, no relief. Just a grey blankness and the familiar sound: *ca-chic-ca-chic-shhhhh, ca-chic-ca-chic-shhhhh.* Over and over again. I pull a few Skittles out of my pocket and chew them down. Still nothing. Frank O'Hara's *Lunch Poems* comes out of my bag and slips through my fingers into the deep grey slush at the curb.

"Oh fuck you too, Frank," I shout into the empty street.

I jam my headphones into my ears and press play on The Cocteau Twins. Keyboards chime, guitars bend. Liz Fraser's falsetto glides up through the mix but nothing happens. I'm still stuck in my body, shivering and aching. I open my garbage bag. Underwear. Socks. Deodorant.

I just need someone to talk to.

I scroll through my contacts looking for a name that doesn't fill me with instant regret. *F-G-H...* The only person I want to call is **My Man-Cellphone** but he won't answer. *Q-R-S...* My hands are shaking. I rifle through my pockets, looking for any scrap of relief. But there's nothing there. It's all over. I finally reach the last name in my phone, the one that Don saved in my contacts: **Xrds MX**. Suddenly, I'm laughing, face turned to the sky. Tears of withdrawal stream over my cheeks. My body slides down the door frame and hits the ground.

When I press *Call*, a woman's voice answers, "Crossroads Mexico, ibogaine clinic."

"Please," I whisper, cupping my hand over the speaker, "can you help me?"

Later that evening, huddling behind a parked car across the street from our apartment, I watch our front door, waiting for Liza to leave. She has a work event tonight. I've kept track of them in my calendar so I know which nights I'll be able to use openly in the comfort of my own home. When she finally steps out, she looks incredible—armored in a lightweight, thigh-length, chain mail dress, shoulders draped in a chic, black trench coat, makeup sophisticated and smoky.

It burns, seeing her like that. I tell myself, *Sometimes appearances are all we have. She probably feels worse than you do.* Taking stock of myself—a man hiding behind an old Toyota Corolla with a garbage bag in his hands—I know it isn't true. She doesn't feel worse than I do. No one does.

When she turns the corner, I run in to grab my passport and fill a small backpack with a sweatshirt, some underwear, and three pairs of clean socks. I pull a Thursday tour laminate from the stack in my closet and loop it around my key chain. It feels right. For a second, I'm in charge. For a second, I'm someone.

In the apartment, all the blinds are closed, all the curtains left shut. No noise seeps in from the street. One of Liza's scarves has fallen from its hook to cover the mirror, extinguishing the last reflective surface in the apartment. It's just as well. I don't think I could stand to see myself right now. No one else is home but the silence in this place is so concentrated, it has a physical presence. Usually, silence this pure only comes to the city in a blizzard. But that kind of silence is expansive, an infinite canvas to paint our dreams on. This silence is a trash compactor, pressing me down into myself.

I grab a book from the shelf: *Brother* by the twin poets Matthew and Michael Dickman, about the suicide of their older brother. I flip through the pages of the book. It's filled with ticket stubs and Polaroids—souvenirs. I like that. It feels like the kind of thing a person would take on a trip that they might never come back from. The book goes into my backpack.

On the way out the door, I turn around for one last look at the apartment. Liza's care and attention clings to every surface. This is it. This is the dream. I hear my eyelids close. The image of the apartment remains fixed. Stable. Every detail is inside me now. My dream house: books on the shelves, mangoes ripening on the counter, bunches of lavender drying above the dresser. I take them with me. I take it all with me.

On the plane, I dip in and out of consciousness, reading and rereading the first poem from *Brother*, over and over, as if for the first time, until my eyes settle on one particular phrase and I put my hand against the page, touching the words to make sure they're real:

I wish I could look down past the burning chandelier inside of me.

Yes, that's it, that's it, that's . . .

I see the grey fabric of the carpet below my feet and the dim strip illuminating the aisles. The world looks like shit so I know I must be awake—awake and coming down. The whole cabin shakes with turbulence.

I sit up. Flight attendants collect empty soda cans with white rubber gloves. A flat plane icon crosses the map on the screen in front of me. Almost there. I pick up the book of poetry again, this time fanning the pages. There's a printout tucked between them. It says *Crossroads Mexico* at the top. I unfold the paper and read: *Ibogaine offers more than just a physical detox and neurological rebalancing. Ibogaine is unique in that it offers people the chance to dive deeply into their own psyche…* but I'm not ready for that so I refold the printout and slide it back into the book's pages.

Just then, a little flit of bookmark or ticket stub falls out from a fold in the book. It lands on the plastic drop-down table top in front of me: a miniature white envelope with the letters RED DEATH printed on it. When did I slip this in here? My man hasn't had RED DEATH for at least six months. I look around but no one else sees, so I take it as a sign from God, open it up, and do the dope right there in my seat.

At altitude, drugs and alcohol hit harder, so this small bag of heroin is a kind of prayer, that the world might be redeemed, here, above the clouds. *Now*, I whisper, *now. Please. Work.* A small vibration starts in the center of my chest, before moving out through my limbs. My heart swells with gratitude. I reach my hand up to buzz for the stewardess but the button's too far away. I need to tell her it was all just a big mistake. They can turn the plane around and take me home now.

Leaning against the window, I look out at the grey clouds. Already they're starting to glow. Already my eyelids are pulling down like heavy curtains. Already the sky is smoothing out and, with it, our plane, sleeping across the darkened face of the earth.

"Sir, are you alright?"

I hear the flight attendant's voice before I open my eyes. When I shake myself awake, she's pursing her lips, making little kissing motions, just like Liza does when she's worried. It takes something out of me.

I smile up at her. "I can honestly say, I'm feeling much better."

She tugs on her ear lobe and leans back in the aisle, whispering across to one of the other flight attendants before turning back to me, "We'll be landing shortly, so you might want to gather yourself."

"I'm good," I tell her, turning to the window. There's a bit of resistance, a sharp pain in my left nostril. Several spots of rust stain the window pane. When I put my hand to my face, I realize there's a dollar bill jammed up my nose. Blood trickles down its length. I pull it out and watch the sky, emptying itself of color. *I'm good*, I whisper to the clouds as they slip by. *I'm good. I'm good.*

"You should start getting acquainted with the others as soon as they arrive. You're all about to go through it," a representative from the clinic tells me at the San Diego International Airport's baggage claim.

Two men from our group arrive on the next flight, carrying camouflage backpacks. They're the same height, an inch or so shorter than I am, but standing tall with a martial, straight-backed posture.

The one directly beside me raises a Styrofoam cup to his lips, spits out a thick brown liquid, and says, "Duane. Marine. How y'all doing?" He stops himself, looks down into his cup. "Well, shoot," he drawls in a soft southern accent. "I'm not sure that was a polite question, considering the circumstances." Though his head is shaved, he has a soft round face and innocent, nearly colorless blue eyes. It's hard to picture Duane carrying an assault rifle.

The man standing next to him adjusts a hunting cap, "Name's John. Happens that I was a Marine as well." John clasps his bony hands together to stop them from shaking and pins them against his chest. Although it's only 7:15 a.m., John has the look of someone who's been working all day at a thankless job. He's still in his thirties but appears much older. When he smiles, his gaunt face fills with creases, only to flatten out again when he looks down at his shaking hands. Unlike Duane, John is easy to picture with an M4 carbine rifle. Maybe his hands only shake when he's without one.

John whispers something to Duane and Duane looks over at me, knitting his brow.

"Hey man," he asks me, "you wearing lipstick?"

I touch my lips. My fingers come away purple. "That's blood."

Duane slaps John on the back, "Well shoot, partner, that's a whole different story."

All the creases come back to John's face. He says, "We're gonna get along just fine."

A third man emerges from the bathroom and lumbers over to the group, with a slow, wide step. His head is bowed in a way that hides his features but his shoulders speak for themselves: if Duane and John are Marines, he's the tank they rode in on. When he pulls his hat off and looks at us, his pupils are pinned, though it's hard to see them below his eyelids, which are half-closed and further obscured by thick black lashes. His golden skin has sharp, regal features that sag slightly on his face. "I'm Faruk," he says, smiling at us, dreamily, before lowering his eyes to attend to a small drop of blood running out from the crook of his arm.

A woman joins our circle just in time to watch the blood make its way down Faruk's arm to the band of his watch. Face expressionless, her features are fixed with a flat ghostly whiteness. But her large, blue eyes radiate a kind of telepathic hunger. She adjusts her sleeves so that they cover the tops of her hands. Then she crosses her arms over her chest and disappears behind a cascade of straight black bangs. "My name is Kate," she sighs. "I'm not a Marine."

Someone just beyond the edge of our circle is shouting, "No, I said *now*, stupid, not in ten minutes. *Now*." She comes out of the ladies' room with large, dark sunglasses covering half her face and long, greasy hair spilling down over the shoulders of a pink hoodie with the words *Queen Bitch* bedazzled across the chest. She enters the circle, with a cellphone pressed to her ear, yelling, "You want to talk about money, asshole? You *know* me."

The representative raises his skinny hands toward the phone, "I'm sorry, Ms. Thompson, but you can't be setting up a drug deal at this airport."

She ducks away, raising an acrylic nail in his face, and takes the phone off her ear to look at it, "Excuse me, *motherfucker*. You think you can hang up on me?"

She takes off her sunglasses. She's twenty-two years old, if that, but already her skin has gone sallow. Even the whites of her eyes are turning yellow.

"It's for the best," the rep tells her. "We're about to cross the Mexican border. At the clinic, your belongings will be searched. There's a screening process; we need to take some blood. Put you each through a battery of tests. Make sure you're healthy enough to survive the treatment."

Faruk's shoulders sag. Our two Marines help steady him.

The rep says, "The search for illicit items is thorough."

"Whatever," she shrugs. "You think I can't find drugs in Mexico?"

We're in an anonymous white van, crawling along the approach to the border, which looms ahead of us in all its prehistoric, shadowed glory. From the passenger seat, I can hear the others whispering behind me. Faces of people in passing cars dissolve in a high glare of morning sun. Walls rise on each side, forcing traffic to flow in only one direction, like a slow, angry river.

I pull my keys out of my back pocket and grasp the old tour laminate firmly in both hands. If I close my eyes, I can almost convince myself that this is all normal, that I'm still on tour, still surrounded by familiar things. I can almost feel Thursday's beat-up van idling roughly beneath me, hear the squeak of its busted shocks, smell Febreze wafting up from the carpeting. In back, Tim, Tom, and Tucker take turns punching each other on the arm. They give off stale sweat and fresh deodorant. I can almost taste the Gold Bond powder in the air. Steve's in the driver's seat, asking if we have our passports ready, checking his pockets, adjusting the radio.

We hit a rumble strip and the picture gets fuzzy. But they're still here with me. I can sense the heat of their bodies. Tucker's got Tom's passport open, asking him how his head's so fucking crooked. Tim can't stop laughing. I can see them all through the haze of time. It's so real. Such a relief.

There's a knock on the window. I open my eyes and a border agent is staring down at us from his booth.

"Passports."

Behind me, the woman in the pink *Queen Bitch* sweatshirt kicks my seat, "Fucking cops."

We arrive at the clinic just after 8:30 in the morning. It's in a strip mall. The rep walks us up to a storefront window. A man in a pair of black-rimmed glasses and neatly pressed dark blue scrubs opens the door and smiles widely, "Please, come inside." His name tag says *Javi*.

The rep waves us in but stays where he is at the door, "This is where I leave you. I wish you all lots of luck."

"*Lots of luck*? Are you serious?" The woman in the pink sweatshirt turns to the rep. "This place is disgusting. Is he even a real doctor?"

"I am a registered nurse," the man in scrubs tells her, adjusting his black-rimmed glasses as he looks around the immaculately clean reception area. "My name is Javier, but you may call me *Javi*." Everything about Javi is healthy and well manicured. His hair is slicked neatly and his smart black mustache is tightly trimmed.

The rep turns to leave, swinging his keychain around his pointer finger, "You're in good hands with Javi. He won't let anything happen to you."

Faruk lowers himself into a plastic chair and immediately begins to slump forward, his body folding until his chin rests on his kneecaps. Fast asleep. Kate looks down at him and licks her lips. The woman in the pink sweatshirt manages to wedge one of her white sneakers under Faruk's armpit. She leans all of her weight into him until his head flops back, exposing an expression of total absence. She snorts, "I know this motherfucker—he's from LA. His family is R-I-C-H. Rich, like *Shahs of Sunset* rich."

Kate props a couch cushion under Faruk's head, "He comes from money?"

The woman in pink turns to John and Duane, "This chick just got wet."

Kate adjusts the pillow, strokes Faruk's forehead, "Hard to believe. All those resources and still he ends up here. He's obviously been disowned. This place is the last resort. For people who've been thrown out. For people with nothing to lose."

The woman in pink raises her voice, "Calling me garbage, lady?" She takes off her pink sweatshirt and drapes it over a plastic chair. "I'll take you out. For free." She stretches her neck, extends her arms out from the sides of her body, raising miles of collapsed veins around her. She looks truly beautiful, like a suspension bridge in its last moment of belief.

Javi steps in front of her, "Not today, Ms. Thompson."

She leans away and hisses, "Did I give you permission to address me, Mr. Nurse?" Then she steps into the hallway bathroom, slamming the door behind her. The walls shake. We stare at her pink sweatshirt, *Queen Bitch* sparkling under the fluorescent lights.

Five minutes later, the bathroom door squeaks open, followed by the sound of rapid footsteps padding down the hallway. John walks to the window, "Not sure who all cares but *Queen Bitch* just hopped in a Mazda Miata with Mexican plates."

Duane asks him, "You seen a state or principality on them plates, partner?"

John reads, "*Charlie-Hotel-India-Hotel.*"

Duane turns to Javi, "Chihuahua. Ain't that where Juarez is?"

Javi pulls out a cell phone, heads for the door.

Duane says, "Shiiiit."

My phone battery is dying but the messages keep coming:
Steve:

> |Don sent us a note to let us know what's up. Sounds pretty intense.

Tim:

> |I had no idea you were going through this, man.

Tucker:

> |You got this, buddy.

Tom:

> |Not gonna lie, I watched some news stories—ibogaine looks scary as fuck.

Nothing new from Liza. The last three texts I sent her sit on the screen with a small check, indicating they've been read.

Still, no answer.

"**Duane, John, Kate,** and *Geo. F. Frey*?" Javi steps into the waiting room, reading our names off a clipboard.

"You can just call me *Geoff*, like *J-e-f-f*."

Javi squints at us, rubbing his mustache with his free hand, "I'll make a note of that, *Jefe*." Javi checks the clipboard again, "It won't be much longer now. Faruk is going to have to recover here in the clinic for a few days. It seems he took too large a dose of heroin before we picked you up at the airport. And we have located Ms. Thompson's telephone through the laptop she left behind. One of our security men is going to pick her up and bring her to meet us at the beach house so she can get the help she so desperately needs. The rest of you should grab your things."

Kate gathers the pink sweatshirt, "Wouldn't want *Queen Bitch* to lose her crown."

Just after noon, Javi pulls the beat-up white van into a garage, where he unloads us through a small door into a large communal room with three red leather couches oriented around a central fireplace. Behind the couches, there are two steps up to a table already set for lunch.

Hardly any of this registers, though, because the house has one dominant feature, which sucks up the attention from all the others: glass walls through which a vast grey ocean breaks against three miles of white sand. Sunlight streams in. Wind pushes through the rooms in short, uneven bursts.

"Welcome to Crossroads," Javi says. Beneath the mantle, the fire jumps. "Each of you has a room. Put away your things. After lunch, we'll have preparatory classes."

Kate raises the *Queen Bitch* sweatshirt up in front of Javi's face, a bright pink question mark.

Javi shakes his head, "Nothing yet."

"**You are sitting** in a canoe," Javi says. "See? Here's the canoe."

The chalk goes scratch, scratch, scratch on the board. A little boat appears. Squiggle, scratch: A stick figure on the boat's left side.

"And here you are, rowing the canoe this way. You are facing this way. Okay?"

Scratch, scratch, scratch. An arrow and two simple oars appear. The stick figure sits in the back of the canoe and rows forward, in the direction he's facing.

"But here is your subconscious mind."

Scratch, scratch. A second stick figure appears in the front of the boat.

"Like a passenger, your subconscious mind is always with you, observing, judging, even recording."

The stick figure on the right gets filled in solid, like a shadow of the one on the left.

"Now, the problem is, in your cases," Javi intones slowly, motioning to the four of us sitting on the couch in front of the chalkboard, "the subconscious mind is rowing this way, against you."

A long scratch and a squeak. He throws the chalk on the desk and folds his arms.

"Can anyone tell me where all that rowing's going to get you?"

I raise my hand but Javi's cell phone rings and he walks to the glass wall to answer it. The stick figures face each other, both leaning away at the same angle, thrusting their oars with equal and opposite force.

Over the sound of the waves, we hear him say, "How did she end up way out there?"

John laughs, "Gotta be *Queen Bitch*. Fifty bucks she's all the way in Chicago. Or New Jersey. Fuck, she might be in France already!"

Duane nods along with him, "The things these people get up to."

Kate pulls the pink sweatshirt into her lap, "I'm keeping it. She can try and fight me, I don't care."

Javi asks, "Was she still breathing?"

It gets quiet.

"I know, I know, I know." Javi continues to repeat the phrase, each one softer than the last until finally he closes the flip phone. Kate finishes folding the sweatshirt and places it on the couch's red leather arm. Javi stares out through the glass wall. "I've got some liability waivers for all of you to sign."

John says, "For what? Is the ibogaine going to kill us?"

Javi turns around, "It is statistically unlikely. Still. I want each of you to think about this carefully tonight: How do you envision your own death? What would it mean to make peace with it? Tomorrow, you're going to come back in here and give me an answer."

Out on the beach, the waves go *ca-chic-ca-chic-shhhhhh, ca-chic-ca-chic-shhhhhh*. Over and over again.

Midnight. I can hear it in the waves falling blind against the shoreline. I can taste it in the black salt air on my tongue. Tonight, the moon is low, drawing only an outline of a palm tree on the deck's glass doors. The water goes slack against the beach, the currents reaching a temporary equilibrium, before the tide turns, again, and drags itself toward the horizon.

I close my eyes to try and call up the comforting Dream House image of my apartment. I see aprons hanging by the front door, records spinning on the turntable. Orange blossoms in the bedroom. Despite the perfect, fixed quality of the Dream House, I keep getting pulled into the heavy gravity of its closed-up cellar. That hidden room is getting stronger, expanding, swallowing up the rest of the House.

Daylight, the common room is blazing. Kate puts on an oversized pair of shiny, black sunglasses as she sinks into the red leather couch.

Javi clears his throat, points at John, "How are you going to die?"

John tells us about some bullet fragments lodged in his skull. "That shit's carcinogenic. I'll probably get some awful cancer that'll fuck me right up."

Duane nods along before adding that he's always had a premonition that he'd be kicked in the head by a horse. He chuckles to himself, "And I love horses. Can you believe that shit?"

"There's a scene in some horror movie where a girl falls into a pit of hypodermic needles," Kate pauses, lifts her sunglasses. "For me, I'll take anything but that."

It's my turn. I clear my throat. "I'm doing this for my girl. Liza. I've broken her trust, over and over again. Letting her down already feels like dying. If ibogaine kills me, at least I know I went out trying to make things right." I look around the room and the others murmur their assent.

"That's a good answer," Duane tells John. "I'm gonna use that one on the wife."

"This is not about other people," Javi says, calmly rapping his fist against the chalkboard. "You are here to confront yourself. Your *true self*. This is the equivalent of one thousand hours of therapy. This is profound exposure." Javi stands, walks to the window. Outside, all of creation carries on without us.

After a few minutes, he finally turns around, "You are heroin addicts. You take your lives into your hands every single day. No matter how perilous this treatment may seem, surely you must see that it's nothing compared to the danger of your current predicament. You have an explicit illustration of the consequences in the case of Ms. Thompson."

Duane turns to John, spits into a Coke bottle, "Is he saying what I think he's saying?"

"People only end up here when every other option has failed. We cannot save everyone. Addicts are their own worst enemies. This is why it is so essential that you ask the ibogaine to reveal yourselves to you. To show you your own *true selves*. This may be your last chance."

I've only ever imagined my *self* as the broken thing that I'm trying to get away from. But what if there's another me: a somehow *heroic* alternate Geoff, buried under the drugs? That comet blaze that Liza saw in me. If I can find *that Geoff*, maybe it's not too late to fix things.

Javi opens the door to the dispensary. I lean in, taking him into my confidence. "Do you know what they've got us watching in there, Javi? *Confronting Your Shadow Persona?* Flashing images of Marilyn Monroe, JFK, and Elvis at us, like we're in *A Clockwork Orange*?"

Javi pulls me into his office. "It's only meant to prime your subconscious, Jefe. Iconographic suggestion. So that your visual language center will have some stable references."

"So someone here might see themselves—deep down—as OJ Simpson?"

"It's an old tape."

I sit down and look out the window. The beach pulls a curtain of water across the sand, whispering in through the window, *shhhhhhh.*

"I read ibogaine sessions can last forty-eight hours."

"Those kinds of experiences are more common in ritual practice. Here, we derive an active compound from the bark to control the dosage. The visionary experience lasts from ten to twelve hours. Then, the reflective period for sixteen to twenty-four hours. At this stage, the emotions return. You may get quite sentimental. The third period is less easily defined. You will find you are no longer physically or psychologically dependent upon heroin."

"I heard it wears you down. Like being worked over in the gym."

Javi looks up from his papers, "The gym?" A big smile breaks over his face, sudden light from a bank of clouds. "Where do you think you are, Jefe? *Club Med?*" He takes the calendar down and shows me our schedule for the week. Under Wednesday: *IBOGAINE SESSION. All Day. Clinic.* Then, in the box for Thursday, there's nothing but a black **X** drawn in thick marker.

"See?" Javi says. "It's a grey day."

I stare at the black **X**. Out the window the ocean plays a janitor, pushing seaweed up a golden sidewalk with its long blue broom.

Javi snaps his fingers in front of my face, "It's okay. Don't be scared."

"I'm not scared. I've taken psychedelics before."

"Mushrooms? A little LSD?" Javi looks back at his papers. "This is nothing like that."

"That's a relief."

The door opens. Juan, an orderly with a shy smile and big round cheeks, walks in and begins whispering to Javi in Spanish. Javi's eyebrows raise up above the black rims of his glasses. He turns to Juan and they continue to whisper, Javi glancing at me with a frown. My stomach sinks. Javi puts his hand up, stopping Juan midsentence.

"He says he caught you trying to get into the dispensary last night after lights out."

My hands are sweating in my lap.

"We have worked with many other addicts before you," Juan says. "We know all the tricks."

"You're an addict. We don't judge you for that. But the real question is," Javi pauses, "how bad do you want this?"

"Do you even want to get better, man?" Juan asks, sounding personally hurt.

"I couldn't sleep. I think from withdrawal."

"Not possible," Javi stops me. "You're on the highest maintenance dose of morphine."

"Before you came here, how much did you use, a day?"

"About 300 dollars' worth."

Javi scrunches up his eyebrows.

Juan shakes his head, "I think you were paying too much money for your drugs, man. Way too much."

"Probably." I think about it for a second. "But I was using about twenty to thirty bags a day."

Javi's watch ticks, *cah-chic, cah-chic*. The ocean breathes out a long, bored sigh.

Juan counts something on his fingers, "It's good that you came here, man. Just take it seriously, okay? No more games."

He turns to leave but Javi leans back in his chair and stops him with a quick volley of Spanish. I can't tell what they're saying but Juan stops in his tracks and turns to me, jaw dropped. Javi bursts into laughter, "I swear to you, I tell him, ibogaine is NOT like LSD and... *èl dice...es un alivio!*"

Juan grins, shakes his head, "No, man. It should not come as a relief. Believe me. Ibogaine is not like LSD. It demands respect. *Muy serio.*"

Javi looks back down at his papers, "He's right, you know. Ibogaine is not for the faint of heart. The drug is an oneirogenic. Can you comprehend what that means?"

I shake my head no.

"The visions are waking dreams. Think of a computer drive that's been corrupted. That's your brain. Ibogaine functions as a program, defragmenting the hard drive. In the process, it opens different memories, different files, and plays them for you. These are all files that have been compromised by wrong actions. When you act against your conscience, your operating system makes a note. Enough of these notes pile up without some internal maintenance and things eventually go wrong with the system: depression, insomnia, drug addiction."

"If it's a psychological reformatting process, how does the clinic deal with the physical symptoms?" I picture gears and disks whirring around inside of me.

Javi smiles, "I told you, *Jefe*, this is not *Club Med*."

We arrive at the clinic just after eight o'clock in the evening. Juan greets us at the front door, wearing a puffy North Face jacket over his scrubs, and leads us into a spacious room, which feels more like a day spa than a hospital ward. There's a row of potted ferns, a table with freshly prepared cucumber water, and a nondescript grey painting of geometric shapes over the couches. In all the low-lit beige, it's easy to miss the heart monitors, wheelchairs, and the two rows of hospital beds along opposite walls.

We're each to choose our own spots now. Kate, John, and myself gather together on one side, John taking the bed in the corner. "Good for operational awareness," he says, peeling off his work boots. Kate sits cross-legged in the bed next to John's and I take the one on the other side of her.

Duane, the only one of us that's done this before, occupies a lone bed across the way. "Don't want to be all on top of y'all when people start losing their lunch," he says, adjusting the recline on his mattress with the remote. "See, I'm easy with this. Slept right through it last time. No puke. No nightmares."

"Lucky bastard," John grumbles. He takes off his beat-up camouflage cap and places it on top of his boots. He crosses his hands in his lap as if he's settling down in front of the TV after a long day's work.

Juan hands each of us a glass of water and a small paper cup with a capsule in it.

"Just the test dose," he says, "to make sure you're not allergic."

I take my sneakers off, then empty my backpack, placing the book of poetry on the bedside table. The lights in the clinic shut off and Javi clicks a device sitting on the floor in the middle of the room, causing a pink pool of light to gather on the ceiling. A bag of saline hangs from a stand on the left side of each bed, where orderlies run lines to the backs of our hands. I imagine that we're all together on a fishing trip: our beds, simple paddle boats, tied to the dock with IV lines. We float around on the water at sunset. The sky, framed by the woods around us, a pink lake projected on the ceiling.

Juan misses my vein. I flinch.

"It's okay, man," he says, quietly. "Don't be scared."

Juan returns with another glass of water, another paper cup. This one has three capsules.

"Feel anything yet? Hear any insects?"

"No," I say.

"Okay. That's okay, man. This is what's known as the *flood dose*. It will start the session."

The first sign of ibogaine kicking in is supposed to be an aural hallucination, usually something primal: wasps, hornets, crickets. I listen for a swarm but hear only Javi's shoes, squeaking on the other side of the room, and the uneven beeping of our heart monitors. I watch the big clock on the wall. Its minute hand slides silently over to thirty-three minutes past eight.

"Oh shit," Kate says. "Hear that?"

It's been half an hour since the test dose.

I see Javi, Juan, and a doctor huddled around Duane's heart monitor. The doctor is nodding her head. I can see small gold hoop earrings glinting behind the tight brown curls of her hair. Javi looks over at the clock and taps her on the shoulder.

They all approach my bed. The doctor asks, "Do you always watch the clock like this?"

"It's just a nervous habit." My eyes flit to the clock then back to their faces.

Juan shoots a serious look at the doctor who bends down and whispers to me, "We find that it's a good idea not to look at clocks while on ibogaine."

"This is especially true inside of the hallucinations," Javi adds.

"Clocks become," the doctor winks at Javi, "very unreliable. It makes some people upset."

"Don't look at calendars either, man," Juan lowers his voice, nodding gravely, while sticking his fists deep into his jacket pockets.

"Try not to worry about time at all," the doctor says, straightening up and fixing me with a reassuring smile. "It has a different motion on ibogaine."

Seven minutes have passed since the flood dose.

"Anything now, Geoffrey?" Javi asks. "Some sounds maybe? An echo? Or some tracers around the lights when you turn your head?" He's got the doctor with him.

"Nothing yet. Unless you think I just haven't noticed."

A scoff escapes from Javi and the doctor slaps him on the shoulder. They look at each other, shaking their heads and stifling laughter, "We'll give you a little bit more."

"Seems like I've had an awful lot already."

"Ah, this is good, then," the doctor reassures me. "After all, there is danger in having too little. Our emotions form a dense forest inside of us. You need enough of the drug to break through the canopy and rise above. This is called the treetop effect. Believe me, the last thing you want is to get tangled up in feelings." Javi unscrews the lid on a brown glass bottle and shakes another capsule out into her hand.

"Whatever you think."

The doctor hands me one last capsule, "Don't worry, Geoffrey, after this, you will definitely *notice*."

I steal a glance at the clock. Twenty-three minutes since the flood dose.

Something's happening. The doctor clicks her pen. An echo replicates and flies away, out over the treetops. I can hear the distant rush of leaves but there's no wind. Down the street, motorcycles burn out across an intersection and turn away. In the distance, their engines merge with the rustling leaves; a cloud of television static at the edge of the world.

Everything's normal again. My fellow patients lie silently in their beds. I listen to the seconds clicking by, punctuating the steady hum of motorcycle engines. It's so faint that I think, *this must be the sound of memory,* as I lay my head back on the pillow.

It's getting hot. Things drip, *drip, drip,* just beyond the edge of my vision. A single cricket chirps in the distance. Nurses huddle in shadows, whispering to one another in a secret medical language.

Someone says, "They're coming back."

Javi laughs. Juan shakes his head.

I can hear a swarm of insects, advancing. But it's unnatural somehow. The sound is mechanical, ultravivid: thousands of engines rev inside tiny abdomens. Rubber tires screech beneath the buzz of wings. I hear them cresting hills, cutting valleys. Now they turn right. Now they turn left. Now they trace the great curve of the earth.

The sound is so clear, I can taste it. A chrome hive on the swarm, closing the distance, pitching engines up, up, always up, even through the downshifts. I hear them circling from both the right and the left. Suddenly, they're everywhere, gears grinding, engines snarling, radios tuned to static. Burning up road. Passing through walls.

I turn to Kate.

She closes her eyes and whispers, "Oh god."

It's inside. It happens in the sliver of a second: a stick through the skin of a drum. I was expecting rockets launching in my head but this feels effervescent, like bubbles rising in a glass of soda.

Flood dose: **two** words that form a cascade, eradicating every imaginable boundary. Ibogaine rushes through my body, a relentless chemical messenger sent to scour my receptors. When I close my eyes, I see it swimming in my system: a trillion black tadpoles, sightless and single minded. Microscopic teeth chew on nerve endings. So I force my eyes open. I lie back in bed, keep still, stare up at the pink light on the ceiling. The world's ending all around me but I feel utterly compelled to remain calm, act naturally.

I turn to look for the book on the table by the side of my bed and, to my enormous relief, the words on the cover are still legible: *Matthew Dickmann / Brother \ Michael Dickmann*. A mixture of honey and motor oil drips from the ceiling. Great clouds of metallic bees migrate around the room.

An orderly next to my bed says, "Don't look at them," in a raspy voice.

The spine of the book makes a crackling noise when I open it to the first poem.

I clear my throat and begin reading.

Turning my head to the facing page, streaks appear in the corners of my eyes. I look up from the book and more streaks appear, refusing to fade when I blink. They stay in place, as if I've dragged a knife across the painted surface of the clinic, exposing bright white canvas underneath.

I ask the orderly standing next to my bed, "Is that supposed to happen?" But then I realize he's only a straight metal stand used to support my IV bag.

Lights flicker. More paint chips crumble off reality's surface. No telling how much time's left before it all falls away, so I fix my attention to the page and continue reading the first poem. Through the white space in the pages, I can see the twin brothers, writing to illuminate what they lost. But light can burn, even as it brightens. I feel heat sleeping in the walls, small flames holding their breath inside the light fixtures. I shake my head and the page is solid once again. Although the room is breaking down all around me, the text remains legible. My eyes settle on a familiar phrase and I put my hand against the page, touching the words like a talisman: *I wish I could look down past the burning chandelier inside me.*

I, too, know what it's like to close my eyes and see nothing past the blinding fires within. Only I can't imagine how it must feel to hold such a precious, fragile thing within you, glittering and clear. No. When I look down inside myself, I see a different kind of fire.

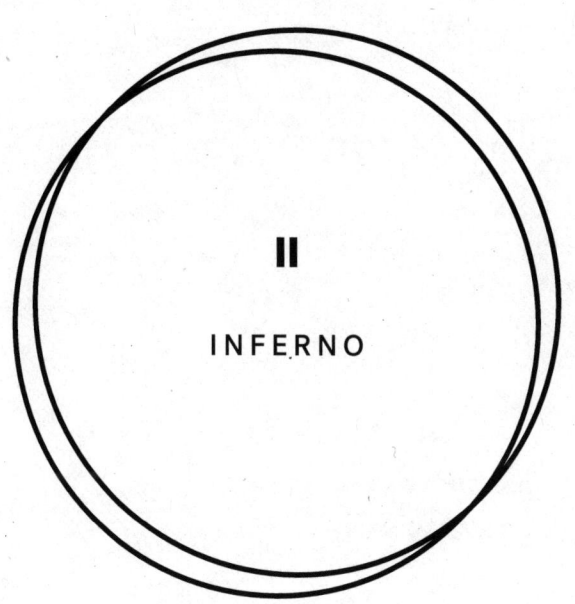

II
INFERNO

I see blood everywhere: rivers of it pouring out my mouth and nose, through my fingers, around the metal screen of the microphone, and down the cable, pooling in thick rusty patches on the hot stage. I see it in a fine pink mist spraying out of my mouth as I'm singing.

I'm thinking, *What song are we even playing? How can I keep singing when there's all this blood?* But the words keep coming, as they've done so many times before.

Only now, every word brings more blood. Blood soaking into the spongy black monitor speakers, which send my voice back up in my face, and blood starting to run in a single rivulet over the edge of the stage, down to the blacktop that's shimmering in the heat of the midsummer sun. And the blood is hissing now on the pavement. And water is hissing out of fire hoses spraying over the crowd. And the security guards have our tour manager surrounded, hissing in his face, "You tell that singer not to come down in the crowd today. If he gets one drop of that blood on us, we'll kill him."

But I can't hear any of it because my head is pounding: not from the loss of blood or the broken nose. My head is pounding with the pulse of the drums, the roar of the guitars, and ten thousand kids screaming my words back at me.

And then it stops.

The world comes rushing back so quickly it makes me nauseous. Suddenly, I can feel the broken nose; I can taste the blood. I look down at my setlist and it's illegible. The stage around me is turning into a giant scab in the 110 degree heat. I blink into the sunlight. "What song are we on?"

It's all so familiar: Tucker waves his sticks in front of my eyes like I'm a plane he's bringing in for a landing. Steve puts his hand on my shoulder and passes me a bottle of water. I take the bottle. "I think I've been here before."

Steve says, "Long Island?"

"No, like, *in this moment*. The show. The blood."

Steve shudders, "Could be a concussion. I tried to tell you to be careful." He stretches his spine and the tendons in his neck rise up against his olive skin. I watch all the little guitar strings tuning up inside of him. He's so tense he almost looks calm. After taking a moment to pat his tightly drawn curls, he drops his hands and resumes carefully wringing the neck of his guitar.

Tom appears over his left shoulder, leaning forward with the loose determination of a puppet whose strings have been cut, "Now that's more like it." He throws an arm over Steve's shoulders. A disposable, threadbare glamor drips from Tom's frame. He's so thin and tall that any tacky garbage looks expensive and alluring on him.

Steve purses his lips and looks down at his guitar, as if there's an exact place where the perfect note lives inside it; all he has to do is pinpoint its precise location and things will be alright. He admits, "Not sure how I feel about this."

Tom shrugs, "It's just a head wound. They bleed. It's what they do." He looks down at his own guitar, a block of marble that he needs to smash himself against until the future falls out.

I look back and forth between the two of them. Perfect opposites. There's something reassuring in the familiarity of it all. But it's not just familiar.

"I've lived this before."

Tom swings his guitar around his back and leans into me, squinting as if I've just spoken a foreign language, "Maybe he *does* need to be more careful."

Suddenly, I'm sitting down on the drum riser and a man in a dark blue uniform is shining a light in my eyes: "How are we feeling? Took a pretty nasty shot to the face with that microphone. Can you tell me your name?"

I press my tongue to my teeth but I can't find the right word.

"This'll go a lot smoother if I have a name, son. Can you tell me who you are?"

Whoever I am, most of me is spilled out on the stage. I keep trying to blink, but the man in the blue uniform is holding my right eye open. I can't see past the little beam of his flashlight but his voice is professional, unhurried.

"Maybe it's time we rethink that, huh? Swinging that microphone way out like that?"

I want to tell him that the microphone sometimes feels like a tiny satellite that I throw deep into space and the cord is the gravitational pull of the earth and when I close my fist, the satellite drops into a perfect little orbit around it. I want to place him there inside my body so he can feel how it feels. But I don't want him to stop the show, so I agree with everything.

He shuffles through a delicate series of motions: tracing the bones of my eye sockets with his thumbs, gently padding at the bridge of my nose with his fingertips.

"Let's take a different tack. Do we know *where* we are?"

"Some hellhole parking lot in hellhole Long Island."

"*Hellhole?*" he says. "So we've never been to Montauk, seen the surf off the cliffs?"

I turn toward the crowd, to the tides of people pushing toward the stage.

"How 'bout this one: Do we remember *what* we're doing here?"

"Headlining a festival," I say. "This is an important day."

"Might want to take up the *headlining* part with the bands who are playing after."

"They're welcome to take it up with me, after a set like the one we're about to have."

The medic chuckles to himself, waves over the rest of my band, "He seems pretty lucid to me. But I'm afraid there may be a more serious underlying condition."

Tom taps his guitar pick against the front of his teeth, "Give it to us straight, doc."

"I'm not a doctor so I wouldn't want to rush a diagnosis. But I'd say he's almost certainly showing signs of being a lead singer. It's a real shame but there's nothing else I can do for him."

Tom's nostrils flare. He takes the guitar pick out of his mouth and places it on his temple, "And that's pretty serious? Medically speaking?"

The medic puts his flashlight in the breast pocket of his shirt and turns to the other members of the band, addressing everyone but Tom, "The bleeding has stopped. We can take a look at the nose later, but if you guys want to finish, I won't get in your way."

Tom and Steve walk back to their amps on opposite sides of the stage. Tim lets his bass strings feed back. The speakers begin to rumble beneath the stage. Tucker leans forward on his drum stool. Already the blood is pulsing. Already the breath is building.

I pick up the microphone and a cheer rises over the crowd, "We're okay if you're okay. Are you okay?" The crowd hisses back at me. The stage thermometer hisses 114 in the corner. The amps hiss radio static, waiting to be brought back to life.

Off mic, I turn to Tucker and ask, "How many songs we got left?"

He adjusts his snare drum, "That was the first one."

I see the road rushing up around me from the horizon, where it runs so flat and straight and long that it makes a mirage of the dry morning light to the windshield, where dotted white lines play tricks on your eyes and every intersection holds the car waiting to jump out and send you to your death.

I see the grass swaying in the breeze as we blast through the middle of Ohio, windows down because the air smells sweet from all the honeysuckle blooming. It makes me miss home, though I leave every chance I get, and, anyway, Tim says it could be jasmine. He taps his feet on the dash, locks into the rhythm of the song on the stereo; a bass player all the way down to the soles of his shoes.

"One of them, you can drink the nectar, the other one is poison," I tell him. "So you have to be sure which flower you've got."

Tim picks at the window's moulding, "Or, then again, for instance, you don't have to drink either, right?" He pulls off a small, black piece of rubber and drops it to the floor before continuing to thump the meaty part of his hand against his chest in time with the song. The motion makes no sound. His frame is as solid as if it had been constructed by a bricklayer.

Tim pops out the Cursive CD and pushes Pinback in and I see myself as a small child, sucking the nectar out of honeysuckle flowers with my parents and cousins in Rhode Island, where I was born. A warm breeze whispers in my ear. Sun shines bright under my eyelids before vanishing behind a bank of clouds.

Now the breeze blows cold through our van's open windows: I'm back on a playground with a little girl—we must've been about five years old—I'm showing her how to suck the nectar out of a flower and I see her putting the flower in her mouth, past some dried grape jelly on her upper lip, and I see an older woman running toward me, waving her arms, *no*.

I roll my window up an inch. Then something hard hits the windshield, fast, and leaves a mark. Tim bolts upright, takes his feet off the dash. The rest of the band, sleeping in back, sit directly up in their seats without stopping to shake off their dreams.

"I was just thinking that you hit someone with the van and you wouldn't stop to help them," Steve murmurs. "Did you do that?"

All I see is empty highway in either direction. No cars or trucks throwing debris. No devastated body twisting on the shoulder. Just heat lines coming off the road, playing tricks on our eyes, making the low horizon look like a cloud of smog or a pool of water. But no overpass, no bridge, no buildings, nothing to account for the object.

"That a bug?" Tim asks, running his fingernail clean along the unsmudged side of the glass. "Left its guts all over the windshield."

I turn my head to look over to the passenger side windshield because there was no way that was a bug. It had weight. It almost shattered our windshield when—*SLAM*—another hits dead in front of me like a softball filled with bright green goo.

And then I see.

No heat lines. No mirage. No patch of smog over rural Ohio. Only black clouds of giant insects. No imaginary pools of water in the dry morning heat. Just a thick black carpet of teeming insects and now we're driving through its center.

We close the windows as fast as we can but there's no escape. They explode against our windshield, smash through the grill, get in our air-conditioning, and start coming through the vents in pieces. After a hundred yards, we've lost all visibility and have to pull over.

Tom wipes at his eyes but it's no use. They're everywhere. Fat black bugs, dripping their hot breath down our necks. A swarm. What a word, *swarm*. So many sticky consonants crammed into a dark, little one-passenger word. I say it to myself just to feel it come out of my mouth, "*Swarm.*"

A pickup pulls over behind us. An older man motions for us to roll down our windows. Tim gets out and, for a second, the van fills with a chorus of jet engines. I hear it in my whole body.

The old man shouts at Tim on the other side of the window but I can't make out what he's saying. All I can think about is that sound. He sets a cloud of bugs into the air, trying to illustrate some point, but all I want is that hungry, restless sound. I lean forward in the driver's seat. Tim opens the door and the sound comes rushing in. He slams it behind him, causing the entire van to shake on its chassis.

"Cicadas," he says, scratching his head. "According to that fine gentleman over there, this is an incredibly rare occurrence—only happens once every seventeen years!"

Tom pushes his knuckles deep into his tear ducts, "This is real."

"No getting around them either. Goes across twenty miles or more. Trick is, go slow, keep your eyes on the road. Eventually, we'll spit out the other side."

Even while Tim is still explaining, I start to roll my window down so I can get closer to that sound. It's glorious. How can something so small make a sound so big? All the windows in the world must be shattering inside them. A noise like that, you could get lost in. If you opened your mouth, it might fill up your lungs. I part my lips, just the length of a breath, and feel the scream pushing past my teeth and over my tongue. I feel it rushing in, scrubbing at my throat, scrubbing at my lungs. And I wonder, how much could a sound really tear away?

I see my bandmates standing on the beach in their dark city clothes, a row of palm trees bending toward the ocean behind them. They're speaking but I can't tell what they're saying. From where I'm standing on the ledge of the hotel roof, everything gets lost in the wind. Tucker pats Steve on the shoulder and now they're all laughing. A red sky over the ocean means nothing if you can't tell dusk from dawn.

From here, the water is shiny black plastic and my band members' faces are empty ellipses. As they catch sight of me on the hotel roof, the ellipses expand, taking in sand, trees, and sky until they contain everything. The world never gathers value, only layers, stacking one desolation inside the next: complimentary airplane bottles of alcohol, pills and rolled-up dollar bills, the ledge of the hotel roof, little paper bags, *Extra Heat, Ice Cold, Str8 Killer.*

"*Do you see what I see? Did you just close your eyes in a hospital bed in Mexico having taken the strongest hallucinogen known to man? Are you far away from home? Does it feel like your last chance? Are you worried that you might see scenes from your own life? Are you wondering how long a night could possibly last? Are you like me?*"

"**Sorry to startle** you," Juan says, softly. "I was just trying to figure out what you were whispering." I open my eyes in the clinic. Juan is standing over me with his puffy winter jacket. He's so close I can see the blood moving through his veins.

"What do you mean?" I ask. "Was I saying something? Out loud?"

"I think you were asking if I *like you*? Or if I *am like you*?" he says. His eyes are missing, so I stare into two long tunnels, set deep in the caves of their sockets. I get vertigo just from looking. I might slip and fall in.

"You heard all that?"

"You seemed to be narrating some sort of biblical story about a river of blood and a plague of insects. I confess, there were some English words that I didn't understand. Are you in a band?" The tunnels in his eyes widen, all his certainty disappearing into them.

"Not anymore." My voice echoes back at me. Might as well be shouting into a well.

"So then, you're noticing the effects now?"

"Well, I'm fucking tripping, aren't I!"

"Excellent, man." He laughs, good naturedly. "One more capsule, just to make sure?"

"Don't give me anymore of that shit. I'm already going out of my mind."

"Going *into* your mind. This is normal. Embrace it. Try closing your eyes now."

"I don't want to fall asleep."

"Fall asleep?" Juan says. "Ibogaine is an oneirogenic: You close your eyes to wake up."

You wake up in Detroit. You wake up in Cincinnati. In Madison. Toledo. You wake up in Twin Falls. You wake up in a dark parking lot outside of Albuquerque. You wake up in Boseman and drive to Missoula. You wake up in El Paso. You watch stray dogs run across an intersection while you look for a place to get coffee. You find a gas station, splash some water on your face.

You wake up in Fresno. In Bakersfield. Sacramento. You wake up in Reno where the neon signs glitter cheaply against the fresh light of a dawning hangover. You find some breakfast in a hotel lobby and shake out a handful of Tylenol. They catch the flicker of the casino lights and dance in your hand.

You wake up on an airstrip in Daytona. You wake up to Federal Marshals. You can explain. You were only looking for a quiet place to park. A war of light and sound as you drive off the tarmac.

You wake up in Mobile. In Memphis. You wake up on the floor of the van, the road roaring up at you. You wake up in Shreveport. In Norman. Wichita. You wake up and Tom's doing ninety, one arm dangling out the window. Steve puts his hands on the dashboard, telling him to slow down, *be careful.*

You wake up to an endless series of highway signs: Salina, Hays, Colby, Aurora. The trailer groaning in slow arcs behind you. You wake up in Denver with a splitting headache. You meet a friend at a diner. He slips a bottle across the table, *OxyContin.* "Cancer's spread," he says, patting the back of your hand. "Can't even digest them anymore."

You wake up on a Saturday morning. You wake up on a Monday. You wake up—it could be Tuesday or Sunday. You stop keeping track. You throw out your calendars and only measure time on maps. Yesterday was Tucson. Tomorrow is Tempe. Time's arrow flies in whichever direction the van's headlights are pointed. You take a Valium and sleep through the Grand Canyon, the Redwood Forest. You sleep across the span of the Hoover Dam.

You wake up hurtling through the endless American midnight. No cellphone, no satellite. Just a twenty-ounce Styrofoam cup of truck stop coffee and a handful of ephedra pills. *Yellow Jackets. White Crosses.* Little black and yellow bullets. Putting them in your mouth feels like loading a gun. You don't care. You're young and healthy and you are never going to die.

You wake up on tour.
You wake up in the driver's seat of the van.
You wake up in Patterson.
You wake up in Conway.
In Texarkana.
In Fort Worth.
Waco.

Round Rock.
You wake up.
You wake up,
you wake up,
you wake up.

"**This depressing music** is gonna get us all killed," Brian, our merch guy, shouts in my ear. "Put on something violent. Get the blood up."

I put on "Full Circle" by Ink & Dagger and crank it. Brian swings his fists, jumping over the middle bench onto Tom and Tucker in back. Tom yelps, throwing his lanky arms up to brace himself. His dinner goes flying against the back window.

"Was that meat you just dumped on me, Tom?" Tucker asks.

"It's a Frito's BBQ Twist, wrapped in a slice of pepperoni and dipped in mayonnaise," Tom says, sadly wiping mayo off the window.

"Disgusting," Tucker says, glaring at him and stiff-arming Brian against the wall.

Tom's shoulders sag over his dinner. "*Five-dollar days.* What do you want?"

"You call this violent?" Brian climbs the seatback. "I want something straight up *ignorant*."

Tom winces. Brian crashes down on him again.

"Glad I'm not a part of that," Tim comments from the seat next to me, slowly pushing a fluorescent orange Cheeto into his mouth.

Brian settles into his seat, uncaps a tube of Chapstick and asks, "Tonight was better, I think?"

"Whole crowd didn't leave during the first song," Tim admits, turning the Cheetos bag upside down to catch the last orange crumbs in his mouth. "It's something."

"How was merch?" I ask.

"It was good. *We'll make it to Kansas City*, as they say," Brian smiles widely, his tousled blonde hair starting to frizz up in the humid summer air.

"Who says that, Brian?"

"No, I'm saying, 'We'll make it to Kansas City,' *as they say*," he repeats, emphatically putting a finger in the air. "It's a euphemism."

I look in the rearview mirror, "A euphemism for what?"

"For going to Kansas City. Obviously," Brian explains, turning his flat palms over like two pieces of blank paper.

"Oh my god. Brian. How much money did we make?" Tucker yells. "Our dicks need to eat!"

"Okay." Brian finally relents. "Who has the keys?"

"Keys for what?"

"For the paddle lock?"

"*PAD-lock*," we all shout.

"Right. Like I said *PADdleLOCK*," Brian looks incredulously at me. He honestly can't pronounce the word. "I need to open the trailer and count the money."

Tim holds his right hand up to the light of the dashboard. His fingertips glow orange with grease and synthetic cheese. He says, "Think we're out of napkins."

"Just streak your orange fingers on the windshield. Leave your cheddary mark as a warning."

"Cheddy Krueger," Tim says, licking the cheese dust off his thumb. "Still figure we're going to make it through the whole year?"

My knuckles go white on the steering wheel, "We made a pact."

Tim turns around in his seat to throw the crumpled Cheetos bag down into the door well.

Steve laughs, "I'm just glad I finished school. You guys are fucked."

"Tom, you're still with me, right?" I look over my shoulder.

"Tallahassee," is all he says back.

Brian holds up an imaginary microphone in front of his mouth, "*Mmmmyello Tallahassee, we're Thursday from New Brunswick, New Jersey...nice to see so many people in the crowd tonight—uh haha, um—for once.*"

"Is that what you think I sound like?"

Tucker says, "I've never seen a room clear so fast."

"*Wait,*" Brian looks around wildly, still holding the invisible microphone, "*where are you all going?*"

Tim leans over the back of his seat, "More people walked out than saw us, the whole tour, combined."

Steve reaches over the bench to stick his finger in Tom's chest, "You're just bent out of shape because you struck out with those girls outside. You tried to give them all copies of our record—for free—and they still didn't take 'em. They didn't want anything from you!"

Tom eyes me in the rearview, Steve's finger still in his chest, "They wanted my last cigarette. That's *something*."

Brian has gone quiet but his face is still darkening from an angry red color to a kind of furious purple. He's really committing to the role and, though he's trying to tell me what a horrible front man I am, I feel a paternal sort of pride for him.

"Don't worry. Every city can't be Tallahassee."

Tim looks at me, "That's inspiring. Should stitch it on a pillow."

"No," Brian gasps back to life and says, almost to himself now, "That wouldn't sell."

Wake up in Hurricane. Wake up in Durango.
Wake up in Mt. Hope. Wake up in Tulsa.
Wake up in Prattville. Wake up in Jenks.
Wake up in Broken Arrow. Wake up in Verdigris.
Wake up in Chapman. Wake up in Dubuque.

Wake up in Ellenboro. Wake up in Menominee.
Wake up in Coleman. Wake up in Amberg.
Wake up in Iron Mountain. Wake up in Silver Cliff.
Wake up in Alpha. Wake up in Mastodon.
Wake up in Crystal Falls. Wake up in Sioux City.
Wake up in Sergeant Bluffs. Wake up in Vermillion.
Wake up in Shiprock. Wake up in Newcomb.
Wake up in Cascade. Wake up in Delhi.
Wake up in Monticello. Wake up in Independence.
Wake up in Strawberry Point. Wake up in Jamestown.
Wake up in Lightfoot. Wake up in Rustic.
Wake up in Great Falls. Wake up in Billings.
Wake up in Oracle. Wake up in Mescal.
Wake up in Vail. Wake up in Red Rock.
Wake up in Maricopa. Wake up in Casa Grande.
Wake up in Carthage. Wake up in Marshall.
Wake up in Scissors. Wake up in McAllen.
Wake up in Pharr. Wake up in Santa Maria.
Wake up in Mission. Wake up—

I keep nodding off. It's hard not to, listening to my band members drop out of the conversation, one by one, as they dip below the waterline of consciousness, settling down into themselves, until they're silent instruments. Alone, I turn the FM dial all the way to the left, where forgotten newsrooms broadcast static. Images of empty offices fill my head. Xerox machines flashing alone in darkened rooms. Televisions glowing test patterns. I turn up the volume and try to focus on the road gently undressing itself in our headlights.

Ahead of us, a cross looms, radiating a profound neon orange aura. I turn off the high beams. Still, the cross keeps shining. When we drive right up to it, the thing is more than nine feet tall and made of reflective material. It's hoisted up on some barricades, detailed with the big black letters *DETOUR* and an arrow pointing to the left. Now, I can see that it's actually an X, barring entry to the road, and not a cross at all. Behind it, there's a concrete pylon. No getting past that.

Below it, a sign says *DANGER*, accompanied by three hands. The first hand is touching a wire—cartoon lightning shooting across the palm—and reads, *Electrical Hazard*. The next hand is being crushed by gears, warning, *Keep Hands Out of Machinery*. The third hand holds an Erlenmeyer flask with a skull and crossbones. *Toxic—Do Not Enter* is written below all three.

Out of the van, everything is still. I pull the parking brake, hit the hazards, and climb up a little on the barricade to see what's ahead, but the night is impenetrable. No little town with its traffic lights blinking at an intersection. No village tavern with candles in the doorway. Not even a single TV shines from a single attic window. Past the edge of the road, America is unspooling: neighborhood after neighborhood of Colonials and Tudors and Victorians, all rolling out in rows of perfectly manicured lawns. But no one's living in any of them. They're houses without dreams. The thought makes me dizzy so I try to steady myself, placing one hand on the metal *DANGER* sign, when a bolt of energy cracks through my body, sparking white in the fillings of my teeth.

I'm in my bed at home with Liza. She's climbing up over my shoulder to kiss me goodnight when a small snap of lightning arcs between her lips and my earlobe, momentarily coloring the sheets with a faint wintergreen light. She's laughing, holding her fingers to the spot on her lip, but my limbs feel like they're covered in wet cement. I can't move. I can barely keep my eyes cracked open. "Sweets," she says, "are you awake?" I try to answer, but the words won't come. I can't breathe. Liza shakes me, "Hey, are you okay?"

The flash passes out through the soles of my feet, down into the earth. A faint buzzing rattles the aluminum sign that reads,

Do Not Enter. Maybe a live wire has coupled with its metal base, deep beneath the concrete. Maybe the sign itself is as dangerous as what lies beyond it.

I get back in the van. Distant lightning briefly appears in the rearview. A storm has been following us since we crossed the Mississippi. I release the parking brake and cut the wheel sharply, turning us down the path of the detour, which narrows abruptly, growing dense with forest. The size of the world continues to shrink until it fits in our headlights. So I push on, following the flicker of the beam where it catches, running from the storm at my back, yet unwilling to face the danger blocking the road ahead of me.

Wake up in Faith. In Red Elm.
La Plant. Gettysburg. Roscoe. Ipswitch.
Minnetonka. St. Cloud. Floodwood.
Esko. Superior. Cable. Rib Lake.
Tomahawk. Antigo. White Pine. Calumet.
Oshkosh. Sun Prairie. New London.
Red Granite. Grand Marsh. Spring Green.
Dodgeville. Highland. Soldiers Grove.
Malta. Sycamore. Lee. Paw Paw.
Meriden. Triumph. Anchor. Normal. Decatur.
Odin. Shields. Muddy. Future City. Cairo.
Dublin. Mounds. Pinhook. Dresden.
Milan. Paris. Friendship. Osceola.
Walnut. Coffeeville. Pope. Sledge. Money.
Macon. Meridien. Stonewall.
Laurel. Collins. Stateline. Citronelle. Crossroads.
New Roads. Natchez. Waterproof. Tallulah.
Epps. Transylvania. Pine Bluff.
Star City. Conway. Kingston. Ozark.
Forum. Stella. Golden City. America City.

White City. Lost Springs. Agenda.
Concordia. Red Cloud. Blue Hill. Overton.
Arcadia. Sparks. Rosebud. Flasher.
Antelope. South Heart. Killdeer. Dodge. Colgate.
Fortuna. Portal. Miles Crossing. Sleeping Buffalo.
Content. Dryer Place. Living Springs.
Big Timber. Sugar City. Blue Dome.
Atomic City. Contact. Carlin. Shanty Town.
Angle City. Mercury. Paradise. Palo Verde.
Imperial. El Centro. Calexico. Dateland.
Why. Coal Point. Rock Valley.
St. James. Thorp. Racine. Coldwater. Salem.
You wake up. You wake up. You wake up. You wake up. Wake up. WAKE UP.

My eyes snap open. The hospital bed lurches. I swing my hand out, reaching for the little plastic bucket on the nightstand. I hate throwing up. Always have. So I fight it. I push the nausea down, trying to focus on the ceiling, on that projected pool of pink light above.

Ataxia is one of ibogaine's most unpleasant side effects. It turns every movement into a rollercoaster loop. Nausea takes over. Can't hold it anymore. I retch into the basket. Thank god my stomach's empty. Nothing comes up but I start coughing, uncontrollably kicking out a small cloud of dust. One of the capsules must not have gotten swallowed all the way. It burns. I spit into the basket, trying to rid myself of the chemical taste. No use. My cough jumps to Kate and now everybody's getting sick.

"Drink some more water," the doctor instructs me, handing over a bottle. The tight curls of her hair bounce as she nods sympathetically.

"Doesn't make any sense," Duane shouts at her between heaves. "I didn't throw up at all the first time."

"It is often much stronger the second time," she replies.

"Oh, great," Duane groans. "Now you tell me."

"You're throwing up demons," she says. "Keep them coming."

Duane looks up at her, wide-eyed, "That a medical diagnosis?"

The doctor smiles at me. "He's okay," she winks. "Everybody throws up on ibogaine. I know I did. But it's nothing to worry about."

"You took ibogaine?"

"We all have to take it before working here so that we know how serious it is and how much care people need when they're taking it." She lifts a cup of orange juice to my mouth, lightly guiding the straw to my lips. I take a pull, gazing up at her.

"It's a long night," she says, adjusting my IV line, "and you have a long way to go, so much to see, so much to learn about yourself."

"There are things down there that I don't want to relive."

"Try to separate yourself. Even by a moment. Say to yourself, *I am the Observer.* Do your breathing exercises. Don't relive. Try to remember. Go in order. This will help you to go deep without getting lost. The more anxious you are, the more the medicine will try to pull you into the moment, to make you believe it is all really happening. When all else fails, try to remind yourself that you can always come back into the clinic and I'll be here." The doctor points up to the pink circle on the ceiling, "All you have to do is follow the light."

"**Been a long** night already, kid. I see that you're tired. Having some doubts. But I know you can do this." The words fade in my headphones. It's a woman's voice. Familiar. I can hear the talkback mic disconnect. It's cold in the vocal booth. I'm all alone.

"Where's the rest of my band?"

The familiar voice tells me, "They're not coming."

The only light in the room comes through two panes of double-reinforced, soundproof glass from the control booth. I pick up the notebook in front of me and trace the words scribbled at the top of the page.

"Did I do something wrong? Is that why they're not here?"

A woman's head pops up in the control booth. I watch through the window as she pushes her curly brown hair back and tucks it behind her ears, revealing a pair of small gold hoop earrings.

"Drink some more water. Even I can't help you if you're not properly hydrated." She nods at me sympathetically as she picks up her own bottle to take a sip. "Do your breathing exercises. Go in order. The more anxious you are, the harder it is to sing."

"Wait," I stop her, "you just told me all this. You're my doctor, right? From the clinic."

The woman squints at me, speaking slowly, "This. Is. A. Recording studio. We're trying to finish a record. They called me in because I'm the *Pitch Doctor*, on account of helping singers find the right pitch. I'm sorry if you were under the impression that I was an actual physician."

She lights a cigarette and exhales a thick cloud into the small control booth. The talkback mic is off but I can hear her sigh through the wall, *Christ*, as she picks a loose piece of tobacco off her tongue with long acrylic nails. Maybe she's not the doctor from Mexico after all. In fact, she doesn't seem like a medical professional of any stripe. I watch her turn a page in her notebook.

The woman's voice crackles back into my studio headphones, "Let me ask you something, you see this line? *I don't want to feel this way forever.* You see that one in your notebook?"

"Yeah?"

"You keep getting stuck on that high note. Can't seem to send your voice up over it."

"I know. It's super high."

I watch her through the control booth window. She tugs on her left earlobe, causing the small gold hoop to glint.

"Not that high," she says. "I mean, I've heard you sing that high plenty of times."

I tap my pen against the page of my notebook, which holds all of the room's faint light. The movement sends soft ripples across its glowing surface.

"I think it's the lyrics that are beating you: *I don't want to feel this way forever...* That line's getting you all choked up."

My handwriting ruins the page, ink blots spreading out over the delicate paper.

"The way I see it, this song's about avoidance. Denial. You're running from something."

It must be a trick of the light but it actually looks as if the ink is moving. I watch the words slither around the page.

"What I'm saying is your voice breaks every time in the same spot. You think it's because you can't sing. I think it's possible that—just maybe—it's a psychological issue."

"Great."

"No, it *is*—it's great," she shakes her head up and down at me through the glass. Her hair comes loose. I can see the tight curls bouncing. I look down. My notebook turns blurry on the music stand, my throat filling with salt water.

"That's a strength. It really is. All these songs are full of so much pain. *That's* your gift. You need to accept that."

I blow air out through my cheeks. The microphone makes it a storm. "Some gift."

"Listen. Your band is made up of way better musicians than you. We can agree on that. But people buy your albums because they relate to *your* pain. It's so raw, when you actually let yourself feel it. Your pain practically glows. Get close to the source of it. If you can do that, this record will work. Trust me. I'll make you a classic record, I *guaran-fucking-tee* it."

The light from the control room window goes kaleidoscopic in my eyes.

I whisper, "*I am the Observer.*"

"You're telling me, kid," she replies softly.

Watercolors run down the surface of the window. I dab at my eyes with the sleeve of my shirt. Things become crisp again.

"Pain is gasoline. Channel it. Use it as fuel or it'll burn up inside you. Trust me. No matter how fast you run, you'll never escape it."

She rewinds the tape and plays it again. Again, I choke. She hits stop. There's a scratchy feeling in the back of my throat.

"Alright," she relents, "take the cans off and get in here. Let me show you."

I shrug the headphones off and head into the control room.

"Look here," she leans over the monitor screen. "Any other singer on the planet, I'd get them close to pitch and just tune the shit out of that note." She places her hand on the screen, tapping the glass with her pink acrylic nails, which are almost the same shade as her sweatshirt. "Here's what a technically perfect singer looks like—in this case, I mean me," she says, straightening up to face me. "See how the notes sit right on the lines for the correct pitch? Smooth." The bedazzled letters on her pink sweatshirt catch the light, sparkling: Q-U-E-E-N-

"Queen Bitch?" I gasp. "Is it really you? I knew you weren't dead."

"It's *QUEEN PITCH*, thank you," she corrects me, pointing to the P with her long pink nail. "I'm the *Pitch Doctor*, as I keep telling you."

"So, you're not strung out? Your last name isn't Thompson?"

"I'm Italian, you couldn't pronounce my last name," she looks up at me and ashes her cigarette on the carpet. "Now, take a look at…this."

The screen pulses. It feels like something is scraping out my throat.

"This, here, is what the computer sees when you scream into that microphone. A hand grenade inside a musical note. Nothing can put that back together."

Fragmented notes overrun the grid. She hits the button to correct the pitch and the program stutters and glitches, bending the fragments inward. We watch them twist and turn in fractal patterns. A few pixels seem to drop from the monitor's screen.

"To the program, it's toxic."

I can see the notes trying to lift off the monitor and take flight, animated by tiny sentient furies. Something's moving around in my throat: a handful of steel wool, trying to scrape its way out.

"It's swarming the program. A plague of locusts. Or a swarm of what do you call it?"

"Cicadas," I say softly.

"Trapped inside, trying to get out."

I steady myself against the door jamb.

"So forget about the pitch. Dig deep, let yourself feel," she balls her fist and pushes it into my stomach. "Open your mouth and let it rip. Just scream it out."

Everything slants off axis. My chest sags against the door, heavy with the weight of so many insects. "I think I need a minute."

"You're not gonna go hang yourself in my bathroom, right? That would seriously ruin my day."

The sun never rises in Jersey City. Not in the studio anyway. I stagger out into the hallway, but the first floor doesn't have any windows. It floats in a kind of perpetual midnight. Coffee is always brewing. Someone's always lying to someone on the phone at the front desk, cigarette smoke in a fog over everything.

In the bathroom, my toiletry kit hides under the sink. There's a half-smoked Marlboro Red drowning in the toilet. Someone has written *REMEMBER* in soap on the mirror. It drips down the cold surface of the glass and collects on the countertop, forming the words *GO DEEPER* in a pool by the paper towels.

From the kit, a bottle of liquid codeine burns with the intensity of a miniature red light district. I take two shots, then two more just to maintain symmetry. My head fills with calculations. Milligrams and titration. Grapefruit juice and potentiation. Every papery grain on the bottle's label comes separately into focus. Each italicized letter arches and turns, making bridges and buildings rise from the label's white ground: *Take 1 teaspoon every 4–6 hours as needed. For the relief of pain. No refills.*

There. It starts at the base of my spine and moves up through the center of my body: that feeling of convergence, storms gathering, clouds descending on the city, turning and turning in tightening spirals. I can almost hear the sound: that *crack of doom from a hydrogen jukebox.* I can see the strings on a black guitar. The inside of a dorm room.

I remember.

Tom breaks the charcoal, leans over, and blows the remnants from the paper. He stops—*shit*—and peers down into the face of the figure he's been shading. I've seen that face around campus; I recognize the features.

"That's Tucker," I say, watching his expression take shape on the paper, a small cloud of detail emerging. The portrait is as clear as a photograph. But it's a photograph that could never possibly be taken, catching the subject in a moment of ecstasy, shadows all around, threatening to reach up and drag him down.

"I want to do the same thing with music."

"Fuck up its eyes?" Tom frowns, pushing a nub of charcoal across the figure's jawline.

"No." It sounds so stupid, even in my head. "I want to find a way to escape every kind of pain. Forever."

Tom never takes his eyes off the paper. His features flutter through a series of thoughtful, twitchy movements. He rubs a drop of sweat from under his eye. It leaves a black streak on his cheekbone.

"We've already started," he tells me, smudging the edge of the paper with his thumb. "Me and Tucker. And now, you too."

I cough; the memory breaks up. I'm in the bathroom again. I should go back, keep working. But I don't want to be here anymore, in this empty studio, standing over a rancid toilet. I don't want to have to keep failing, alone in that cold, dark room. I don't want to find the source of my pain. I want to be back with Tom, finding a way to escape it. I want to hear those songs again. Even if they're only echoes. Even if I have to keep replaying them on a worn-out record in my head.

I grab the codeine and take another shot. The feeling of convergence starts again. The room turns in spirals around me. I hold on to the rim of the sink and close my eyes.

Tucker answers the door. Tom nods in my direction, "This is our singer." Tucker pushes the screen door out with his shoulder and squints, "Nice to meet you, *Singer*. Want anything to drink?"

I take a can of soda and hold it against my ears to try and cool my sudden excitement. Tom called me a singer. I try to picture it. Lights flashing. Microphone in my hand. I take a sip and let the carbonation fizzle in my mouth.

Tucker leads us upstairs.

In a small attic room, the two of them begin warming up. Tucker's mood lightens the faster they play. When he put his sticks down and swivels the seat of his drum stool, changing its height, Tom flexes his recently broken wrist.

"This is what we're working on now. It seems like the start of something."

They look at each other and take a breath.

And then it's over. I haven't heard a thing.

So I make them play it again. And again. A sudden explosion of color and movement. The chords are rich and orchestral but the texture is ragged, as if the song has been torn from an ornate tapestry and set ablaze in protest, the burning flag of some beautiful, forgotten country.

They turn to me, expectantly. I look Tom in the eyes. Then Tucker.

I tell them, "We are going to be fucking awesome."

And they laugh at me, but I know it's true.

The bottle of codeine falls off the sink. Picking it up, I notice a yellow warning sticker: *DANGER: Toxic*, with a hand holding an Erlenmeyer flask. The bathroom feels warm and damp and used.

"Is there someone else in here?"

The mirror fogs up. Words appear in finger-smudged streaks: *FOLLOW THE LIGHT*.

The bulb above my head sputters and pops, taking the last of the room's visibility with it. "Hello?" I run my hand along the surface of the door but can't find a knob.

I am the Observer, I whisper to myself. *I am the Observer.*

The mouth of the bottle flickers dimly. I hold it right up to my eye and cup my hands around the opening. Inside there's an entire universe of light. I tip it back and swallow the whole thing.

Back in Tom's dorm room, I try to stall. "I think I may be tone-deaf."

He claps a hand down on my shoulder, "Well, I guess it's time to figure something out then. Because you're in and there's no getting out. You're one of us now." Out of a sock drawer he pulls a prescription bottle, tall and thick as a beer can. He opens the cap. Inside there are dozens of flat, luminescent discs with little plus signs on one side.

"Percocet," he says, flexing his bad wrist. He shakes a few out in my palm and turns back to the small TV to look for a VHS tape. *Akira* finds its way into the VCR. I swallow the pills and yell, "Tetsuooooooo!"

We turn the volume down and sit on the couch with his guitar. As the Percocets come on, the song opens itself to me. All the notes in the guitar chords separate in the air between us: the suspended 7th shimmering between the root note and its octave, a combination of parallel lights. Tom starts humming a little spring breeze melody and pink petals rain down on an endless green lawn.

I exhale dreamily, *I am the Observer.*

Tom leans forward and shakes me, "Enough of that shit. Be here with me."

The moment has its own mass, its own gravity. We're falling together, but we're still falling. There's no parachute to pull, no stopping. I've always been the Observer, even inside the walls of my own life. Other people make decisions while I stand back and watch the consequences rearrange the furniture. But here is a chance to align my will with the path that's been chosen for me. I try to let go absolutely, adding the force of my desire to the gravity of the moment. I'm in the band. *I am the Singer.* I stand up and stretch my arms toward the ceiling, releasing all the pressure from my spine. Acceptance can feel like freedom if you're desperate enough to believe. And that's how I feel. Desperate and free. My fingers reach upward so sincerely that I grow half an inch. Still, fear never really leaves, it only changes color. I can't shake the notion that Tom has chosen the wrong person to be in the band—a singer who can't sing at all. I push the thought down, out of sight, somewhere the Observer won't find it.

We spend the rest of the night together, playing the song over and over, trying to nail down the structure, the rhythm, the melody. Then we play it again, just to play it.

But something happens on the screen. Tetsuo's expression changes. His face fills with the horror of the new. I understand. Life will come, but not in the way we imagined it. Everything becomes possible after it happens, not before. We're not the type of people who make friends easily or start bands. We're not the type of people to critique art or stay up all night watching Japanese anime, high on painkillers. Until one day, we do, and then, suddenly, we are.

On the screen, Tetsuo is finally understanding that he's the type of person that abuses Akira's abilities and, as a result, turns into a disgusting monster. His desire for power was boundless when he was small and weak, and so, Akira grants him that power, boundlessly. We watch it obliterate the boundaries of his body, stretching his anatomy until the flesh fills a stadium, overruns a city. It's beyond any belief or understanding, as all new things are.

When I was small, I wanted Akira's power too. But there's a power in ordinary things—it's called meaning and, together, Tom and I have found it. I can feel all that meaning and the painkillers making me confident and new.

A fire alarm rings and we leave Tom's small glowing dorm room, but we take the light with us. As we wander through the faceless crowd in the quad, we carry it like a secret or a superpower—a small seed, a sign of things to come.

I step out of the bathroom, blazing into the hallway. I'm cinematic, photogenic, ready for my close-up. That moment in Tom's room had always been leading to this one. When I enter the vocal booth, Pitch Doctor dims the overheads but the room stays lit. I watch her lean into the glass, unable to see past the glare of the window. She engages the talkback mic and asks, "Are you okay in there, kid? You look a little strange. Want me to call your manager? See if he can get some of your bandmates down here?"

"Roll the tape. I can do it without them."

"That's the spirit. Higher than heaven and twice as bright."

She presses play on the Studer 24-track. Reels turn, gaining speed as magnets press into audio tape. I take a breath and the sound gathers itself, rushing away from my fingertips, draining from my legs, and converging in my chest. I can feel it concentrating into a ball of compressed luminescence, growing stronger and smaller as it moves up my throat. By the time it reaches my vocal cords, it's no bigger than an atom.

"Alright," she says, "here it comes."

I open my mouth to sing and the atom splits. A white flash hits the audio tape, spilling out of the studio, filling the world with a brief, bold thought, and annihilating everything in its path. For me, that flash contains all my possible selves, all my possible endings, beyond which life is as fundamentally unknowable as death. I decide I'll live forever in that glow, in that moment where nothing can hurt me. I am the sun. I am a star.

The light moves slowly at first, as a wave of heat and music, expanding out from the studio at the speed of our van's headlights, crawling down Kennedy Boulevard. My consciousness burns. The Observer is looking out the window but, in here, the sound gathers momentum. My thoughts accelerate with nothing to stop them. I slip my hand into Tom's backpack and grab the last of his painkillers. The band drives on, unaware, moving along the highway to the beat of sodium lamps coming on, one after the next. I can feel the life force pushing through power lines. New eyes keep opening, synapses flashing between them until the entire interstate sparkles under silver strands of electric tinsel.

Swallowing a Percocet in the back of the van, I watch the light circle the clover leaf where Route 4 meets 17. Our record, now finished, blasts from the van's stereo. My thoughts race ahead at the speed of production—passing incandescent through couriers' hands, through security, through customs. Moving through the cabin of the 747, along photoluminescent strips that line the aisles, and into the cockpit where they smolder, reddening the pilots' faces before takeoff.

We pass Newark Airport. Chewing down a handful of 222's, I keep my eyes on my bandmates. The Observer becomes distracted and follows a plane taxiing down the runway. Jets fire. Then, up into the air, a signal flare is shot into the sky. Our van races along below as it burns out over the Atlantic. By now, the record must be headed to the deeper parts of Europe for duplication. Mass production. The sound comes on fluorescent. In rows and banks. In the sparks of heavy machinery. In small, dense lasers.

Dissolving the time-release coating on some OxyContin in a bottle of orange juice, I wait. Compact discs are packed, wrapped and barcoded, covered in marketing stickers, and shipped out to twinkle from the racks of suburban strip malls. I check on the little red pills floating in my orange juice.

Dissolve, I whisper. *Just dissolve*. Suddenly, my face appears on every television set in America. We watch it glowing through a repair shop window in Union City. The owner comes out and shouts, "Hey, is that you on the TV?" But I'm not sure if it is. I'm having trouble remembering who's the Observer and who's the little red disc floating in orange juice. My bandmates laugh and laugh and laugh. It sounds like, *dissolve, dissolve, dissolve*.

My thoughts are moving faster now, spreading out ahead of me on a current of heat and light and music. It can't be contained. But the band keeps something hidden, a secret. They travel in a pack around me, park the van in Hoboken, and take me underground to the PATH train, where they hold me by the shoulders. They tell me it's going to be okay. I just need some rest. We're leaving our old van behind and getting on a nice plush tour bus. We'll each have our own beds. On the train, we move through the bedrock under the Hudson River. Darkness below 9th Street. Below 14th.

At 23rd, I drink some orange juice, knowing the Oxys have dissolved and the opiates are finally free from their time-release coatings. The train doors open and I begin to rise. Up from the platform, up the stairs, to the street. Up 6th Avenue to the building where we rehearse. Past the brand-new tour bus, waiting for us at the curb. And up again. Up the stairs to Ultrasound Studios where I crush a Roxanol with the heavy base of a whiskey tumbler. Here it comes, again, the heat, the light, the music, trickling down the hallway, through the double doors into studio B, flipping power switches on, flooding mixing boards. Graphic equalizers, maxed out with a spasm—green, yellow, red—now back to black at rest. Heat, light, music, meaning—all of it gathering with the mist inside amplifiers. Glinting from guitar jacks. Sparking when they're plugged in. Waiting to explode at the moment we first hit.

We're back in five.

"Alright, you look great. Now try not to sweat off all this foundation."

"It's the lights," I squint up at the makeup person. "Too bright. I can't take it."

He says, "That's live TV for you."

"Do you have a Valium or something to take the edge off?"

"A Valium? Are you for real? This is late night national television, not white wine spritzers with your auntie in the Hamptons.

Stop squinting and get back to the stage. Conan will intro you as soon as we get back from break."

"These lights are killing me. Can't see a thing. Where's the rest of my band?"

"Already out there. And don't worry about not being able to see anything. Remember, what's important is everyone seeing you."

I cup a hand over my eyes, blocking the lights. Where's Liza? This is such an important moment, she should be here. But we haven't even met yet. For a second, I think I see her in the audience but the PAR Cans fire up and I lose her again. Time feels all out of order. Conan is standing at his desk with a copy of our new record, *War All the Time*, tucked under his arm. He's reading a cue card for the next segment. His lips are moving but I can't hear what he's saying.

I check my pockets for something to get me through. But there's nothing: no Oxy, no morphine sulphate, not even a Valium or Xanax to smooth things out. I whisper to myself, *I am the O—*, but I can't finish the phrase.

"*I am the O...*"

"What's that, sugar?"

"I can't remember what I am. It starts with an *O*."

"Oblivious," the makeup artist suggests. "Objectionable."

A camera operator pushes equipment toward our backline to frame up a shot of the drum set. "Scoot," the makeup artist says, snapping a towel. My band members huddle around Tom's amplifier. I hurry over, but they're so wrapped up in what they're doing that they don't even notice me.

On top of his amp, Tom has a sketchbook open. He's putting the finishing touches on a drawing of the TV studio. On one side of the page, Conan lurks over the desk, a caricature of himself with exaggerated cheekbones and a pompadour. He's pointing to the band. A speech bubble says, "Who the fuck booked these guys?" On our side of the page, Tom has us all lined up at our stations: Tucker, standing on a stack of dictionaries, trying to see over the top of his drum set; Steve, glaring at Tom with murderous intensity; Tom's self-portrait is oblivious, staring into space with two crooked eyes; and Tim, somehow, looks just exactly how Tim looks in real life: solid, reasonable.

In the center of it all, Tom sketches a figure with a microphone. A military uniform takes shape, complete with suspenders and an armband. Tom draws a hard part in the figure's hair and a furious expression on his face. With his free hand, the figure is performing a Nazi salute. A speech bubble says, "Schnell! Schnell!" over the character's head as he urges the band to play "*Faster! Faster!*" in German. Tom adds a gap between the figure's two front teeth. Somehow he found all the fear that I pushed down inside me when we started the band and sketched it out in sharp detail. *I am the Object*, I whisper to myself. *I am the Opening*. Tom erases the speech bubble and pencils in, "*I am the Oberführer*." My band members huddle around him, giggling.

"Thirty seconds," booms the speaker at our feet and everyone pulls themselves together. We take our positions. The producer counts us in. Quartz lamps flare. It gets incredibly bright.

Conan introduces us over the swell of the audience, "... Thursday, who debuted in the Billboard Top 10 with their new album, *War All the Time*..."

My eyes are open but I can't see. The world is a flat, white field and I'm all alone. From somewhere far away, I hear Tucker counting off the intro. Tom steps on his tuning pedal, unmutes his guitar, and starts strumming in time with Tucker's hi-hat. Steve swells his volume. Tim drops a single bass note into the pattern. Conan smirks and snaps his fingers to the beat.

Everything slows and comes to a stop. The light stutters from a strobe and streaks back into its fixture. I watch the fire jump off the stage and burn through the gels on its way back inside the parabolic lamps. The red *EXIT* sign over the stage door turns itself into an entrance.

And I feel it happening inside me too. It's as if someone hit a switch and my polarity flipped. The microphone still works but I can't understand the words coming out of my mouth. A teleprompter near the foot of the stage scrolls through a monologue:

Star death occurs when the core runs out of helium, which it needs for fuel, and starts to form heavier elements like neon and magnesium. The magnitude of gravity upon the dying star increases in such a way that the outer layers crush in on the core until its entire radius scrunches down from something the size of the earth to a little rock barely as big as Manhattan. Then it heats up billions of degrees until it explodes—

The collapsing place inside my chest is pulling everything back toward itself. It wants more, more, always more. I can't stop thinking about the pills sitting in my bunk, calling to me from all the way out on the tour bus. I can picture them in their bottle, a twinkling pocket galaxy. The band keeps playing. The studio audience keeps clapping. Everything has changed. Only no one has noticed. It might be a billion years before anyone could even see the difference.

When we finish our song, the house lights come up so that we can get a look at the audience. A massive glass chandelier hangs over their heads. Its light comes down in branches, where crystals burn against a red, velvet sky. A cannon goes off, soaking the air with color. As the confetti clears, cue cards and camera men disappear, replaced with gold balustrades, Tiffany glass, red marble colonnades. I'm standing on the stage of an old theater: The Los Angeles Wiltern or the Detroit Fox. I have no idea how I got here. In the balcony, people fill the aisles, pushing past one another, until their bodies flood the staircase, spilling over the railing and falling silently to the dance floor. A sea of outstretched hands reaches for the lip of the stage, grabbing and grasping. I don't recognize one person in the entire place, only a crowd, singular and predatory, like a giant open mouth. Applause roars at us from beyond the barricade and the sound is devouring.

Unable to get that sound out of my head, I slink back to the bus, get in my bunk, and put on my headphones. But that gnawing, devouring sound is still there. It actually seems louder now, like maybe it's coming from inside my head or someplace deeper. Maybe another mouth, with sharp black teeth, has opened somewhere down in my stomach and begun chewing all of me, starting with my attention.

I shake a Xanax out from a bottle of assorted pills and hold it in my palm where it catches all the light, concentrating it. I swallow the pill dry. It moves down along my digestive tract until it reaches my stomach, where it's swallowed again.

I put another pill in my mouth. And another.

And another.

But I picture it like this, I'm firing neutrons through the long subterranean track of the particle accelerator under Switzerland. Just to see what will happen. Will the universe suddenly reveal its scaffolding to me here beneath the blankets? Will reality be altered in some inexplicable, permanent way? My chemist father told me that one of the top physicists in the world sent a good luck note to the team at CERN the day that they fired up the Large Hadron Collider. It had one line: *Don't feed the black holes.*

Nevertheless, they continued, though there was a not-insignificant chance that they were gambling away existence itself. At the time, I thought they were crazy. But now, I understand. Who doesn't want to feel how it feels when matter and antimatter meet in the vacuum of space?

Who doesn't seek oblivion?

Eyelids flutter open, then closed. Blues and greens and blacks strobe past. My head throbs, stuck between worlds. Road sounds float in through the vents in my bunk. I roll over and look up at the blinking, red LCD light on the alarm clock above my bed. Our bus continues to glide through the night but all interior power must have gone out, possibly from a short in the generator. The rest of my band is sleeping, but it feels personal, as if they've abandoned me after *Conan*.

The little red light on the alarm clock blinks *ON*, blinks *OFF*. *ON*, *OFF*.

ON.

I reach out my hand to touch it, but the perspective is wrong. My arm is fully extended, still the dot is beyond my grasp. The darkness of my bunk is infinite, unbounded. Time stands still. I can't sense the texture of my sheets, the cushion of the mattress beneath me. The red dot is all there is. What if, rather than near and small, it's actually enormous and very far away? It would have to be massive, planetary, a dead star, a red giant.

I grab for the distant red dot and, through the vacuum of space, I feel myself floating toward it. It gets closer. Brighter. I see my fingers reaching for the center.

I lean forward.

I'm rising.

My hand gets caught. Two worlds are blinking back and forth: red dot on the alarm clock, pink light on the ceiling. Javi leans into my field of vision, puts a hand on my chest.

He's saying, "No."

Pink rings of light blaze on the ceiling above us, a projection.

He's saying, "Stay in the bed now, Jefe."

He's holding a needle. Blood's running down my arm from the back of my hand.

He's saying, "You pulled out your IV."

Pink light on the ceiling. Blood on my hands.

My body lifting from the bed.

Javi places one firm hand against my collarbone and presses down until my shoulder touches the mattress, "Calm down, close your eyes."

I'm falling. The black is fast and endless on all sides. I can feel darkness coiling around me, and in the center, my bed dropping straight through the fabric of the world, down through the elevator shaft of night, down, down through the dream, but I can't catch hold of a breath, have no relative sense of the direction I'm falling in.

Then—*slap*—I land in a pile of sheets on the mattress. The mattress lands in the center of the bunk. The bunk lands on the floor of the tour bus. Two other bunks land above me in a stack. Our bus lands on the highway and keeps moving, driving on. My alarm clock lands on the stand above my head and goes blank. Everything settles.

I open the curtain and step out into the corridor. All the bunks are dark. Our crew is asleep. But cutting through the quiet are distinct, repetitive inhalations—each one the length of a powdery white line. Credit cards tap against hand mirrors. Cans of Coors split open in silvery sighs.

While half the bus dreams of distant undiscovered cities, beautiful impossible mathematics, or the shape of their own bed, there's a half that stays closed up in their closets of sleep, though they haven't slept in days. They're the half that cuts cocaine into little lines and watches it glint and gleam like fresh snowfall in the endless black morning of their own private winter. The half that bites their nails and taps their toes, nodding to themselves repeatedly with the perfect assurance that their secrets are safe.

"Do you have any idea what time it is?" I whisper.

An arm shoots out into the aisle above me, dangling an eight ball of coke.

"Get some rest, Tucker. Big show tonight."

I can hear him grinding his teeth.

"Big show every night." He opens the curtain, slips out of his bunk, and blocks my way, shuffling his fingers anxiously.

"No," I start backing away. "I'm too tired."

Each muscle in his jaw strains. All the blood in his body rushes to his face. He presses his forehead against my chest and takes a step forward. I let him back me down the aisle, several paces, before jumping into my bunk and closing the curtain.

"Hold on," Tucker cries, slipping under the curtain with me. Face sagging slightly, he loosens his jaw. His eyes are sore and tired. His voice fills with passion, "I just wanted to tell you that I love you, Big Man."

I pull the comforter tight under my chin.

He wipes his nose, sniffles into his fist, "We don't say it enough."

"Tucker, I can't do this right now. You're high and I'm…" I look down at the empty pill bottle on my mattress. "I'm in no state to deal with anything."

"We're brothers," he pleads with me. "Don't you remember what that means?"

"It means I can tell when you're fucked past the point of conversation."

"What about you? You've got a bag of Skittles in your bed. What are you, five years old?"

Tucker reaches his hand across my chest. "Wait—" I tell him. But he grabs the bag and it rips. Both of us freeze. Skittles go everywhere. Tucker looks at the ripped bag in his hand. He frowns, seeing an engineering problem that he can't quite solve. I twist open the empty pill bottle and start gathering up loose Skittles, one by one.

Tucker picks a red one off my pillow and tosses it in his mouth, "What happened out there? You were terrible. Don't tell me you let Tom's stupid drawing get to you."

"It wasn't that."

"You don't even look like Hitler."

I'm the Obsessive, I whisper, collecting stray Skittles. *I am the Absurder.* "It wasn't the caricature. It was that long strange passage on the teleprompter—about black holes and star death. Did you see that?"

"I saw it." Tucker stops chewing. "Looked like one of those letters your dad's always sending you."

"Exactly. My dad and those random notes. So totally disconnected from real life."

Tucker watches my mouth moving, "Is that what you think?"

"It's like having a subscription to *Scientific American* instead of a father."

Tucker spits a clump of Skittle into his palm, "Except they're all just personal notes, written in code. Please tell me you know that and you're just fucking with me."

"Wait," I pause to watch the candy dyeing Tucker's palm red, "what?"

"Like, for instance, when MTV started playing us and the band blew up, he sent you a note about the Big Bang. And before we went in to start recording *War All the Time*, he sent the one about rockets and the conservation of linear momentum. The Big Bang? Momentum? Hello."

"Okay, sure, those two."

"But lately you must've noticed that the tone has changed. Now his notes are all about dark energy and the eventual heat death of the universe." Tucker shuffles his fingers. The red clump glistens in his palm. "He's obviously worried about you. Only natural. We haven't been home much in the last few years."

I put a purple Skittle in my mouth but there's something wrong with it, so I spit it into Tucker's hand. He licks his lips, watching the colors mix together, "The rainbow tastes like shit, right?"

"Okay. Let's just say you're right and my dad snuck into the control room to send me that message through the teleprompter. He mentions the collapse of a star and the formation of a singularity. What's that all about then?"

Tucker looks down at the mattress. His voice cracks, "You selfish piece of shit." He opens the curtain and throws the sticky red candy against the door to the front lounge. "You're thinking about going solar."

"Going *solar*?"

"Without us."

Our driver stomps on the gas pedal. A great accumulation of speed presses my head back against the pillow. So I upend the pill bottle, dumping the rest of the Skittles into my mouth. I swallow them, without chewing, without knowing what flavors they are, and imagine all the separate colors of the rainbow melting back together as they slide down that dark tunnel inside me.

Tucker stops talking and clenches his jaw. The bus is shuddering now. We must be doing a hundred miles per hour. It feels as if the entire thing might fly apart at any second. I look into Tucker's eyes. I can see the blood pulsing in his temples, hear his heartbeat louder than my own. But he looks strangely calm. I feel calm too. Maybe velocity can be a kind of drug if you're going fast enough. I close my eyes and listen to the cold air hissing through the vents.

Tires squeal in the distance. But that's outside of the bus, somewhere beyond the dark corridor of our bunks, somewhere above my soft sheets. A beer bottle smashes; a window breaks. But that's out there. Far away.

I am the Overreactor, I whisper. *I am the Overwhelmed.*

Gravity turns and the direction of down changes. Everything is louder and closer. A heavy thud, followed by a scream of metal, summer rain rushing in through the wall's open zipper.

We land in a pile against the door to the bus's front lounge. Everything hurts. Bare feet squish against the hallway's wet carpet. From the tangle, someone sticks a knee in my ribs, pinning me against the door. We can't get it open. This is all wrong. We need to get out front. See what's happened.

Move back. Slide the door.

There's a man standing in the wreck. "Don't come up here—stay back, goddamnit!" It's our driver. He looks freshly murdered.

The whole passenger side of the bus has been ripped open. It's actually kind of pretty: the metal loops and curls in silver ribbons through the dark red birthday present of the front lounge. Not much else about it is pretty though. Blood covers the walls—you wouldn't say it's *dripping* exactly. It hangs from the ceiling in long black ropes.

We crawl through the bus's guts and out into the grasslands on the side of the highway to wait for help. But I don't recognize anyone. I'm surrounded by children. One of them, a skinny, lanky kid saunters over, bowlegged, and stands next to me, pointing to the shredded side of the bus. He looks back and forth between me and the bus, tapping his finger against his front teeth, "It's like that song, 'Understanding in a Car Crash'—but like with a bus. Am I right?"

I squint at him. He looks vaguely familiar. "Am I still dreaming?"

He pinches me, hard, and I pull away.

"Nope," his nostrils flare. "Don't think so."

"Where's my band? Tucker? Tom? Steve?"

A bigger kid with tight curled hair walks up behind us. "Didn't the band, like, break up?"

"Yeah," the skinny kid's face is twitching. "Isn't that why you're here?"

"I need to wake up, but for real. I need to *wake up*, wake up."

"This dude needs the medic," the bigger kid chuckles, lightly patting his tight curls to make sure they're still in place after the accident. He looks me up and down, as if there's an exact place where the damage lives inside me, as if all he has to do is pinpoint its precise location and things will be alright. "He musta hit his head."

The skinny kid tugs on the bigger kid's sleeve, "It's just a head wound. They bleed. It's what they do."

"Nope. This isn't real."

The skinny kid laughs, "Maybe he *does* need the medic."

Our bus is split open. I watch as it leaks fuel. The tour medic arrives and checks out the driver. "Hit a horse," he tells her, waving at the pile of meat strewn across the road. "Nine hundred-pound thoroughbred, spooked by the thunderstorm, broke its gates."

When the medic finds me, I'm stuck in a loop: reliving the crash, watching the red Skittle of the horse exploding in the metal teeth of our bus, over and over again. She snaps her fingers in front of my face, passes me a bottle of whiskey. Wind shivers the grass. Rain takes the horse blood from my hands, in slices. I turn my face up to the sky.

"This ought to help," the medic tells me, placing three pills in a paper cup.

A tall, middle-aged man in skate shoes comes up behind her. "Hey doc, mind if I holler at you for a sec?"

"I'm busy, Crisco," she stands up and tucks a loose strand of hair behind her ear. The man in the skate shoes—*Crisco*, apparently—watches her walk away. He tips his Volcom trucker hat in my general direction, as an alternative to an actual greeting. His bleach blond hair is in desperate need of a touch-up. He slides a pack of Newports from the thigh pocket of his cargo shorts, adjusts his Oakley sunglasses, looks around, and coughs without covering his mouth, before motioning toward my bus with the unlit tip of a fresh cigarette, "Fucking gnarly."

I look down at the paper cup and toss three pills to the back of my mouth.

"Woah, bro," Crisco says, taking off his sunglasses. "I think we've got a contestant."

I tip the whiskey back to wash the pills down.

Crisco's eyes go wide, "Yes! Climb up on that *Chandelier*, bro. Take her for a ride!"

I swallow the pills in a hot, paint-thinner gulp, "Can't understand you."

"The *Chandelier*, bro," he tells me, pointing into my paper cup with the tip of his cigarette. "Ibogaine hydrochloride? That's its street name: *The Burning Chandelier*... You know, like, *I wish I could look down past the burning chandelier inside me*? What do you think he's talking about, bro? It's ibogaine. You just took a shit load of it too."

"The medic told me it would help."

"Yeah, I bet, man," he says, finally lighting his cigarette.

"I just hit a horse," I try to explain.

He takes a drag on his cigarette and puts his sunglasses back on.

"No shit. I saw that. You hit that Horse super fucking hard. Though," he seems to contemplate this, "I don't know if you should be so proud about it."

"What?"

"The *Horse*," he says. "Why were you hitting it so hard in the first place? I mean, bro, do you have some serious deep-seated, unexamined childhood trauma or some shit like that? You know, for most people, *Horse* is a line they just won't cross."

"*Horse is a line?*" I repeat.

"Sure, man. You know—smash some *skunk*, splat a little *kitty kat*... Fuck it, I been known to smoke a couple *speckled birds* in my time. But *Horse*? Come on."

"Yeah, but, the *Horse*? That was just an accident. That wasn't my fault."

"Yeah," he agrees, "I know. That's what they all say. But you better hold tight to that *Chandelier*, bro. When it gets a-swinging, you won't be able to hide from the pain anymore. You'll have to look yourself in the eye."

He turns back to my bus and all the dimension disappears from his features, as if his face has been printed on a piece of paper. I see the edge of his head as he turns and there's nothing behind it: he's a mask of a man.

"You're kind of a flat character, aren't you?"

"You tryna start something?" He flexes his muscles. They make a crumpling sound.

"You are literally made of paper."

He leans into my face and stares down deep into my pupils.

"Ohhhh, I get it. The *shit* is kicking in."

"No, Crisco, you don't get it. I took ibogaine a few hours ago in Tijuana and all of this, even you, is in my head."

"Holy shit," he takes a long drag from his cigarette, "you're telling me you took *Mexican ibogaine* a few hours ago and now you just took some more?"

Is he right about that? I hesitate for a second. Up above the rain clouds, I see the storm-blown branches of pine trees undulating across the sky in a deep green tapestry.

"Are those coniferous clouds?" I ask him.

"Bro," he whispers into my pupils, "you are tripping *so* hard."

The rain comes into focus on my hands. The horse blood has been strafed off, but now my skin is covered in deep green needles. I feel a new mentholated sting with each drop.

"It's raining needles. Needles from the sky."

He starts laughing but accidentally inhales too much smoke and begins to choke, "*Hhhhh*—yeah, bro—*ckk*—, that's what I'm talking about. Ride it."

Now he's doubled over, coughing and laughing.

It sounds like, "*cornerstork.*"

It sounds like, "*halfalfasprouts.*"

The cigarette drops out of his hand. He's trying to catch his breath but he can't stop laughing. His coughs are gathering power, unionizing, and threatening to turn against him. The cigarette rolls a couple inches and touches the edge of his foot but he's made of paper so the foot immediately catches fire. Now he's coughing and laughing and he's trying to put out the fire on his leg. Instead, it spreads to his hands. Before long, he's engulfed in flames—entirely—laughing and coughing and he's yelling, "Bro, you gotta ride that *Chandelier*. Like this. Watch me. I'll show you, bro."

He moves in great, galloping circles. Maybe he believes that he's at a rodeo and that the fire is a more sensible animal to ride than a horse. Pine needles crack and sparkle in the flames around his head, producing a thin, minty smoke, so that the air becomes an ad for Newport cigarettes. The world is alive with pleasure.

The bus catches flame. Grass burns in the field beyond it. Even the sky seems to scintillate. It needs to breathe or reproduce, and the trees must feel the waxy seals around their hearts begin to melt because they start dropping their pine cones down through the atmosphere. The whole scene swells into a pornography of light and heat before disappearing in a bright chemical flash.

Smoke clears, revealing a sky that's blue and very far away. The highway has been swept clean. There isn't a single scrap of debris or drop of blood anywhere on it. But I wouldn't notice it if there were.

All I can see is a gleaming gate: a shining door, set in the center of a forty-foot-high, metal wall, which curves away in both directions. Sunlight polishes the gate until it's as blue as the sky, giving the impression of a heavenly city encased within.

A perfectly round insignia has been stamped into the metal surrounding the door latch.

When I step up to the gate's threshold, the latch unfastens and the doors begin to part. A calm sense of relief settles over the countryside. As I walk through the entrance and into the walls of the city, I notice two pillars flanking the opening, each topped with a giant silver cicada, and these words, cut high into the arch above:

> *It is the desperate moment when we discover that the empire, which had seemed to us the sum of all wonders, is an endless, formless ruin...* (Italo Calvino, *Invisible Cities*)

II

ii. THE GATE

Ruins. A city stands, intricately broken. Its gates clang shut behind me. Cylinders turn in their locks. From the inside, there are no latches. No handles or seams in the walls. Nothing to indicate the transgression of a boundary. The gate keeps its secrets. But there's no mistaking it: this is a new world. Here, the sky billows with smoke, rising out of a charred landscape. Above the fumes, distant birds make letters with their black wings: v's and f's and capital T's, wheeling out over the wreckage in sentinel arcs.

The city unwinds in a series of nested circles, each road curving within the outline of the one preceding it, each circle descending just a bit deeper into the earth. There's nothing random or coincidental. Everything has been laid out meticulously. Each design element shares a common purpose: the burying of something so deep that it will never be found.

All paths seem to lead equally to the center, but that's a lie. Simply choose one road to follow and observe how it doubles back and returns, covering the same ground, time and again, before closing off into nothing. Every road is a dead end and every dead end holds a painful memory. There are too many roads to choose from and too many bad memories to avoid. Escape is equally impossible in all directions. This is civil engineering in the image of a children's maze. But am I the child or am I the silver ball? And does that distinction even matter anymore?

No. Inside the maze, the only question that matters is sprayed in five-foot-tall, metallic red letters across a torn billboard. It's a question that I've been asked many times over the years; a question that seems simple enough on its surface but opens into an entire hidden world when viewed from within:

"Why don't you just stop?"

Why don't you *just stop hiding things? Why don't you just stop sneaking out of the house before dawn? Why don't you just stop listening to that song if it makes you so sad? Why don't you just stop cracking your knuckles? Why don't you just stop saying you were at an NA meeting when everyone saw you standing on the corner? Why don't you just stop sweating? Why don't you just stop singing if you hate the sound of your voice? Why don't you just stop asking to borrow money? Why don't you just stop nodding off at dinner with our friends? Why don't you just stop throwing up after eating anything at all? Why don't you just stop muttering to yourself in public? Why don't you just stop falling down? Why don't you just stop lying? Why don't you throw away that bag and just stop using for ninety days? Why don't you just stop using heroin for one single week?*

An individual can quit anything if they put their mind to it and have a little faith. A little determination. They could stop breathing for twenty minutes. They could stop being a person. It's not so hard. Go ahead. *Why don't you just stop?*

This question opens a million little doors in my heart and freezes me between them. It strands me in blind alleys, down endlessly curling lanes of shame and self-doubt. Though it is a question of the mind and not a question of the body, this *question of the mind* is one that I feel reverberating through my consciousness and into my body lying in a bed in Mexico, causing an immediate physical reaction: blood pumps hard, contracting the heart muscles so rapidly that my pulse becomes an act of violence my body inflicts on itself.

Pressure builds. My inner violence jumps into the physical world of the clinic, where it sets off an alert on the cardiogram. Doctors adjust beds, check pulses. An alarm sounds, echoing down through the nervous system, where it reaches the metal walls of the city gates, producing a deep resonant hum. Panic deepens. Pulse quickens, further reinforcing the cardiogram's feedback loop. Doctors scramble. Body senses danger. Flames leap into the air. Cardiogram reads 167 beats per minute. Orderlies shout. Bits of burning coal rain down.

Why don't you just stop?

Shaking. My body can't stop. Someone rubs a damp cloth across my forehead. Someone holds my hand.

Someone whispers, "Just breathe. That's all you need to do now."

Someone raises the sheets. Someone pats my shoulder.

"In. 1-2-3-4. Out. 1-2-3-4-5-6-7-8. Good. That's good. Go slowly."

A cool breeze passes through the ruins, clearing the smoke. My pulse begins to normalize. Sparrowhawks, black kites, and peregrine falcons beat their dark wings against the sky, casting off black letters. Their typographic shadows fall on the cracked concrete, leading me to the entrance of an alley where an LP record sits, propped against the curb. I pick it up and examine its cover, adorned with the silhouette of a dove. Inside its dust jacket, the record looks newly pressed. On the back sleeve there are several songs listed, each one named after the city it was recorded in. I wander into the alley, reading a block of text typed out above the name of the first song.

Every city is a system, an alphabet of possibilities, limited by design, yet ordered in a way that provides infinite varieties of movement within its walls. The only meaningful engagement with an alphabet is to form words and speak, as the only way to situate oneself in a city is to choose a path and walk.

Ten paces down the alley, a cement wall blocks any further progress.

"...*choose a path and walk*. I have to choose a path."

I scan the record sleeve and speak the name of the first song, "Barcelona."

My breath moves through the dark alley, sending wavelets through the cement wall. I place my palm against it. It's not cement, only soft grey fabric; not a wall but a curtain. Beyond it, a winding path unfolds in complete silence. Stepping under the curtain, I speak the song's lyrics, filling the alley with sound.

Barcelona, the ancient *seat of Catalonia, rises out of the Balearic Sea every morning in a new configuration, and though its beaches are dotted with ports and shipping routes, the path is circuitous, labyrinthine. It can only truly be reached by taking the long, thin road that turns like a maze through the center of all ruins.*

Though it's true that this path runs through parks and plazas, passing under red-bricked arches and into secret markets, hidden along temporary alleyways, it must be noted that these places are carved as much from sunlight as stone. Any stray thought can open up new directions in which to get lost. One may find themselves trapped forever in spirals of contemplation, distracted by the milk steaming off a cortado, the vanilla seeds speckling pads of cold butter, meals sleeved between the splits of fresh baguettes, the sea's sweet voice in the green grapes of the region with their briny echoes of white wine, and, most of all, in the elaborate stories spun out by charming pickpockets up and down the constantly shifting Avinguda Diagonal.

Steps along this path are best measured in paving stones, hydraulic cement, and intricate tiled roses; an entire unspoken history unfurling ahead of every stride.

When the Carrer de la Marina finally intersects the Carrer de Mallorca, the Placa de Gaudi opens into an oasis on the right. At this same intersection, on the left-hand path, a many-steepled church melts into the ground; saints kneel beneath four honeycombed spires. Stone drips off the facade, onto their shoulders. The Sagrada Familia, Gaudi's unfinished temple, towers above everything else, even inside the traveler's mind.

"**Welcome back,**" **a** familiar, dispassionate voice echoes down through the alley. I look up from the record's jacket. Somehow the small lane has wound its way into the aisle of a cathedral. Red carpet softens the fall of my sneakers. Liturgical incense threads a hush through everything.

I follow the carpet through the pews, up to the altar, where my old roommate wields a heavy brush, covering a stained glass window in matte black paint. Around him, white stones glimmer from the transept's facade. Above the plinth, past the marble columns, row after row of blackened windows line the walls.

"Did you do all of this, Don?"

Don mumbles, "Just picking up a little work on the side. This project has been going on since way before I came into the picture."

I walk to one of the windows on the church's eastern wall, "What's under the paint?"

"It's not paint," Don hesitates. "And you don't want to know."

A multipurpose razor sits on the ledge of the nearest window. I pick it up and retract its cover. The blade feels soft going into the paint. Starting at the bottom right, it glides across the stained glass, revealing first a darkened stage, then a gaunt figure bent around a guitar. It's slow work but I keep scraping. Blond hair falls over the figure's face. Emaciated ribs show through the holes in his shirt. Behind him, a man with a microphone flickers in the shadows.

"This supposed to be you and me?" I call across the transept.

Don stops painting and slinks over to examine the window, "It's me with the guitar but that's not you with the microphone. That's Sean. You're really having a hard time seeing yourself for who you are, huh?"

"I am the *Observer*." The phrase suddenly crystalizes in my mind.

"Not in here, you're not," Don brushes his hair from his eyes. "Once you stepped through those gates, you inverted that relationship. Out there you were the Observer, in here you're the Observed. This place is the Panopticon, the all-seeing eye, waiting and watching."

"How did the Panopticon even get in my head? That's where we are, right? It's the ibogaine, I bet—mind control—I read about it in the brochure. The CIA studied ibogaine in the 1950s, for an op, targeting delinquent drug users. Psychological warfare and such."

Holding the razor blade up to the light, I notice a small embossment on the handle: *Property of the Central Bureau.*

"Clinic might even be a CIA front."

Don shakes his head, "Quite the opposite. They're a liberating army. Truth is, it's not the ibogaine you need to worry about. Your whole mind is an op. You've always been in prison; ibogaine just showed you the bars. We all internalize. We all make miniatures. Once you know you're being watched, you begin to watch yourself, trying to police your own actions—your own thoughts and feelings—for any wrong move. A functioning carceral state needs no cages."

I step back. There must be hundreds of windows, some still wet. Others chipped and cracked from years of neglect. "So, this cathedral we're in, it's a place where secrets are hidden from the police state?"

"A sanctuary, in the original sense," Don leans against the wall. "But in this case, you're the state. And the police."

"Okay."

"And the criminal."

"Alright, I get it already."

Don leans back, searching the vaulted ceiling, "And maybe the victim of the crime too?"

"This was Philly," I interrupt, pointing to a plaque on the window's heavy, black frame. *First Unitarian Church. Ink & Dagger circa '97. The greatest hardcore band of all time."*

Don shrugs, "Those are your words, not mine."

"For me, that show was life changing."

"Then why you got me in here blacking it out?" Don asks.

"It was one of the best experiences of my life. I don't want to forget it."

"You're concealing something from yourself. Scrape out the next two panes."

I put the blade to the glass and scrape. A round wooden table appears. Two lines of cocaine, a joint, and a bottle of Jack Daniels. The blade slips. "Shit," I whisper. In the next pane, another stage. Another scene with Don bent around his guitar. In this one, I'm standing next to him, holding the microphone, eyes rolling back in my head.

Don holds the paint can under one arm, "Our set at This Is Hardcore. *In memory of Sean Patrick McCabe. Rest in Peace.* Don't want to remember that one, huh? Guess you were pretty fucked up."

We stare at the window. It slowly begins to move. A mess of limbs churns in front of the stage. People dive on one another, walk across each other's heads. I watch myself swaying on the stage, barely able to stand.

"I was so fucking scared. Sean was my idol. I didn't want to disgrace his memory by being too timid. So I tried to channel some of his chaos."

"He was your idol," Don dips the brush in the can, soaking its bristles, "but he was my best friend. Did you think following him down that same path to an early death wouldn't affect me? Did you think I wouldn't blame myself?"

A camera flashes in the crowd. I watch a ribbon of light slide along the surface of the glass in a slow wave. Don pushes past me to the next window and drops his brush into the can. His shoulders slump. He adjusts his glasses and sighs, "Not this one again. How many times am I going to have to treat the same pane?"

In the stained glass, a freight train is stopped dead behind an orange-brick school building. Its steel tracks are painted arterial red for a stretch of about twenty feet, trailing the first car. The conductor sits in the grass, staring up at the bruised, purple clouds, wondering how such a small boy's body could hold all that blood.

"You've painted this window before, Don?"

"Many times," Don places the brush at the top of the scene and makes gentle fanning motions down the surface of the glass until it's covered once more. "But it never stays."

We watch the black slide off onto the stone below. First the purple returns to the clouds, then the iron to the train resting on those rusty, red tracks. A small, yellow cassette tape player once again sits in the freshly greened grass.

Don points to it, "Every time I cover this window, I wonder what the deal is with that Walkman. The thing's so bright, it's no wonder that kid didn't see the train coming."

"He was my French partner. A transfer student. His Dad was the new vice principal, total hard-ass. The kid got bullied bad. Used to ask my advice all the time. I got tired of listening to it, so I passed him that Walkman and a Pixies tape. Told him, *Don't let it get to you.* Some fucking help I was. When he sat down on those tracks and the train went over him, that Walkman was totally untouched, like he threw it clear. So thoughtful."

Don adjusts his glasses, "*Don't let it get to you.* Incredible stuff. Ever consider a career path in professional counseling?"

"Exactly what kind of paint is this, Don?"

"Keep telling you. It's not paint. Just a treatment. To cover the glass. Here," Don stops just ahead of me. Sunlight stripes his face, red and white and tropical orange, from an untouched window. Its glass is intricately cut and stained: palm trees, seashells, millions of delicate cuts, graded with infinitesimal color variations in sand and water.

Don says, "Hand me the atlas."

I can't take my eyes off the stained glass, "The atlas?"

Don slides the record out from under my arm, flips it over, and reads off the names of the songs, "Barcelona, Manila... *Sydney.* Looks about right." He reaches across the window panel and flips the iron latch. Miles of golden sunlight and cobalt elements shine from the window's glass beach.

"Don't open it. The picture—it's so beautiful—I want to hold on to it."

"It's not a picture," Don tells me, pushing the windowpane. "See?"

I reach my hand through the opening into warm salt air. The beach continues to glimmer. Don hands me the LP jacket, "Speak its name."

"Sydney."

Between the vast Indian Ocean and the Coral Sea, a merciless patch of red clay and rock floats on the back of a giant sea turtle named Australia. The turtle sleeps as it drifts through the ocean, dreaming of the perfect city. In this metropolis of dreams, buildings can grow up to be anything: an opera house can transform into a ship with ivory sails and float into the bay, just as a tower can point up at the sky until it pierces the clouds, its cell tower becoming a long thin needle.

The inhabitants of this city love the gentle turtle and love living inside a place formed entirely of dreams, and yet, they are under a constant existential threat: the threat of the turtle waking up. Without continuous slumber, the turtle may drift up through the murky waters of consciousness and forget about the city entirely or, even worse, fall asleep again, this time dreaming of a similar city, missing only the slightest yet most sublime details: the soft blossoms of the Jacaranda tree, the sound of rain in the banana leaves, and the morning Yum Cha carts full of steaming rice noodles, fragrant lotus cakes, and juicy pork and leek dumplings.

We step out of the cool, dark interior of the church into absolute white. The sun pops its flashbulb, blasting the flat, black outline of the ragged cliffs past the tightening lasso of our pupils. Our eyes settle and the scene develops slowly, like a photograph fixing in a chemical bath. The light lands gently now and rests on the surface of the water, stark and sparkling.

We stand silent for a moment, taking it in. A railing stands in front of us, demarcating a sheer drop of 3,000 feet.

At the edge, Don says, "Look down."

My eyes shift focus, expecting to see the Sydney beachfront, but the basement drops out of the world. Vertigo overtakes me, so I cover my eyes and back away.

"What is that?" I whisper.

"It's just the Visual Cliff," Don pats me on the back. "The ibogaine is overloading your system. We're entering the zone where brain damage is likely. I needed to check on some of your neurological capacities to make sure we weren't in danger of losing any higher functions. But you passed. Congratulations, you have the healthy visual response of a seven-month-old infant."

"What about Sydney? What about the beach?"

"Uncover your eyes."

I drop my hands. The beachfront reappears in the shape of a crescent moon. My focus has adjusted, sharpening everything. Once again, the sun crashes on water like broken glass. It's so blue I want to jump in. I look over my shoulder and recognize the Royal Botanical Gardens. Birds scream from the tops of trees. Giant spiders spin webs between them, casting monstrous shadows at our feet. Just ahead of me, Don strolls the boardwalk, drinking the most refreshing-looking cup of iced coffee I've ever seen.

"Where'd you get that?"

"Sort of a notorious little spot around the way. It doesn't look like much," Don shakes the cup and holds it up to the sun, "but the secret is that they make the ice from espresso. Doesn't water down."

"I'm so thirsty."

"It's the hole in the ozone," Don nods, taking another sip. "Tremendous heat."

Heavy waves crest and pound the far shore. Closer, at our end of the beach, a gentle tide pushes ghostly objects up the dunes, where they float briefly around our ankles, before pulling them back with the water. A video game console—tethered by wires to a small, blocky television set—floats up, rests one plastic controller on the boardwalk, and tumbles back down the beach.

"We had a PlayStation in the Thursday van. So much Tony Hawk."

"All we had was an UNO deck," Don glances at the remaining coffee in his cup and tosses the whole thing into the ocean.

"Didn't you hear me when I said I was thirsty, Don?"

Don tilts into the sun, shielding his eyes, "I did."

A red-sunburst Rickenbacker 330 washes up. Don points at it, "That's the guitar you bought with the equipment budget for your third album."

"I loved that thing."

"You sold it five years ago to buy heroin."

A wave smashes over the railing of the boardwalk, dropping a photo album at our feet. Before I have a chance to pick it up, a smaller capillary wave snatches it out of my reach. Old Polaroids spill out. In one, I'm sitting on the stage at Fireside Bowl, in Chicago, laughing my ass off, blood running down one side of my face. "Tim accidentally split my eye socket open with the head of his bass. The whole crowd gasped. I could hear it above the music before I felt anything."

A beer floats by, leaving a rusty trail in the water behind it.

Don asks, "Have you ever heard the phrase, *these are the golden days?*"

I shrug.

"Well, these are them," he says, waving at my guitar. "*Bye-bye.*"

"Glad this is so fucking funny to you. My life reduced to garbage in the sand."

Don grabs hold of my shoulder, "Don't take everything so seriously. This is for the best."

I taste warm saline in the back of my throat.

Don tightens his grip, "You're not going to cry, are you?"

I slap his hand away, "Of course not. I'm just thirsty."

Don grabs a cup from under the waves and collects some seawater. I can smell the salt in the air. "Drink this." He pushes the cup in my face.

"That's disgusting."

He cups my chin in his hand, "You said you were thirsty. Now drink it."

He's right. I am still so thirsty.

I put the cup to my lips, expecting warm salt water. But the liquid is thick and sweet. "It's good."

"Drink up."

The first sip tastes of milk and honey and warmth and human kindness. But as I swallow it all down, my molars begin to ache. The liquid is starting to feel more like wet cement. Afraid I might choke on it, I spit some out.

Don presses the cup to my lips, "You need to drink it all. Don't waste a drop."

I struggle, but Don holds my mouth open and pours it down my throat. I can't seem to get free so I let my body go limp.

"You wanted it," He tells me. "Here it is."

I push the cup away and vomit into the ocean. Little flecks of gold and silver shine out from the cloudy, amber liquid: broken guitar strings, crushed pennies, the keys to my first apartment.

"Good," Don tells me. "Get it out."

In between heaves, a faint jingle echoes from the far end of the beach. Don releases me and turns to look. I hear soft, metallic sounds moving up the boardwalk as I wash my hands in the ocean. Thousands of silver bells rain a dull chorus against the wooden planks at our feet. The sand speckles with indentations.

"That's it," Don shouts, covering his head with his hands. "Let it all out."

I kneel down and pick up one of the bells. It's an engagement band. There are millions of them, shining out from the sand, dropping into the ocean in brief wet blips.

"This is the ring I bought for Liza when I decided to propose. But it was a rough time. Shit happened with Martin. My record label fell apart. I needed cash."

Don touches the paintbrush to some pictures lying on the ground. They turn black.

"So I brought the ring to the pawn shop. Just for a loan. Just for a week."

Don kneels down and starts working on the guitar. When it's completely covered in dull black, he throws it into the waves. It sinks.

"I barely got enough for two weeks of dope."

I open my hand. Don touches his brush to the ring and it darkens. The band breaks apart in my palm as the rain intensifies.

"If these are the golden days, why are you painting them black? Shouldn't you only paint over the stuff that I need to forget?"

Don holds the can up, "It's *all purpose.*" He taps his finger against the can's white label, which reads, *Hero-in-a-Can Brand All-Purpose Window Treatment and Curing Fixative.* "This stuff'll cover everything."

I turn my face to the sky and let the rain wash over me. The tide is rising. All around us, typhonic waves pound the shoreline. A forty-foot swell breaks on the side of a skyscraper. It tumbles into the surf.

Don shouts, "Time to move along. We've still got to climb the Visual Cliff."

We sprint up the stairs with the ocean at our heels. Further down the boardwalk, waves crash over the dome of the Opera House, pushing its granite sails into the sea. Water pours through the supports of the Harbour Bridge.

"Don't stop now," Don yells, taking the stairs two at a time. St. Mary's and the Queen Victoria Building go under. There's no point in looking down anymore. I can feel the ocean spray on the back of my ankles. When we reach the top, Don kneels down and dips his brush in the water. "You're scared. Only natural. But I believe in total power and dynamic," he tells me. "Sharp angles. Danger." The sea levels out. A small puddle darkens around the bristles. When Don lifts the brush, a black slick spreads. Already, I can't recall what it is I've lost.

I hand Don the record. He examines the sleeve and runs his fingers down the list of songs, mouthing the names of cities, *Barcelona, Sydney*... He stops and looks up at me, "I think you'll appreciate where we're heading. We can stop by our old apartment, drink a couple beers." He hands the record back, "Check it out."

This is the city of cities: New York. *Novum Caput Mundi:* "Capital of the world."

Its blueprints present a marvel of civil engineering. Viewing them all together, one is struck by the grid of numbered streets, the organization and forethought. Trace these fine details with a finger: here the waters of Canal Street run not only through the consecutive blocks of Elizabeth, Mott, and Mulberry but also through Chinatown and Little Italy. Six blocks north to Little Australia and north again, through the remains of the Village, to the spot where West 32nd Street unfolds block after block into Koreatown, then Murray Hill.

The plans are clear, comprehensive. However, when the traveler arrives within the city itself, blueprints and street numbers will provide no guidance. Because New York is not a physical place at all, but the psychological embodiment of every city. All the traveller needs to do to confirm this is retrace their own steps, winding impossibly from Barcelona to Sydney to Brooklyn.

Rise above the ruins and view them from one of the city's innumerable lookout points. Contrary to the clean lines and clear indications of blueprints, the streets are, in fact, laid out in a series of concentric circles, rather than a grid, and the numbers count down as the traveller moves toward the center. Finally, the traveller comprehends that the path through the ruins has only ever stretched through a single city, one that exists solely within the walls of one's own mind.

Shade falls across the text. When I look up from the album sleeve, we're walking through a deep canyon. Apartment buildings with darkened faces. Don leads the way, his feet falling steadily on the double yellow line that splits the street.

"People from LA talk about the Santa Anas driving them crazy, the devil in the breeze, the secret undoing that gathers in the back of the throat."

Wind picks up, throwing a trio of garbage cans down the sidewalk. Pages from the *New York Post* and the *New York Times* whip along after them. Stiff, rippling sounds fill the air.

"But at least their wind has a name..."

A fern gets blown from a fire escape. Its ceramic pot cracks against the curb, spilling earth out on the concrete.

"Here, in New York, our desert wind has no name."

"And no desert," I remind him.

He pauses in the middle of the street. "Every city has a desert. We just have to find yours."

"Our old apartment," Don points to a second-floor window.

"Your old place was so much nicer."

Don puts the black brush back to his lips, "I only took the room because I thought you might off yourself after your band broke up."

"I wasn't going to *off myself*."

"That bag of heroin you showed me. The one that your dealer slipped in for free with your usual pills. I warned you not to fuck with that shit," Don gets quiet. "I took it and threw it in the fucking garbage."

"Found it in the trash after you went to sleep. Tacked it up on the wall in my bedroom."

Don shakes his head, "That was a mistake."

"Be honest, man, you knew."

"Okay, I'll be honest," he puts *honest* in air quotes like honesty is an imaginary concept. "When you showed me that bag of heroin, I was almost proud of you. For once in your life, you weren't being such a fucking pussy. You were actually committing. Jumping in at the deep end of the pool, as it were."

I throw my hands up in the air.

"But that story never ends well. People nod out and melt their faces off on space heaters. Accidentally smother their kids. Crash cars. Drown in tubs. They die. Or worse. Take it from me."

We walk down Newton Street and turn on Graham, then left at Norman. Bees swarm in angry, yellow clouds at the Nassau Avenue stop for the G train. Down Manhattan Avenue, the Peter Pan Donut Shop is missing. There's no florist, no diner. We turn right at Banker and walk to a corner that should be West. A street sign reads, *END*. Don points to a big, red-brick building overlooking the East River from the Brooklyn side.

"Your old office."

Wind blows against the face of the building. Black liquid oozes out its windows, running down over the brick facade, flowing onto the pavement. Don tosses his paint can to the curb. "Guess we won't be needing that."

A pink slip flutters against the front door. It reads, NEW YORK NOTICE TO QUIT, To: *COLLECT RECORDS, LLC*. Don pulls it off the glass and opens the door, "This is where I leave you."

"You're not coming in?"

"This is as far as I can go. Besides," Don glances at the LP sleeve before handing it to me, "record's almost done."

The streets flood with black paint. Don opens the door of his car and gets in. I watch the front wheels dip below the paint, into the pavement. Don adjusts the mirror, releases the parking brake. The car sinks to its door handle. Its rear end wobbles a bit and goes under. Don looks calm as he rolls the window down.

"Hold up. Before I go, you're scared to find out the truth but here's what I believe: You have important work to do and a long life ahead of you. Fuck all the noise. Get through it. When you're out of here, hit the real Don up, he'll help you out—more than you might think."

Inside the building's lobby, a thin membrane of ice coats every window. Faded notices hang on the cork board next to a photograph of this same lobby full of people.

A bell dings brightly at the arrival of the elevator. Doors slide open on a smartly dressed man whose skin shines with the alluring health of expensive blond woods. The sides of his head are shaved close while the top is pomaded into an impeccable pompadour.

"Norman!" I shout, jumping into the elevator to embrace him.

"It's me," he laughs. "Your favorite employee."

"Employee? You should be running this place. You're better at it than I ever was."

"Who am I to argue?" Norman steps back, waves a hand in my face. "Can I just ask where you've been? We're on deadline."

Suddenly, I'm holding a coffee.

"How'd you do that?"

Norman pushes a button for the fourth floor. When the doors close behind him, he leans back and smiles, "You said it yourself: I'm really good at my job."

I take a sip, "God, this place is a ghost town."

"Mmmm. It is a shame this is all ending before we get a chance to release that," Norman says, pointing to the record in my hands. "Our in-house designer embossed the logo onto the back cover and when you press down on it, time stops. It's some of his best work."

"Did you say it can stop time?" I ask.

"I told him not to," Norman says, holding his hands up, fingers outstretched. "It adds seven dollars to the unit price."

"Seven dollars? And it stops time?"

"Seven dollars *per unit*," Norman clarifies. His eyes go wide. The elevator lurches up.

"Wow," I say, running my fingers over the embossed cardstock.

"I know." Norman shakes his head. "The man upstairs will never go for a suggested retail price of $37.99. But our designer won't listen. You want to try and explain it to him?"

The elevator's bell goes *ding* and the doors open. We step into the hallway, causing energy efficient bulbs to click on, one after the other, down the length of the corridor. Each office becomes entirely visible through the building's glass walls. At the end of the hallway, we come to the Collect Records office but our automatic light doesn't switch on. Norman taps on the glass, "Yuck, where is he? I just left him here for a second. He knows he's in deep shit for designing this expensive packaging."

I press my face against the glass, shielding my eyes from the glare. At the design station, a monitor is on but no one is in the seat. In the computer screen's glow, I can see a rolled-up dollar bill by the keyboard. There's a small red rubber band sitting on an open sketchbook.

"Do you want to explain that?" Norman asks me.

"That's not mine."

Under the desk, I see a body, lying face up, skin like last week's unsold raw fish. The young man's eyelids sag down over his soft hazel eyes.

Norman yells through the glass, "Are you sleeping? We're on a deadline."

I bang on the glass wall, "Can you hear us? Please try to wake up."

Norman sighs as he slumps against the glass wall, "I know you're struggling. But did it ever occur to you what effect it might have on other addicts in recovery to work for a boss who's getting high all day at work?"

The designer's lips are turning purple. In combination with his hazel eyes, the effect is striking. He has an impeccable sense of color and balance.

"Ok. Do me a favor," Norman's body tenses, "don't turn around."

"Well now I've got to," I sigh. "I have no self-control."

Across the hallway, behind the glass partition, someone pulls back a floor-length curtain and the hallway lights up. Through the glass, there's a living room. I recognize the ugly beige couch, the record player. I recognize the pictures on the walls. I walk closer to the glass.

Norman says, "I think this is a bad idea."

There's movement on the carpet. Liza jumps up from a set of crunches. She's looking right at me. A cluster of freckles around her left eye trembles a bit before she breaks into the biggest, warmest smile I've ever seen.

"Hi, sweets," I whisper, feeling all the blood rush into my head. The hallway heats up. Liza remains silent. I watch the freckles trembling around her eyes. Her smile drops.

"Don't think she can hear you," Norman tells me. "She definitely can't see you. There's a glare."

Liza turns her head, keeping her eyes trained on the glass. She scoops her hair back, twisting it into a knot at the top of her head.

"I always knew she'd be okay, no matter what happens to me. She's the epitome of a well-balanced individual. She loves herself. She knows her boundaries."

Her phone beeps and she checks her messages, smiling briefly and then not at all.

"It's probably a guy. Heard I'm out of the picture so he's taking his shot."

Norman checks his watch, "We should go."

"She'll have no trouble moving on. She's not like me. She doesn't let stuff eat at her."

Norman places his hand on my shoulder, "There are times when I think you must be one of the most perceptive people I've ever met. Now is not one of those times."

Liza bows her head as she exhales, loudly. She releases her hair from the knot and shakes it out, making worried little kissing motions. Past her, in the apartment, I can see water running down the walls in heavy streams. Norman leans in to get a better look. He presses his hand to the glass where the waterline is rising. The room is filling up like a fish tank. Liza's ankles are already submerged, but she doesn't notice. It moves quickly. Over her calves to her kneecaps.

"We should really be going," Norman tugs me back from the glass. "We're on deadline."

Liza composes herself, turning away from her reflection. She walks through the apartment, straightening up as she goes. I watch her take a book off the coffee table and place it neatly on the shelf. She straightens a chair, adjusts a picture frame. Still, no acknowledgement of the water, though it's almost to her waist. She walks to the vanity mirror over her makeup desk and stands there, staring at her reflection.

"She's got to get out of there."

Norman sighs, "That's what we all keep telling her."

"This is serious," I slap my hand against the glass. The sound gets swallowed up by the noise of the running water. "She's going to drown."

Norman pulls me gently back, "She's a captain. They go down with the ship. They drown. It's what they do."

"This is where I stay," Norman tells me at the elevator door. "You, however, are going to…this one." He pushes a button marked PH. It lights up.

"Since when does this building have a penthouse?"

The doors open and Norman waves me in, "Time to see the man upstairs."

"God?"

Norman rolls his eyes, "Martin Shkreli is a lot of things but a god is not one of them."

"This goes to Martin? And you're not coming with me?"

"You know I love you, I really do. But, in a literal sense, you couldn't pay me enough. I hope you remembered to bring your name!"

"My name?"

He pats me on the chest, quickly withdrawing his hand before the doors slide closed.

The elevator opens to an aerial view of the city.

"There he is!" a thin, boyish voice calls from somewhere behind me in a light New York accent. We're above the cloud line. Across the street, buildings crowd a construction site's perimeter like a row of crooked teeth. A massive space separates the two tallest towers. I put my hand up to the gap between my two front teeth and run the tips of my fingers along the rough edges.

"Are we in Manhattan?" I call over my shoulder.

"Well, we're not in Brooklyn anymore, that's for sure." I turn around. Martin's sitting behind a thick oak desk. He's tossing a small Nerf football from one hand to the other, swiveling back and forth in a massive chair that looks as if it might swallow him at any moment. Several banks of TV screens click on along the adjacent wall, creating a cacophony of voices as news anchors compete for attention from their separate boxes.

"*Martin Shkreli, a lightning rod for growing outrage over soaring prescription drug prices, is back in the headlines...*"

"*A judge, having revoked the young CEO's bail over an offer to buy a lock of Hillary Clinton's hair...*"

"*The search to find impartial jurors in the Martin Shkreli fraud case continues. Among the potential candidates' chief complaints? 'He looks like a dick' and 'He disrespected the Wu-Tang Clan.'*"

Martin pushes a button on the tablet embedded in his desk. All the screens blink off, simultaneously, silencing the room. Martin sighs, "What can I say? They love me."

The chair across the desk from Martin is empty. As I scoot it forward, he smirks. The expression exaggerates every sharp angle in his face, making him appear both sinister and childish. He has a little boy haircut offset by cold, intelligent eyes. He catches me examining him. I quickly scan the desk for something to focus on.

"What's that?" I ask, pointing to a small, complex-looking typewriter housed in an open wooden box.

"It's an Enigma machine," Martin puts down the football. "Do you know what that is?"

"No."

"You don't know," Martin snorts. "That's funny." He swivels his chair to face the windows, twirling his hair absently. He leans forward, bracing one hand flat against the glass while examining the decaying buildings, "You really gotta start taking better care of your teeth, man."

"You're one to talk." A drop of mercury rises in my blood.

Martin puts a finger in his mouth and runs it along the top of his teeth. "My teeth are okay."

"No, Martin. I mean maybe you shouldn't lecture me about taking care of things. Like you've done such a great job taking care of your company or the patients who rely on you for medicine that can mean the difference between life or death."

"I guess that does make more sense," Martin says. "My teeth are perfect, so…" He seems very far away, gazing out the window.

"I don't understand how you could do this. How you could let the company you built fall apart, how you could leave all those patients twisting in the wind… How you could adopt this super villain persona instead of apologizing and adjusting the price of the drug?"

"Look, it's not for us to understand why Harambe had to die for our sins. It is only for us to take our dicks out in remembrance. Right?"

"What?"

Martin shakes his head and blows a lock of hair from his forehead. "It's a meme. Never mind. Look. There's a lot more to this than the public would ever even want to know. Be glad you don't understand. Be glad there are people like me to do this stuff for you. You'd shit yourself if you understood how healthcare works, what innovation needs to prosper."

"Martin, I'm sure it's a dirty business, that even competing in that field leaves its mark on you. But you had a chance to explain this all to Congress. You could have brought down the whole shitty system but you just sat there taking the fifth and smirking at them. That's what I don't get."

"What? Congress?" Martin scoffs. "That was just a meme." He sits up straight and swivels his chair, folding his hands on the desk before him. He makes a serious face. He rolls his eyes sarcastically.

"See?" He says. "A meme." He looks forward, cocks his head, raises his left eyebrow. "Get it? A meme." He smirks. He feigns sleep against the desk. He puts up both his middle fingers. He says, "Meme, meme, meme. It's a legal strategy."

There's a guitar on the wall behind him. He pulls it down and starts playing, looking out the window again, distracted by a passing sparrow.

"Why didn't you just show some humanity, meet this thing head on? Make *that* the meme?"

"That's not how memes work, man. You really don't get it, do you?" he starts playing "Understanding in a Car Crash" sarcastically, with exaggerated note bends. The unplugged electric guitar sounds like a banjo in his hands.

"Funny," I look down at the Enigma machine. Its ivory numbers gleam, set in their round onyx keys.

"Getting warmer," he says, leering at me from across the desk. "You wanna try it out?"

"What I *want* is to know how you could do that to me. To all the bands on the label. If it was always going to go this way, couldn't you have just stayed away?"

"Please. If you need someone to blame, then you're looking in the wrong direction. In case you haven't figured things out yet, this isn't *A Christmas Carol* and I'm not your Jacob Marley."

"I'm pretty sure you'd be Scrooge."

"Wow," Martin says, putting the guitar down, "named after Chaucer and he doesn't even get the point of Dickens. Classic." He turns to his computer and does a theatrical shrug, winking into the webcam.

"Are you live-streaming this?"

"I'm a psychological projection!" he yells. "Look at me. I don't have blue eyes. You do! My office doesn't overlook the river on the east side and it certainly doesn't overlook that steaming mess you've created to represent your anxiety over the decay of your teeth. A classic problem for heroin addicts, I might add."

The building shudders. We feel the floor shaking beneath our feet.

"Think about why you're here," he says. "In a pharmaceutical office. Think about how you got started on opiates. Think about decay. Moral, physical, spiritual. Why am I here? What do I represent? Am I a villain or a scapegoat? Are you really just an *Observer*? Or is there something more for you to do here? I mean, think about it. There's a fucking Enigma machine on my desk that you can't stop staring at. Fuck!" He reaches down behind his desk. When he emerges again, he has a 7-Eleven Big Gulp in his hands. He sucks a mouthful of Mountain Dew through the straw, gets up, and paces the room.

"How do I use it?" I ask, running my fingers over the smooth divots on the face of the machine.

"Type in a question. Then follow the instructions on the ledger," he's staring out the window. His voice comes to me, reflected off the glass. "I mean, truthfully? That's not even how Enigma machines work. But what do you care, right? You've never been a *cinéma vérité* guy anyway. So just type in your big question."

I pause, trying to think of the right question, trying to imagine the answer I need.

"There's this question that they told us was important. 'Ask the ibogaine to show you your true self.' I guess I should do that. I want to look down inside myself and see clearly."

"Sure," Martin says to the window. "Knock yourself out."

Carefully, I type the letters in, one at a time—

S-

H-

O-

W-

Martin comes up behind my chair and leans over to watch. I hunch forward, continuing to enter the letters:

-M-E-

-M-Y-

-T-R-U-E-

-S-E-L-F—

I set the machine's dials to the position indicated on the ledger. There's a freshly sharpened pencil sitting on a pad of white-lined paper. When the machine is ready, I push a button—*S*—and record the resulting letter on the paper: *N*. Then, I push the button for the second letter of the question—*H*—and record the letter that lights up: *O*. There are sixteen letters in the question and sixteen letters in the answer:

N-O-N-O-N-O-N-O-N-O-N-O-N-O-N-O

The two of us look at the letters, waiting for them to resolve into a secret meaning, a binary code of *N*'s and *O*'s, carrying a revelation about the hidden nature of my heart.

I lean back in my chair and look at Martin, "Did it just tell me *no*?"

Martin looks at the pad, then the little wooden machine, and finally, at me. When his eyes rest on my face, his features light up with a cheerful, violent expression.

"Ahahaha, you're kidding," he grabs both sides of his head, like he's in a cartoon. "It won't tell you. This is rich! You have absolutely no idea who you are. You don't even know your own name!"

"Quit dicking around, Martin. What am I to you—a joke?" I throw down the pencil. It rolls across the desk, falls over the side. "Seriously, fuck off." I pick up the record in its sleeve and walk to the elevator.

"Go ahead," Martin sings after me, still holding his head, doing a little dance in the spot where he stands. "Keep on running. Deny the truth. Keep blaming me. Whatever makes you happy, dude!"

Buildings are crumbling across the street. The floor shakes. Martin jumps up on his desk, grabbing his guitar by the neck. The elevator doors ripple open. Martin swings the guitar in a smooth arc over his head and its body smashes against the rim of his desk. "Look at me," he shouts. "I'm a rock star." Inside the elevator, a sinking feeling overtakes me. Then, the drop.

Outside is a black jewel. Cars gleam against the curb: jet, tourmaline, obsidian, onyx. What little color remains in the world concentrates around Thursday's beat-up tour van, which stands vivid in white and dented silver. Directly above, the unopened rosebud of a Cardinal perches on an electrical wire. Attention is being drawn with a spotlight, shouting, *look here, look here, look here.*

The van's side panel opens and Steve jumps out. "You made it," he says, crushing me in a big hug. "You doing okay in here? Finding the answers to your questions? You figure out how to beat this thing yet?"

"Hold up. You know where you are?"

Steve checks his watch, "Your subconscious mind is starting to figure out what's going on. You should be able to talk to yourself a little more clearly now. Without all the *Observer* prompts and *Follow the Light* emergency exits. Consider me a messenger from a purer state of being."

"So, you're not really Steve then? You're *me*?"

"I'm your understanding of Steve. A little bit Steve and a little bit you. It's not that different from the way things are in waking life, to be honest. We see what we want to see about each other. I'm conceptually anchored in your mind as a kind of older brother or authority figure. As you've moved through your anger, denial, and resentment, you've stopped seeing me as a bully and have reclassified my conceptual center as *tough love*. So here I am."

"I see."

He checks his watch again, "We better get out of here while we still can."

"If only we had some idea of which direction to go."

"Give me the map," Steve tells me. "I'll show you." He grabs the record from under my arm, pulls it from out of its sleeve, and begins counting the rings, starting at the outside edge,

"*Barcelona, Sydney, Brooklyn… We are…*" Steve runs his fingers along its vinyl surface. "Here."

I follow the path of Steve's finger. Where it rests, the grooves magnify, my vision telescoping down into blind black valleys of sound. A miniature world pulls its walls up around me. I recognize a microscopic version of the street we're standing on, a black scene in a black city: a black sidewalk lined with black-brick buildings, the roadway flowing with a river of vinyl between them.

"Everything you've seen down here, the circular maze you've been lost in and the road winding through those memories—your whole experience on ibogaine—is shaped like this record. The arc of your story is progressive, slow, but circular; the song plays and the needle travels forward, in time, but it also moves inward, toward the center of the record, toward the center of your *self*.

"Javi tried to explain this encoded experience, this quality of memory, as a computer's hard drive. He told you that your hard drive had been corrupted by actions that went against your operating system and that the ibogaine would defrag the drive. But you're not much of a tech guy. So the ibogaine has shown you a record with the wrong actions scratched across the path of the song. You experience them as skips in time."

He runs his finger along the surface, pulling my vision back through the black streets, back through the all-night drives and endless studio sessions. "Let's see where you've been." A black Brooklyn rushes past, followed by the black beaches of Australia, with their black waters spilling out on the black sand, the waves' hands reaching up their black gloves to slap at the black boardwalk. Black Barcelona, black—

Steve pulls his finger off the record and my vision rushes out from the grooves. I grab his shoulder for balance as the world finds focus in small patches of color: our white van at the curb, the red streak of a cardinal finding flight in the high blue sky.

"You've covered some ground," Steve tells me, "but at this pace, you'll never reach the center. You'll never find your way out of the maze."

"Eventually I'll wake up."

"Not at this pace," Steve counts the rings on the record. "When the time runs out, that's it. This whole place is going to collapse on itself."

"And if I haven't found my way out of the maze?"

"You knew the risks when you signed up for this: some people can't handle the effects of ibogaine in their system. Their hearts give out. That's why the rigorous screening process. That's why the hospital. But there are other factors: an increased uptake of serotonin in the brain can cause a serious problem too. It's called a serotonin storm. You've seen one moving at the edges of your vision. You've heard the thunder, felt the lightning raising the small hairs at the back of your neck. Get caught up in that and you might go into seizure or shock. It can be fatal. There's one other thing," Steve points to a stranger's face looking at me through the van's rear window. "Recognize this guy?"

"Not really," I tell him, as I try to get a better look. "What's he doing in our van?"

"Tell me something," Steve leans in close, "what's he look like to you?"

"He's sort of a creepy white guy with a bad haircut," I tell him, watching the guy squinting back at me through the window. "Too skinny, bad posture, bad teeth. I think he's mocking me."

"That's what I was afraid of," Steve waves his free hand in front of the window. "It's mirrored glass. That's your reflection."

"But he looks nothing like me."

"Your self-image is breaking down," Steve motions to the guy's blue eyes, the gap between his front teeth. "I'm afraid it's probably brain damage."

I look again at the man in the van window. His image seems degraded in some minor, critical way. I wave at him and he waves back, but there's a slight lag.

"How about this: do you remember who you are?"

"Sure, I'm—" I search my reflection's face, growing increasingly uncertain.

"Just your name," Steve continues gently. "Can you give me that?"

"I don't think I can."

Steve checks his watch, looks over his shoulder, "This is worse than I thought."

"So what do we do now?"

Steve raises the record again, "Don told you there's a desert at the heart of every city, the barren place that keeps us from finding ourselves. You still have to cross that. So far, you've been following the needle's groove and the memories have been playing for you in a chronologically ordered way. But if you want a shot at making it out of here with some higher brain functions intact, you're going to have to cut across the natural progression of the dream." He drags his nail across the record. "It might not be too pleasant."

Steve hands me the record and gets in the tour van. My band is in there, waiting for me. Tom throws a shiny, silver Pop-Tarts wrapper out through the open door and waves me over. I get in and start the engine.

"What you got there?" Tom asks, Pop-Tarts crumbs sputtering from his lips.

I slide the record out of its sleeve and hold it up to the windshield, "I think it's my life: the travels, the shows, my family, you guys, Liza. All of it."

Tim says, "Don't seem like all that much when you really look at it."

He's right. It's so small. Could an entire existence be written on the two opposing faces of the same black coin? Could life be so thin? I hold it sideways and trace its edge with my fingertips. "Let's take it for a spin and find out."

II

iii. THE RED PLACE

Texas is endless. I've heard that it takes a whole day to cross, but now that we're here, that actually seems optimistic. We've already been driving for some time. How long? Well, what time is it now? Our van's roof blocks out the sun but it must be sitting high: the light has a cruel affect and even the cacti tuck their shadows between their legs. Yes, it's definitely daytime, but which day? I can't recall the date or, for that matter, what year it is. Roads are ageless. Especially in the desert. It could be 2001 or 2011. I spent so many years traveling—this could be any one of them.

I suppose it doesn't surprise me to find myself back on these roads. It's not necessarily a bad thing. No state has ever felt as true to me as the transitional one. I enjoy the ride. I feel free.

The van is in motion. We're clocking miles, doing ninety as long as I can remember. Still, the fuel gauge says *full*. I bang my fist on the dashboard and the needle stays where it is, cruising comfortably in the green. The speakers are humming with a pleasant sound. Nothing recognizable. A shifting palette of gentle consonants fills the air. I take a sip of lemonade and it's ice cold, though it's been sitting in direct sunlight all morning.

My band members dream contentedly into the afternoon. Tucker yawns and turns over on the middle bench. Steve starts a movie on his laptop and settles in, crossing his arms skeptically over his chest. Tom raises his hands to his headphones, pressing them down hard over both ears, like he's trying to hear something vital. He scrunches his nose up and lets it go. Tim sits shotgun and chews on one of his fingers, distractedly, while reading a book of short stories.

I follow the highway with my eyes. It continues out past the edge of the visible world. There's a black line on the horizon, redacting everything beyond it.

"How much more desert can there be?"

I must have said it out loud. Tim smiles and looks up from the page.

"And where are the crossroads? Right? I mean, doesn't really give you any options, does it? I'm not saying I mind. I'd happily stay right here, with you guys, the sun in our eyes and the road rushing by."

Tim looks back down at his book.

"I'm serious. I could stay right here forever."

Check it out. Here I am, sitting on the bed in my little apartment I share with Don in Greenpoint, staring at that packet of heroin as the night comes on. Why did I dig it out of the garbage? I'm too scared to use it. But I can't stop thinking about that little paper bag. There's a brand name stamped in red cursive on one side: *Lamborghini* with a cartoon race car. So strange. I wonder who manufactures such small bags. What purpose could they serve, aside from selling heroin?

I haven't been sleeping much since Liza and I split up. Don's sick of hearing about it—about this girl I've only known for a year, who I fell head over heels for, who said she fell for me and then broke my heart anyway. He's sick of hearing it and I'm sick of saying it, so I spend a lot of nights keeping myself awake, staring at the wall. And now I'm staring at this little bag of heroin. But I don't know what to do with it. Have no idea how strong heroin is compared to the pharmaceuticals I've been abusing. I'm not even sure whether you have to prepare it specially or if you can just take it *as is*. I go online, searching for advice, as casually as if I am trying to fix my stereo. It's easy. There are drug forums where people trade tips and tell harrowing stories.

The first message reads: *Snort it, smoke it, pop it, shoot it! SWIM says you can't go wrong.* I scan the rest of the page. Several other people mention SWIM. I guess it must be a small community. Everyone knowing everyone. *SWIM says snorting is a goddamn waste of time. If you're gonna snort, you might as well pop, and if you're gonna pop, you might as well go all the way.*

As I push on through the forums, my mind reels at the staggering number of posts, the staggering number of members these forums have. All of them passing along the tips, tricks, and trials of someone they call *SWIM*.

I come to find out *SWIM* is an acronym: *Someone Who Isn't Me*. Users of drug forums falsely believe that they can legally avoid self-incrimination by referring to themselves as *SWIM*. But *SWIM* can't protect them from the law, just as *SWIM* can't protect them from the effects of addiction. Anyone can see that—anyone who isn't them.

I put away my laptop. I've never had an addictive personality and I know I never will. I have too much self-control for that. So I turn the envelope over in my hands, eventually pinning it up on my wall as a reminder that it's there if I ever need it. There's so much to lose, things that have taken me years to build, and there's no rush after all. I'm no junkie, telling stories on drug forums. That's for people who had abusive parents, unhappy childhoods. That's for victims of the criminal justice system, the disenfranchised. That's for tortured artists and beat poets. Someone who isn't me.

"This road must have an end, right?" I drink lemonade, press my foot down hard on the gas, but the needle stays maxed out at ninety. The black line on the horizon seems larger than it did before. I squint into the distance. It's as remote and inevitable as death.

"Wasn't there something I was supposed to remember about that storm?"

I flip the visor down to block the sunlight. The black band on the horizon swells, almost imperceptibly. There's no turning around; there is no avoiding it. No matter how long it takes us, ten hours or ten years, we'll reach the storm eventually.

I stare into the distance. What a sad place.

I turn to Tim, "Are you scared?"

He smiles and looks up at the road. He can't see what's coming. But I can. I can see it all.

Check it out. Here I am, throwing a bottle of OxyContin in my bag, leaving for a party down the street. This little paper packet can stay here, safe, pinned to the wall, where it won't hurt anyone. If I'm not going to sleep, I might as well be social.

Everyone's already pretty fucked up at the party. The guitarist of a young band that I love asks me if I'm going to join the others doing cocaine inside. He asks if I'm going to "turn up." I tell him that I'm more the type to turn down.

He says, "But how far down do you turn?"

I give him the only answer I can think of: "All the way."

He says, "Fuck yes," whips out a couple lines and tells me it's "H."

"Horse."

"Heroin." I tense up.

He laughs, "Relax. It's not such a big deal."

I take an Oxy from my bag and crush it with the edge of my phone. He says, "Suit yourself, big spender." We pass a cut straw back and forth, each snorting from our own little piles. Soon the pill is coming on, so I grab my stuff and take off for home, across McCarren Park.

I can't help but wonder what Liza is doing at this very moment. Is she home in bed? Is she alone in her apartment, just beyond the edge of the park? Is she thinking of me, like I'm thinking of her? Or has she met somebody new? Is it too late to swing by and ring her bell or would that just freak her out? If it only took one conversation to split us apart, couldn't one conversation glue us back together?

Someone yells, "Hold up," and comes from behind to sling his arm around my shoulder in a warm, friendly gesture. He's tall. It's dark. Only shadows register under the brim of his baseball cap. I figure it's someone from the party, so I try to shake Liza out of my head and act casual, like, "Hi."

"Just keep walking," he says. "Give me your bag."

I start laughing. It's a funny thing to say. Though he doesn't seem to think it's funny. He adjusts something cold in my rib cage and repeats, "Give me your bag."

When I look at the thing pressing into my ribs, my knees buckle and the stranger has to catch me.

He says, "It's okay, I got you," even while the gunmetal flashes under the streetlight. I pass him my bag. It has my phone and wallet along with my rent in cash and my entire supply of opiates. "Can I just have my medication?" I ask him.

He pushes me away, takes a step back, "You sick or something?" Then he noses the barrel of the gun down into my backpack and taps it against the pill bottle. When he looks back up at me, he smiles, "Ain't getting these back, no way. Now close your eyes and turn around. Count to 100 while I decide whether or not to shoot you in the motherfucking head."

"**It's the end** of the world." The darkness ahead is a physical barrier in the road. Like the day just falls off a cliff.

In the rearview mirror, Steve presses play on a movie and crosses his arms. Tom adjusts his headphones. Tucker yawns and turns over. I look at Tim. He chews on one of his fingers, distractedly, reading his book. The storm swallows the sky. I push my seat up so I'm right against the windshield and I watch it come.

Check it out. Morning breaks. I'm sitting on my bed, staring at the heroin packet pinned to my wall. *It's not such a big deal.* My friend at the party said exactly that. *It's not such a big deal.* Maybe he's right. I'm starting to wonder if anything is a big deal anymore. The man with the gun granted me something. He also took something away. I just can't work out which is which.

Some days life feels like punishment. Others, like permission. First the band splits up, then Liza and I split up too. Now I'm flat broke and scared to go outside, seeing gunmen on every corner. With the band, at least I had seen it coming. No surprises there. But Liza and I were just getting started. We had both blown up our entire worlds, just for a shot at being together. Our thing began unexpectedly in the aisles of a kitchen store. She was buying a spatula and I was selling them. Her friends said I was just a phase, some fly-by-night charmer in a rock band. Her family said I was evil, a home-wrecker. My ex said my problem is I fall in love with everyone I meet. My parents said I should talk to a priest. But when all was said and done, I did the only thing I could. I loved her. No one could stop me. I didn't listen to caution. I didn't heed warnings. The thing is, Liza did. And we haven't spoken since.

I pull the heroin packet off my wall and sit on the bed, turning it over. The sun lands on the windowsill with all the glory of a discarded penny, making everything around it look cheap in its dull copper light. I grab a mirror and draw two lines, pointing at the horizon of my bedroom window, like a single highway lane taking me the only direction I want to go.

    I've already been on the road that led me here for miles.

    Maybe I've been on it my whole life.

Steve presses play on a movie and crosses his arms. Tom adjusts his headphones. I look over at Tim. He chews on one of his fingers, distractedly, reading his book. The stereo hums softly and then I hear it. Right before Tucker yawns and rolls over on the bench seat, I hear a pop. In the recording studio, we call this an audio artifact. If you make a digital edit to a recording, it doesn't make a sound. It's clean. But still, even an untrained ear will hear the edit if it's looped enough times. Your brain is always listening, always analyzing sounds for emotional and spatial cues. The trick is, don't listen for what's there; listen for what's missing.

    I hear the pop and it all becomes obvious. I look in the rearview mirror.

    "Steve presses play on that movie and crosses his arms," I say it out loud and then I watch it happen. "Tom scrunch your nose up. Wait, wait... There it is."

    I listen to the familiar sounds of the van.

    "Tucker," I find him in the rearview, "yawn and roll over."

    He does it. I hear the loop as it clicks over and starts again. The record is skipping. Ahead of me, the darkness has grown apocalyptic. As we close the distance, I see the boundary of the storm, a metal grate of rain, slamming down over street-level windows. Fear must've dragged me into a memory, a loop I could stay in, to run out the ibogaine's clock instead of facing myself.

    I know what I have to do.

    The record is sitting on the dash. I grab the sleeve.

"If this thing can stop time, maybe it can unstop it too." The sleeve is cool and smooth against my palm. I slide the record out and smash it against the dashboard. It shatters, scattering shiny black plastic pieces on the van's floor.

I turn to Tim. "Here it comes. Are you ready?"

He looks up at the road and smiles.

Check it out. I'm leaning over this mirror, putting a rolled-up dollar bill under my left nostril. One line of heroin disappears. I move to the other side and repeat the motion. It takes a little less than five seconds.

I want to experience some shit like the birth of the universe. Like the space behind my eyes tearing open, showing me the door to eternity. I want to be a god, towering and empty. But it's not like that. Instead, it's like remembering a grocery list of things that hurt. Not just your back and your knees and your joints and your teeth. But your skin and your blood and your breath and your memory and all those people you've known. Then the list gets longer and you remember more shit than could ever be listed: the sound of rain on windows, the cool clink of ice in a glass of water, the way your mom used to rub your back when you were too young to even know why you were crying, that song you heard coming out of a car radio and how you chased that car down the street just to hear the song a little bit longer, the smile from that girl in the kitchen store and the electric shock when she brushed her hand against yours and how you fell in love and thought it would last forever but then it didn't, and so, the list of hurts stretches on and on because that's the secret—everything hurts all the time—and it all just goes on hurting like that until my fear disappears and my body disappears and I look down into the empty mirror below me, finding only my two eyes, and then the shit really kicks in and the hurt disappears too.

SOMEONE WHO ISN'T ME

The front end of the van enters the storm like it's smashing through a window—first not at all, then all at once. The rain shatters against the hood, making a grey kaleidoscope of our windshield. Everything inside the van appears to float, as if we've plunged into the sea.

Daylight retreats in the rearview, two car lengths behind us, now three. It slips out of reach, just like that, and the storm slams down behind, sealing us inside. The wipers snap into action, raking water in unstable arcs. A hidden world reveals itself for a moment at a time—road, then sky, then storm—each a wafer-thin slice of consensual reality.

The air sizzles, rich with the smell of ozone. An acrid, chemical taste rises in the back of my throat.

"Hey, does anyone else smell that?"

My bandmates slump unconsciously in their seats, heads lolling back and forth in unison.

The hair on my arms stands up. A handful of lightning reaches down and slaps the hood of our van. Thunder cracks its knuckles in my ear. Our struts buckle. The suspension sends us into the air for a moment.

I see myself throwing up in the only stall of the men's room at work, then rolling to the ground next to the toilet, feet sticking out under the partition door. Wads of paper towels litter the floor, spilling out from an overfilled garbage can. I'm trying to negotiate the situation, telling the floor, *This room is for waste.* But I'm not getting anywhere. The floor's giving me talk back, *It's true, this room is for waste, so you must've been thrown out, partner.* Water runs through pipes. I watch a parade of employees from down the hall come in, one after the other. I see the door open. I see their legs as they walk in. I see the tags on their expensive sneakers. I see them stop. I watch their shiny sneakers turn around and walk out the door.

No time has passed in the van. We're still up, just off the ground, everything as it was, except now there's a high-frequency tone ringing in my ears, stealing the impact from our landing.

Without its sound, the storm becomes a kind of pantomime. Jagged branches of pure white touch down in balletic turns all around us.

In the Crif Dogs bathroom, I watch my last bag fall in the toilet. It lands on a big pile of shit that's not even mine. But it's my last bag, so I reach my hand in and pull it out, and what do you know, the fucking paper is soaked in piss, too wet to even snort, so I put the whole thing in my mouth—piss, shit, and all—and let it dissolve. It makes my eyes get all blurry and wet; it tastes so bad and, fuck, it turns out I had another bag in my pocket anyway, might as well snort it, but, of course, of-fucking-course, I rip the bag and it spills out on the floor and, honestly, at this point, what does it even matter? I get down on the ground and sniff it off the filthy floor of the goddamn bathroom of Crif Dogs, shit still sitting in the toilet behind me, when—are you fucking kidding me? I locked it, I totally locked it—the bathroom door opens and the sweet twenty-year-old who works the counter is looking down at me, no comment on my pants being down around my ankles or anything like that, thank god, just kind of shaking up and down.

"Could you please leave and maybe don't come back?"

Thunder rolls. Van rumbles. Rain comes down. Wipers keep wiping. Road, sky, storm. Another bolt of lightning splits the seams of reality. Rip, rip, rip.

I see myself offering sixty dollars to anyone on Bedford Avenue who might piss in a cup for me, and, no, I'm not blind, I see their reactions, one after the next, yes, I see their disgust, their shame, their anger, not just that I'd ask them such a rude and insane question but that I'd even try to talk to them in the first place, since they see that I'm not like them, no, I'm obviously a fucking maniac, a subhuman, a junkie, and I see my own thoughts running through my head like a bunch of lunatics running through the streets, so that my own reaction mirrors the disgust of the Bedford Avenue crowd, heartless goddamn consumers and gentrifiers, the world's biggest fucking circle jerk of a neighborhood, so yeah, I'm a fucking junkie but at least I can see the goddamn truth of it, at least I can admit what kind of an insane and heartless world this is, what a suicidal, selfish world we all live in, and none of it fucking matters, none of it lasts a single fiscal quarter, to put it in terms that you'd understand, to put it so you fucking get it, in other words, I'm saying, it doesn't last long, not the thing but how much the thing matters, it lasts for a second if it ever mattered, what I'm asking is, did it ever matter? Do you think anyone cares that I'm, what? A junkie? And you're? Like? A fucking green tech billionaire or something? Give me your piss or Fuck OFF.

I shudder in the driver's seat, causing the van to swerve slightly in its lane.
"Got no recollection of any of that."
Fast asleep, my band members sway with the road's contours.
"Doesn't really seem like me, though, does it?"
I lean my forehead against the windshield. Silver phosphors flare in the belly of the storm, where lightning unravels in incandescent threads, spidering along the underside of the clouds. As we advance along the road, the light advances along the sky.
"What else have you got buried in those clouds?"

Don's phone rings. It's Liza. For me.

"Saw you on the news. Local rock star mugged at gunpoint. You okay?"

"Only made the news because the guy started an Instagram account on my phone and it accidentally tagged all my friends. 'Criminals—they're just like us,' right?"

"I want to see you."

I look at the empty bag of heroin on the mirror, "Don't know if that's a good idea."

"I made a huge mistake. My family, my friends. They don't know you like I do."

"Some amount of stuff has come up. I got involved in something I shouldn't have."

"It's okay. I was lonely too. That guy I've been hanging out with. That was a mistake."

So it was true. She had moved on. I pick up the empty bag and rip it open. I lick the seams, then suck on the wet paper. Little by little, the ache in my stomach disappears. Little by little, I can see the future opening up before me. Liza still loves me. I hear it in her voice. This will be the last time I do heroin. Why would I ever need it again, now that life is beautiful and nothing hurts? Now that I'm not alone. Now that I don't have to kill myself. I'll quit for her. I'll do it. No problem.

"I'm free," I tell her. "Want to buy me dinner?"

Three lightning strikes converge just over the road's shoulder. A luminous sphere of magnesium-white forms at its center. Hovering just ahead of our van, the ball of lightning fills with imagery. I see so many scenes all spilling open, side by side now, coming together to form a bigger picture, and, for the first time, I can see clearly who I've become in the last five years: I see it on my friends' faces, like when I told Norman, in a meeting with our record distributor, about how long I had been clean and how proud I was of myself. I told him that—and I meant it, I really did—even though at the time I was nodding in and out of consciousness at the head of the table. I see now that he knew I was high, he always knew, of course he did.

I see my parents, looking hopeful and sincere, like when I explained that I just needed a little help to get clean—just a little help, I mean *financially*—to get through this year. Even though they didn't want to, even though they fought it, they knew—maybe they didn't even consciously realize it, but they knew I was lying to them—and they helped me anyway. I see how good everyone has been to me, how hard they've tried to love me, even as the person they knew disappeared.

"This is it, isn't it? My *true self*." I look at Steve, suspended in position by his seatbelt. "Is this how you see me? Is this who I really am?"

The sky cracks open in a blinding flash. Lightning splinters the clouds, a thousand bright fractures crawling from a central point, through which my doubts disappear like a child through the thin surface of a frozen pond.

Someone who isn't me stands alone in front of a mirror. It's the stranger from the reflection in the van's window. Could that be me? I see the back of the head, the shoulders. In the mirror, I see the blue eyes, the bad teeth. Without a doubt, the person is me. I watch his right arm swing out to the side, his hand clenched in a fist. It comes fast, smashing into his face with a loud crunch. But there's no reaction. Just a thousand-yard stare. Then, his left fist connects with his nose. Blood pours out his left nostril. Still no reaction. The punches come more quickly now. I watch him slap and scratch at his face, his chest, and hear the words, streaming past his lips, just above a whisper, "fucking fuck, piece of shit, fucking piece of fucking shit," but, still, no reaction registers in the eyes in the mirror. I'm too far away; I want to see what he sees. So I move closer, I put my hand up to try and reach into his body.

My vision goes black. I see a familiar highway sign. A hand getting zapped. *DANGER.* Big white letters. *Risk of Electrical Shock: Do Not Enter.* I push in anyway. I feel myself enter the body like a charge. My eyes open. A black and white portrait comes into view. It's old and grainy but instantly recognizable. I squint at the portrait, trying to bring it into focus, because I know. This is it: this is how I see myself. The charge continues to build, only reaching its limit as the portrait comes into focus and I recognize it, I see the picture, but it's—it's—

It's Hitler.

I open my eyes, jump out of the body, and step back from the mirror.

I open my eyes. The van swerves into the shoulder, jumps the median.

I gasp through the surface of consciousness.

"Oh fuck—Am I Hitler?"

Javi stops writing and looks up from his desk.

"Sorry," I whisper. "It must've been some kind of mistake." The room wobbles. Javi leans forward in his chair, adjusts his thick, black-rimmed glasses.

"Está bien?" he asks.

"Don't worry," I smile, weakly, "I'm not really Hitler. I'm 90 percent sure."

He narrows his eyes at me, clicks his pen.

"Okay, 80 percent." I take a deep breath and close my eyes.

Distant flickers hint at the shifting texture of the storm. In one moment, the rain solidifies into a swarm of cicadas. In the next, it crystallizes into a hail of diamonds, fragile and fine. The wind shouts itself out, growing increasingly hoarse until the last of its breath is spent, and the day falls silent, suddenly uncertain of its own fury.

Everything is high gloss; the rain must have been a kind of lacquer. Highway merges with beltway, curving around some distant point, like a massive traffic circle. All of it slick, all of it wet. It looks like we're driving on a giant record, each lane a different groove. And up above, the sky mirrors the road, changing from the thick grey plumes of storm cloud into something smooth and reflective. I can feel a rumbling beneath us. I know we're moving but the absence of any landmark makes it appear that the record spins, beneath us, while our van remains completely still: a needle held in place by a hidden hand.

A column of light breaks through an opening in the clouds at the center of the storm: the central spoke of the record, the point around which everything turns. I bank the wheel, crossing three highway lines and jumping the median in the process. We travel perpendicular to the intended flow of traffic, gouging a deep trail, making a sound like a stylus scratching across vinyl. The noise tears all rational thought from my mind. Then it stops. The ground runs smooth. We stall, coast for twenty feet, then come to rest against a curb. I roll the window down. Over the engine's dry hiss, I hear that maddening, empty sound:

ca-chic-ca-chic-shhhhhh
ca-chic-ca-chic-shhhhhh

"This is it? This is the runout groove? Where the music finally stops?"

All the guys in back are out cold. Tim slumps against the passenger window. I grab a sleeping bag from the floor and drape it across his lap.

"It's alright. Only talking to myself anyway."

In the eye of the storm, everything is calm. Sunlight bathes a fresh green lawn and lights up a red house with white trim. No cars in the driveway but my old bike leans against the porch. This is the house I grew up in. It must be the record's center label, the place beyond sound and time. I step out of the van and cross the lawn.

There's a spare key to the front door waiting for me under a flower pot on the porch. The key turns, but the door sticks. Its wooden frame must be swollen from the humid air. I throw my shoulder against it and the house opens into the kitchen with a squeak.

No one is home. I can tell right away. All empty houses sound the same.

It takes no time at all to walk around the ground floor, with its circular layout: kitchen giving way to living room and then to dining room, before emptying back into the kitchen, where I came in. Taken all at once, the house is fairly small. All of it surrounds a central staircase, which leads to my bedroom upstairs. I take the stairs up to my old room, two at a time, first leaning over to brush my fingertips against the worn red carpeting on its steps.

Everything is just as it was: the shade of light coming from the second-floor landing, the texture of the tan wallpaper on my left. Even the massive oak tree, growing up through the center of the stairwell, is somehow familiar, even though I don't remember it ever being here. Reaching the second floor, I see that the tree has been felled, cut clear across its center, the top of its trunk resembling a large round table. I place my hand on the smooth wooden surface and count the rings, starting at the outer edge: ten, twenty, thirty… by the time I've hit a hundred, I've barely started. There must be five thousand rings, maybe ten thousand.

I move around the oak, take a breath, and open the door to my old bedroom.

Everything is exactly the way I had it when I was a little kid: ET bed sheets; hollow, wooden crucifix on the wall; desk in the corner, absolutely covered in white-lined paper; and toys. They're everywhere. Teddy Ruxpin, MASK, M.U.S.C.L.E. MEN. Even a Millennium Falcon with the gun turret snapped off. I remember the day I got it. I threw it up in the air to see if it could fly. It couldn't.

This room is identical to my childhood bedroom in every detail except one: this room is on fire. It burns internally, without any smoke, as if the place itself were the reincarnation of flame. White ash lines the walls, synthetic yellow carpet steams in patches, veins of molten rock run through everything. Action figures sink through the floor in pools of molten plastic that were once their legs—looks of agony dripping from their faces—and comic books burn—sending flecks of fire up into the air, where they pirouette, unbound from pages.

In the center of the room, it's me. Just me.

Little five-year-old me in red polyester footie pajamas. Overgrown bowl cut hanging down over his trusting blue eyes. Runny nose. Chocolate-stained hands. Holding a stuffed Oscar the Grouch doll to his chest with such tenderness. Whispering in its ear and laughing at whatever Oscar whispers back.

He walks over to the bed, peers at me through Oscar's matted green fur, and asks, "What's your name?"

I touch my fingers to my lips, "My name is—"

He looks up at me, expectantly, but I can't think of anything to say. Children need reassurance. Stability. I wish there were someone here to help me, someone who isn't me.

"My name is taking a nap inside my mouth," I say.

He nods, slowly, "Naps are for babies. I'm five."

"That's really grown up."

"Five and three quarters," he raises five outstretched fingers on his left hand and adds the pointer finger on his right, holding it up between us like a talisman. "Almost six. And... My... Name... Is—"

"Geoff," I blurt out, crouching in front of him. "That's your name."

He twirls his pointer finger and boops my nose, "That's your name too. Did you forget?"

"I forgot, completely and totally."

"That's so silly," he sets down Oscar and takes my hand.

Little Geoff leads me back out to the landing.

"Let me show you," he says. He climbs up the tree stump and stands in the center. "See?" He points to the innermost ring between his feet.

Looking down, I see a pebble thrown in a wooden pond, the years rippling out in waves around it. A record of damage displaced. Charred black streaks where the bark was pierced on the northern side. Scars from a forest fire that burned entire years off its body.

"Is this the tree of life?"

"No," little Geoff laughs, sticking his fingers in his mouth.

"Is it dead?"

"What? Noooooo," he starts jumping up and down in frustration, "you don't get it."

"But this tree has been cut down."

"Not cut *down*," he corrects me, pointing up to a hole in the ceiling, "cut *open*."

I climb onto the tree stump and look up through the hole in the roof. High above, in the upper atmosphere, a vast canopy of oak branches out across the sky, stippling the air gold and green under the feathery shadows of leaves. The canopy stretches from a central trunk that floats directly above me. I see its cross section: smooth polished wood. I can count its rings, identify the damage. It's the same tree as the one that I'm standing on.

"Are we inside of it," little Geoff asks me, "or is it inside of us?"

Pointing to the centermost ring, he shouts, "It's me!" Now that he mentions it, he does kind of look like a sapling. "And that one is you," he points to a ring further out. The wind picks up, blowing through the canopy. It looks like breathing, the way the leaves blur and bloom in slow motion.

Softly through the branches, a fresh snowfall begins. Big white flakes flutter down, glowing with a powdery light. I watch them tumbling, end over end, until one somersaults through the hole in the ceiling, into my hand. The flake is cold but has the texture of starched paper. It makes a crinkling noise as I close my fist around it. When I open my hand again to examine it, I see that it's not a snowflake at all but a small, white paper bag with a cartoon tree printed on it in black ink with the words *Forest Fire*.

My younger self reaches up to touch the bag, where it sits in my palm. He looks up at me, "It hurts." I drop the bag and slide my hands under his arms. He's so light, he's almost no weight at all.

"It's okay," I tell him, hugging his little body against my chest. "I've got you." Deep reds and bright yellows ignite in the branches above us. Burnt orange and coffee-tinged browns go sparking through the leaves.

"No," he says, "the tree is sick."

Everything is wilting. Desiccated grey branches fall. Sunlight crashes through the canopy. Beneath my feet, the wood feels soft and mushy. Out the southern window, the storm continues to turn in black spirals around us. I watch the lawn disappearing, inch by inch, everything squeezing in on the house.

"We better get out of here," I hold the boy and try to run but my feet have sunk into the rotten wood. I can't free myself.

"No," he cries, "we can't go out. Only in." The atmospheric pressure is enormous. I can feel the air pushing down on us. A scratching sound starts up on the other side of the wall, armies of termites in the wooden supports.

"Doctor," I shout at the ceiling. "Nurse, can anybody hear us?" The embers of the room brighten as if they've been blown on, but no answer comes. An emptiness opens up inside me, deeper than a hole in the ground, so deep that I can feel it in the house's bones, in its foundation, so deep, it must be inside and under everything.

The boy points down into the tree, "We have to go inside."

"What's in there?"

Emptiness floods in through the windows, *ca-chic-ca-chic-shhhhhh*. I can hear it rolling over the horizon. The boy hiccups in my face, "The dream." Out the window, the ruins are closing, one by one, whole city blocks compressing in accordion bellows.

I feel panic rising. The house is gone now. We're sunk up to our shoulders in the rings of the tree. My friends are all gone. I'll never see Liza again. I'll never make things right.

Immense waves of heat crash through the opening in the ceiling, accompanied by a crackling noise. The low winter sun opens its mouth and a tongue of flame leaps to the tree's canopy. Fire spreads, dancing through the dry leaves in slow circles. Now everything is passion. We sink down through the tree, our heads bowed under the golden crown of the burning world.

"This is the dream," the boy tells me. Everything is black. His small face is very close. It's all I can see. His blue eyes are completely open—innocent and defenseless. As he speaks, I watch the story animate his features, "In the dream, there's a maze and there's a person standing in it."

He points at me, "You're the person."

"Inside the maze, the light changes depending on which turn you take. And every choice you make is wrong. But there's no way to turn back," The boy waves his arms around him, "because everything keeps changing. If you go through a door in the maze and then you decide to turn around, the room might not be there anymore—maybe just a hallway where a room once was or a staircase or a wall—and that's just the start."

The boy pauses and touches his fingers to his lips, reflecting. I wonder if he isn't older than I initially thought. Perhaps eleven or twelve.

"What about the change that the light makes to the person as it flickers over them?" he asks. "The one who enters the maze becomes unrecognizable to themselves within even a few turns. You might become an orphan or a widow in the maze. You might lose your job. You might become desperate in the maze; see yourself a liar, a cheat in the maze; become a murderer or a thief. You may lose yourself completely."

The boys stops and takes a breath. He looks down, evasively, and when he looks back up at me, he winces. He must be a teenager, at least. Possibly even seventeen or eighteen.

"So, you're walking through the maze and the light is changing, and you're changing, and, no matter which direction you pick, the light lets you know that you picked wrong, so that the further you go into the maze, the further wrong you become, and every direction has one thing in common, it points further into the maze, so that you are always traveling deeper and the light dims so completely that you become estranged from yourself, to the point that you begin to shout, 'Hello? Is anyone there? Am I even here?'"

The boy continues aging. Stubble appears on his cheeks. He gains weight.

"While, at the same time," he laughs, "you hear the questions reflected back through the corridors and ask yourself, 'Who is that shouting? Is there someone in here? What do you want?'"

The boy looks over his shoulder into the darkness. When he returns to the story, there are dark circles beneath his eyes.

"Hearing the words reflected back to you, as if for the first time, you perceive the escalating aggression of the questions, the rising tenor of the voice, and you know, suddenly, that you must find the source of this voice—you must find the person who is speaking—and you must kill them."

The boy is thinning out again. He looks tired. His pupils are pinned.

"So now you're running, searching for the person that you must kill, though moments ago you were not a killer, and the maze is changing more quickly and the light is dimming and you are panting and you're getting agitated. Confused. You're doubled over, gasping. Still, it comes to you in a flash: the oxygen levels in the air correspond to the light levels in the maze."

The boy doesn't look in my eyes anymore; he just stares through, at a point somewhere behind me.

"So you're panting and you're lost and desperate and you must kill someone who is looking for you at this very moment, but, also, have the walls been closing in, is the ceiling getting lower?"

His eyelids begin to sag. He's not looking at anything anymore. The words spill out of his mouth, without any internal editing. Is he even listening to himself?

"These are the questions spinning through your oxygen-starved mind, when you see the figure running just ahead of you. But you know this is the point now, don't get distracted, as you take off after this person, but suddenly—miraculously, you think—the figure turns toward a doorway that has wide-open light streaming through it and you hear them gasping into the light, drinking it down, and you run fast to catch them, no, forget about them, you sprint toward the light, the air, the exit, but your elation turns to horror, where the opening, the escape, the air, and the light empties out over the side of a cliff and you watch the person plunging to their death. And you realize that they saw the cliff, that they knew they were choosing a moment of light—a moment of air out in the open—over continuing to live in the maze and you feel a bit of envy but mostly you feel thankful that you have not made such a rash and permanent decision."

The boy seems to wake up. He raises his line of sight.

"And then you remember that the person is you."

For the first time, I see myself clearly.

"The person is me."

And it hurts so fucking much.

III

BORDERLANDS

Bodies can fail in all different kinds of ways. Proponents of medical science claim that if you ignore the circumstances leading to a death and examine instead the mechanism of failure at work, there are basically four ways to die: oxygen starvation, lethal temperature, chemical toxins, and physical damage.

Oxygen starvation. Lethal temperature. They have such beautiful clinical terms. But I've never seen anyone die in clinical terms. Suffocation. Stroke. Aneurysm. Car crash. That's how people die in the world I grew up in.

When my friends talk about death, they talk about a gunshot, a twist of the knife in the center of the guts. But I'm from the suburbs. I saw a lot of people just forgetting what it takes to stay alive. Falling down the stairs. Slipping through thin ice on a frozen lake. Falling asleep in the raging fire of their own homes. The difference between two Tylenol and twenty.

It's not rare. It happens all the time.

Even a relatively minor injury can keep you from continuing to exist. People go into shock. People bleed out. All it takes is four pints. Lose that much blood all at once and you might think gravity is getting stronger, pushing down on you until even breathing gets hard and your limbs drag against the ground, until the color runs off the walls into the gutter, taking the living world with it soon after.

Blunt force trauma. Electrocution. When my uncle used to work in a home for troubled youths, he pulled a boy off a wall socket where the kid had jammed a fork, making a circuit of death. The boy's body turned off like a light switch before the medic showed up and turned it back on.

I once saw a body in the woods near Allison Park. That's up in the Palisade Cliffs. My buddy James noticed it first. He spotted its red right arm sticking out from under the brown leaves, hand curled in a fist, with just the last two fingers outstretched. We argued about what it looked like, a gang sign or a distress signal. But we were both wrong. It looked like a piece of bruised fruit someone threw in the garbage.

Bodies can fail on purpose. It's not hard. Take a bottle of sleeping pills and never wake up. Throw yourself off a roof and the ground will stop your body but the rest of you will just keep on going, deep into the hidden place below.

In high school, my French partner's body failed to stop a train on the tracks behind the football field. He just sat down on them and didn't get up. I had to step, every morning, over the stain of his blood just to get to school on time. When I got there that first day after it happened, I spent first period French class staring at his empty chair as my teacher called out *Christian, Christian,* repeatedly, with no answer. Eventually someone told her why he was gone and she walked right out of the classroom. We saw her smoking a cigarette in the parking lot through our second-floor windows.

Oxygen starvation. Lethal temperature. Chemical toxins. Physical damage.

Bodies can fail in all different kinds of ways. But some ways happen more frequently than others. Statistics tell us that drug overdoses currently kill more people in the United States every year than gun homicides and car crashes combined. Opiate painkillers, in particular, along with their synthetic analogues make up the fastest growing segment of drug-related deaths, increasing at twice the rate as any previous year of the last decade. Current figures indicate no signs of stopping or even slowing down. In fact, looking at a bar graph that charts the rise of opiate-related overdose deaths year over year from the last two decades is like staring up at a series of cliffs that are too steep to climb.

But when junkies talk about death, we don't rely on statistics. We don't say *overdose*. We don't say *it was an accident*. In the world we live in, death sits down for breakfast with us every morning and still no dose is ever over the limit. You can't take too much. In the world we live in, getting heroin in your body is never an accident.

No. When someone dies in our world, we say, *they fell out*. We say, *they dropped*. As if life were a tall window, set high above some glittering city, that we perch along, leaning further and further out to get a glimpse.

When one of us dies, we tell ourselves, *they crashed*, each of us imagining our own body as a heavy piece of machinery that must be steered around a high canyon pass at heart-stopping speeds. We say, *they just slipped away*, as if existence were a dinner party that we keep excusing ourselves from, one by one. Or we adopt the even tone of the doctors, announcing, *they didn't make it*, as we attempt to hide our hurt at being forgotten, once and for all, by our fellow travelers.

My friend K, who showed me where to score dope out in Oakland, used to reminisce about the people he used to see out there, on the street; people he didn't see anymore. He said, "They turned all the way down," as if our bodies were expensive stereos and life was a song that lasted only as long as we could hear it.

Michael, who worked in the dean's office of a prestigious college, would obsessively list the names of the recently dead every time he took me down that long, dark hallway in Chinatown. He'd snap his fingers and tell me, "They got burned." To him, each day was another bag we had to buy from a dealer, just to get by, and eventually everyone got a bad batch. He did.

Melissa from the NA group around the corner used to say, "Gone." No explanation was necessary. Nothing happened. They were here and now they're not. "Just gone," she'd say, from her plastic chair, in the days when we were both trying to kick, but that was before she got back with her drug-dealing ex-boyfriend and now she doesn't even say that.

Fell out. Slipped away. Didn't make it. Junkies have such soft words to describe violence. So much so, that these words are often in direct contradiction with the scenes unfolding right in front of our eyes.

I remember copping once at the 42nd Street/Port Authority Bus Terminal in the exact spot a man had died just a day earlier. My drug dealer saw the whole thing. Apparently the guy had told him he'd "had enough of drifting around like a leaf in the wind" when he bought his last bag. Then he disappeared into the second-story public men's room. The one with the heavy doors and deadbolt locks on the stalls. Twenty minutes later, he was dead in the middle of the thoroughfare. My dealer threw down an empty pistachio shell to solemnly mark the spot. "Here lies the stone that split the river." But the river looked unchanged to me. The stream of people carried on as before. No one had even noticed him until rush hour ended.

If the words we use to describe violence seem soft, please understand that this grace does not extend to all things. No, for heroin users, the smallest misunderstanding will often stretch to operatic heights. This owes to a basic inversion common to all drug addicts. While we are in the grips of addiction, we can still see the life beyond us, but we see it through the looking glass of the drug, which flips the image of the world as it really is and shows us something that we can accept. In this way, our bodies fail to process reality.

When I say that my body failed too—it failed to hold up to the stresses of ibogaine in my system—and that I died right there in that hospital bed in Tijuana, adding my name to the long list of drug statistics, this is not a lie. This is a liberty that I can only take because I am still alive.

An orderly shakes me by the shoulder. I open my eyes and life returns. I exist. My body has not failed. Gradually, the orderly's features come into focus and I recognize Juan. But something's off. His eyes are small fires, set deep in the cave of their sockets. I feel like a marshmallow, roasting under his gaze.

"Take your shirt," he tells me, face flickering against the grey morning light. "The visions are over but… Next part is like. So much heat."

I look past him. "Yes. I see."

The clinic smolders at the edges. I wonder if maybe the ibogaine has slipped its container and set our world ablaze. It's no worse than my childhood room had been, moments ago. But that was just a dream and this, apparently, is my new reality.

"This might take some getting used to."

"You'll be okay," he says. "Trust me." He smiles at me, face rising with woodsmoke and spark. I look deep into his blazing eyes.

"How did you get your pupils to do that?" I lean toward him. "Did you sneak a little ibogaine for yourself?"

He backs away from me, showing his teeth in the imitation of a smile, but all the warmth has left his features. Things just get worse for him when he reaches the other side of the room and bumps up against Duane's bed.

"Hey Juan," Duane shouts, "just want to know: Did I die here? Or back in Kandahar?" I watch them out of the corner of my eye. Juan says, *oh, oh, oh* and walks off to find a doctor.

"Oh sure, just go about your business," Duane continues. "Meanwhile, I'm dead over here. And no one is even taking me out with the trash." But it's a peripheral matter. Everything is now. If Duane's dead, that's his business.

"Wow. Did you hear? Duane *died*," Kate whispers from the bed next to me. I turn my head and the two-dimensional inferno of the room shatters and reassembles itself, in a series of dull photographs, until she's in the center of my field of vision. "See, I thought I died too," she adds, "but I was just *tripping*. Poor Duane. I guess he's really dead. And John is completely covered in crickets."

I look past Kate and see John with his head thrown back in a deep sleep. His snoring echoes and distorts. It all seems digitized: Every movement pixelates and reforms. The signal is lagging. I can't see any crickets on him but the persistent chirping sound has become a kind of low-level hum underneath everything. I accept it as a permanent development.

"Guess that makes us the only two survivors."

Kate looks around and clears her throat, "Huh. I guess it does."

"Can I ask you something? Did you ask to see your true self?"

Kate puts a hand up to her mouth and laughs into her fist, with a little cough, "I'm Cleopatra." She glows quietly in her skin and then asks, "How about you?"

"Don't know. I thought I was Hitler or the Devil or something terrible like that... But I could just be a lonely little kid."

"Uh huh," she nods, still smiling. "I see it."

About halfway between the living and the dead, the nervous system steps away from the world and its surroundings and runs on a parallel track for three days, so as to shrink away from a certain desolate feeling that the body produces after an ibogaine trip. This is Grey Time—the despondent day when all the used-up light from the fantastic hallucinatory night crumbles and falls over the world, like a shroud, reducing every color to charcoal and cloud cover, when dust gathers on every surface, revealing not just grey tables, grey chairs, grey hospital beds and operating tables but also fully functioning grey machines—grey heart monitors and grey brain scans and grey blips—watched over by the ghostly grey shadows of orderlies. Occasionally, an emergency issues from one of the machines in a desperate red alarm and a patient rises in sudden color from their grey bed and immediately the grey doctors surround them with their syringes full of leaden sleep. The patient leans back on the pillow and the doctor tucks a heather-grey blanket under their chin and the entire hospital slips back into dust.

"How many people kill themselves in the comedown from ibogaine?" John asks Javi. "One in four? One in five? Have you ever lost a whole group?"

This is back at the beach house, all of us sitting on a trio of grey leather couches around a grey fire. There's a giant pot of chicken pozole steaming on the stove in the kitchen. I would maybe eat some of it but I'm wrapped up in a grey blanket and can't imagine how to get out.

"When did we leave the clinic?" I ask.

"See what I'm saying?" John motions at me with the brim of his cap. "He'll be the first to go. He's barely holding on."

Javi asks me, "What's the last thing you remember?"

I cough. Water drips off my hair and runs down my face. "Why is my hair wet?"

They all look at Javi like, *Should we tell him?* He shakes his head, *No*.

"I remember John was still sleeping, and Duane," I tell them, "well, Duane was yelling about being dead."

Duane spits out a little chew into an empty Coke bottle, "Mmm, I did think I was dead. Saw the body on a slab and everything. But that was more a, whatdoyacallit, *premonition*... of what'll happen if I keep drinking. That really your last recollection?"

I nod.

Kate brushes her hair back and gives me a sad smile, "Oh, honey, that was two days ago."

"Have I just been sleeping it off?"

They all turn to Javi. He leans back and smoothes his mustache.

Duane shrugs, "Juan said you haven't slept since Monday. We took ibogaine on Tuesday night."

John crosses his arms, "Today is Friday."

Javi interjects, "Which means I'm almost out of time with you all. So..."

"Right," John says, "sorry. So, as I was saying, I used to think it was more just a matter of circumstance. You pick up because you're bored, sitting around in the green zone all day. Then, you keep using because the shit makes you invincible, you know, when you're out there—"

"When you were in the war zone?" Javi suggests. John looks over at Duane. They both laugh.

"Yeah," John says, "the *war zone*, sure."

"Like they put some tape around it," Duane says.

"*Have your war here,*" John smirks back. "But, you know, now I see that there was trauma happening all the time over there. And back here, you know? Life doesn't wait for you. It just keeps on flying by."

Duane breaks in, "My unit was stuck in a firefight—*boxed in* is what I'd call it—and a bullet doesn't just make a hole, even with all that tactical gear. It tears a man open. Things fall out, things fly off the body. The rational mind don't know what to do, so you try and put 'em back together. I held my buddy's stomach in place while he died in sections, bullets skipping in through the walls."

John picks up the story, again, "What you might not understand is how easy it is to get heroin over in Afghanistan. The locals practically slip it into your pockets as you pass. And your fellow Marines? Everyone is either numbing down or speeding up. But mostly we're all walking in circles waiting to kill something or get killed our own selves."

"That's perfectly understandable," Javi tells him. "You were put in an impossible situation. Whatever happened over there. It doesn't define who you are. You are both allowed to come home."

Kate shudders a little at the word *home*.

"Kate?" Javi asks.

"I'm not sure I want to go home," she tells him, nervously adjusting the sleeves of her hoodie. "What do you do when the trauma happened *at home*?" When she pulls her hair back, I can see rows of track marks, in various stages of healing, all up and down her arms.

"Are you scared to go back to your husband?" Javi asks. "Has he hurt you?"

"No... What?" Kate snaps, growing frustrated with her sweatshirt before finally deciding to take it off. "No. It's just what I have to tell him. It will hurt him. It hurts me. I was very small. Before we took the ibogaine you tried to prepare me. You said *a lot of women* uncover this kind of trauma when they take ibogaine. I just assumed you meant a lot of *other* women…"

I tilt my whole body over toward her and whisper, "It's going to be okay."

She leans away, turning her head to get a better view, "You look ridiculous."

Javi uncrosses his legs and scoots forward in his chair, "What about you, Geoff? Where does your pain come from?"

Kate dabs her eyes.

Duane spits into the bottle.

John cracks his knuckles.

Where do we locate the origin of pain?

Medical science locates pain at the intersection between intense or damaging stimuli and the body's nervous system. Evolutionary theory positions it as the motivational urge to protect oneself from harm, whereas biochemistry links all pain back to a basic inflammatory reaction.

But what about trauma—pain that leaves a mark? Where do we locate the origin of inexplicable, irreversible personal damage? David Lynch locates the origin of American trauma as July 16, 1945, in White Sands, New Mexico, 5:29 a.m., at the exact moment that we detonated the first atom bomb. It would be another month before our Air Force would drop a pair of these weapons on two cities in Japan, ending over 100,000 lives. But Lynch places the origin of the trauma in the test, when we first opened our eyes to the idea.

I'm not so sure.

There was murder in America before the atom bomb. Matricide, patricide, genocide. Our foundational myths are all soaked in the blood of the people whose land we built our homes on top of. And let's not pretend that trauma is an American product. We imported it, like just about everything else in this country.

One hundred years before his compatriots would "discover" the American continent, the Italian scholar Petrarch located the birth of trauma at the fall of the Roman Empire. He saw the Dark Ages dawning all around him. We tend to think of this trauma in terms of a bloody physical brutality but Petrarch was talking about the trauma of ignorance, the paucity of ideas, the loss of humanity that comes with a crumbling Church.

Though, as far as the Church is concerned, the Bible places trauma much earlier. The first man born to woman, Cain, murdered his own brother, Abel, and yet Genesis 3 posits the fall of man earlier, still, in the eating of the forbidden fruit from the tree of knowledge. God finds the couple cowering from him, covering their own nudity and punishes them, telling Adam, *Cursed is the ground because of you; / through painful toil you will eat food from it / all the days of your life / It will produce thorns and thistles for you, / and you will eat the plants of the field. / By the sweat of your brow / you will eat your food, / until you return to the ground / since from it you were taken; / for dust you are / and to dust you will return*—thereby conflating the creation of work with the creation of death, forever, in one small pronouncement.

But I think the birth of trauma comes earlier in the Bible. The snake in the garden pushes Eve to eat the forbidden fruit, telling her, "When you eat from it, your eyes will be opened, and you will be like God, knowing good and evil."

Knowing good and evil.

That sounds like pain to me.

In which case, the birth of trauma was at the first moment of conscious thought. Not the first death. Not the original murder. Not even when Adam and Eve got caught. But the moment the idea opened its eyes.

Well.

I can remember my mother telling me it wasn't natural. She said, "A young kid shouldn't lose so many of his peers." It was "too much." I remember our entire French class bursting into tears when we heard the train's ghost whistle the Monday morning after losing our classmate. It was the same day that the school let us out early for his funeral. We were all wearing our black suits and dresses. "Nice outfit," one of the kids a year below me joked as I walked up the lawn before first period, "who died?" I thought he was being sarcastic. I thought he was being cruel. So I pushed his head through a hole in the fence. But he wasn't being cruel.

He just didn't know.

Before that, around my eighth birthday, there were the older kids with their suicide pact in Bergenfield. Blamed on heavy metal music by the cops and newspapers. But really just the end result of shame and survivor's guilt from an earlier tragedy: The previous September they had all gotten drunk up in the cliffs and one of them fell. They blamed themselves. How could they not? Everyone else did. I'm sure I would've done what they did too.

I almost did.

A couple times.

The guitarist from my first band, Mike, died of an overdose just recently. But we all got in pretty deep, even as kids. My French partner, the one who killed himself on the tracks? He wasn't the only one. Another member of our little group dropped a birthday present on those same tracks not long after. Everyone told her to leave it. *It's not worth it.* But she had to try. None of us were rich. Some of us couldn't explain it, if we brought misfortune home, no matter how small. Excuses didn't buy new winter jackets. Excuses didn't pay medical bills. Only parents could do that.

I used to imagine trauma was a force of motion, something that sat heavy in the freight cars that came barreling through the center of our town. I used to sit up all night, listening to its metallic song, clanging out: *ca-chic-ca-chic-shhhhhh, ca-chic-ca-chic-shhhhhh.* You didn't have to be standing on the tracks for the train to hit you either. It could find you in the headlights of an oncoming car or in the tip of a needle. It could find you in the closet of your own home.

When I was still in elementary school, that train found its way into the hands of my best friends in the barrel of an old service revolver, lying around in a cluttered attic. They passed it around, felt the danger sleeping in its chamber, until finally K squeezed the trigger as a joke, *fuck you—bang—you're dead*, but it went off in his hand, for real, and then, all at once, S was dead, forever. And K was the kid who killed his best friend. And I was the kid who had gotten into a fistfight with S just three days before. And in those three days, I'd prayed to God, every hour, on the hour, to kill S—to kill him dead.

And then, he did.

Should I locate the origin of pain in K's gunshot or my prayer?

I'm still not sure.

When I was little, just seven or eight years old, my mother told me, "If I don't wake up tomorrow, just know it's not your fault." She had broken her back in a wreck that split her car open and dumped her over the guard rail. Her recovery was a slow, painful process. I was scared a lot of the time after that accident, but, until that night, it never occurred to me that any of it might've been my fault. That, all this time, the train might've been me.

Well.

Was it?

A single, lost moth circles the lightbulb over our heads. Desire will burn all the dust off its body. I raise two fingers as a perch for the insect to land on. Its soft body collides with the hot glass and drops to the ground.

John says, "What did I tell you? Not long for this world."

Then I'm on the stairs.

Then I'm lying half-awake in my bed on the cold lower level of the beach house, waiting for the night to come in a deeper shade.

And then it does.

"If you hear people screaming, it's okay. I screamed too. It's just the ego trying to hold on."

I hear Javi starting the morning session without me as I top the stairs and come into the main room, overlooking the beach. I can smell the ocean, hear the waves crashing against the shore.

"Hold up!"

Kate makes a spot for me on the couch. The fire burns behind its screen under the mantel. Sun rays flood the room in a blinding gold color, catching prismatically in wisps of amber smoke.

"Goddamn! It lives," John says, passing me a worn red blanket with little purple tassels on one end.

"Howdy-do, partner," Duane calls, pantomiming a cowboy riding a horse. I can see a bulge of dip, tucked in under his lower lip, when he smiles. Kate dissolves into laughter, pulling her sleeves over her fists to dab the corners of her eyes.

"I wasn't really myself these last few days," I apologize.

"No, man, you *were*," Duane replies. "That's why it was so funny. Wish you coulda seen yourself on that horse. With all them black New York clothes and your hair flopping around. Hell."

"I was back on *Horse*? Where did I get it from?"

"Horse*back riding*," Duane pronounces each syllable slowly.

"Don't remember any of that."

"How about gettin' dumped in the creek? You remember that?" John asks me.

"This really happened?"

John opens his hand, "You owe me five dollars, my man."

"Aw, sheee-itttt…" Duane drawls.

I look into the fireplace. At least the flames have been swept into a container once again. The clock reads 7:57 a.m.

"What's on the schedule, Javi?"

"We're prepping for your session with the Toad."

"That sounds pretty satanic. Especially with all this incense burning."

"I know, it's like fucking church in here," John says, scrunching his face up.

Javi holds up one hand, "The smoke is coming from downstairs, where the shaman is performing a purification ritual in preparation for your meeting with the Toad."

"Who's the Toad?" The fire swells against a quick gust of ocean wind.

"The toad medicine," Kate says. "DMT."

"That's right," Javi reassures us. "5-meo-DMT occurs naturally in the venom of the *Bufo alvarious toad*. They're native to the Sonoran Desert, right nearby."

"You kill the toads?" Kate asks, eyes still watering.

"Milk them," Javi clarifies.

"That doesn't sound vegan."

"We hope to provoke a transpersonal experience by inducing a temporary, controlled ego death. Some call it *Unity with God*; others, *Enlightenment* or *Absolute Unitary Being*; I, personally, like the Sufi term *Lifting the Veil of Consciousness*."

"Do you remember the movie we watched yesterday?" Kate asks me. "*The Spirit Molecule*?"

"Was it some mystical shit, narrated by the UFC guy?"

"Joe Rogan," John says, snapping his fingers. "He's actually super deep. You should hear his podcast. It's how I learned about ibogaine."

"It's a pretty good show," Duane agrees, "once you get past the unholy amount of Fleshlight commercials at the top. Try listening to that at work. *N-S-Fuckin-W.*"

"The Shaman," Javi interrupts, "will see you each, one at a time, for your session. They'll last about forty minutes. We're going in this order: Kate, then John, then Duane. Geoff, you're last. Then we eat."

"You guys just have Shamans, like, *on call*?" I ask him, hand-raised, grade-school style.

"It's just Juan," Duane shrugs. "No big deal."

When it's my turn, Javi stands me in the doorway and fans me with burning sage. Juan bends himself to the task, lips pursed in concentration. Javi fiddles with a lighter, examining the small pipe. There's a black, plastic CD boom box in the corner but no music plays. Deeply patterned quilts cover the floor of the meditation room. Walking on them feels soft and comforting.

"Okay," Juan says, "come sit down."

I sit. They lay me back, for a moment, to adjust the pillow under my head. "Comfortable, Jefe?" Javi asks. I look up at their faces, huddling over me, and indicate that I am. They gaze down at me as if I'm injured, as if I'm dying.

Juan says, "Let's begin. We will sit you up and all practice some deep breathing together.

After the second deep breath, you will breathe in the medicine from the pipe. Do you smoke?"

"Never had a taste for it."

"That's okay," Javi reassures me. "Sip it, like a straw. Take in as much as your lungs can hold. Then lie back on the pillow and we will tell you when to exhale. Are you ready?"

I had seen the others return, smiling and crying, unable to speak. Something had happened to them in here. Something serious. It scared me. I squeeze both of the men's hands. They hold me steady.

"I'm ready."

"Okay," Juan starts counting, "in for 1-2-3-4."

Before I came downstairs, Javi told me that 5-meo-DMT reliably produced mystical states. He said, "Total transpersonal experience is reached 70 percent of the time."

"Hold it; 1-2-3-4," Juan whispers.

I challenged Javi on the numbers, "So if the three people before me all reached that state, then statistically speaking, I should be in the 30 percent that doesn't get there, right?"

"Breathe out; 8-7-6-5-4-3-2-1," Juan whispers.

Javi scratched his forehead, "Try not to overthink it. This is a good group. And I know good groups."

"In," Juan says.

"What happens if I don't break through?" I asked. "Anything?"

"Hold—"

"Maybe nothing," Javi replied.

"Out—"

"Maybe?" I asked. He shrugged.

Juan slips the stem of the pipe in my mouth, "Here we go. Sip, sip, sip."

"Do you know why I picked you to go last?" Javi asked me. I had no idea. He shook his head. "I've been doing this a long time. When I asked you where your pain comes from, you seemed so lost. As if not knowing would prevent you from ever getting clean."

"Keep going," Juan urges me along. "Sip, sip—good." He starts giggling. "Holy shit. He's getting so much."

"But the truth is probably as simple as this, you use drugs because you're an addict. It doesn't matter why. It matters what you do now."

"Don't. Stop," Juan yells. "A little more. In. In."

"While you were at the clinic, I found a piece of paper outside your room. It was so faded, almost illegible. But I recognized it. I knew right away what it was from, so I printed up a new copy for you. When this is all over, I want you to take a look at this paper and then go find a group that you can work on it with."

"Hold it. Hold it," Juan says. He lays me back on the pillow. I close my eyes. "I'll count you down and then you exhale."

Javi handed me the paper. I felt something tighten in the pit of my stomach as I began to read, some pang of recognition: *Here are the steps we took—*

Juan says, "TEN."

"NINE."

"EIGHT."

"SEVEN."

"SIX."

"FIVE."

"FOUR."

"THREE."

"TWO."

"ONE."

"LET IT OUT."

I feel my mind plunge down an elevator shaft and smash against the bottom floor of my subconscious. All the pieces of my story, all the attachments of my personality shatter off, falling away until all that's left is a single point—a single period in the sentence of my life, breaking free from the format of my body, smashing past the typesetting, sprinting along the top edge of the page, ignoring margins, getting away from sense and sanity, stretching its own elastic—though finite—boundaries, gathering the world into a single breath in the back of my throat—and all I can think is, wait a second, am I going to be okay? Because I feel like oh my God, I'm about to die or something worse—the last little bit of me is about to slip away out of existence—but, just now, as if in response, Juan says, "It's okay, let it out." And—

I feel myself dissolve in a crystal shiver, rocketing out of my body, up through the cloud of smoke released from my lungs and into the humid twilight of the darkened room, released not just from the bounds of body but from the bonds of space, time, self, and soul, the shiver rushes up through the tiles of the ceiling and in through the fibers of insulation between the walls, briefly sparkling like cotton candy, before dissolving in the mouth of the morning, out into the sky above Rosarito Beach, over the too-blue water and the dark-green depths alike, over the dog with the coat like a Siberian snowstorm and eyes like the ocean: one shallow blue and the other shining bright black from out of the depths, and the shiver ceases moving up and commences, instead, traveling in a direction best described as out, spreading out from the center point above the beach house, a shiver the size and shape of a mushroom cloud, a megaton blast of consciousness, reaching out in every direction at once, touching a red bicycle with white plastic handle bars, touching the pedals as they turn and touching the cream white Converse sneakers that push the pedals, all of it turning, the pedals, the chain of the bicycle, the wheels, the world below, the thoughts cycling through the mind of the kid riding down through the little canyon behind the creak, the kid with the coffee-colored hair blowing against his forehead in the breeze, the canyon with the path over those big rocks at one end and the wall with the big green and yellow spray-painted letters, MXXC, at the other, and out too in the opposite direction, past Tijuana, past the clinic, something happened there—for three days and nights, a burning in the fabric of the world—but to whom did it happen and when? Out over the ocean, over schools of fish, fins moving dorsally, moving densely, over the dolphins, who ascend and break the surface, looking up at the shiver traveling up into the atmosphere, into the dome of the sky, traveling out over everything, and the dolphins laugh at the small thing, at the fragile human mind, trying to hold on to its body with everything and look at the shiver, so thin, and so stretched, unraveled all the way, and they pause and follow it back to its source with their eyes, see its full shape, like an umbrella—yes, they know of umbrellas, they find them floating in the sea all the time—and they see the shiver tethered down to the earth by the thinnest thread, by a kite string of consciousness, really, and they watch it tremble at the edge of its ability to hold on, and they tremble too with excitement and they start to scream, yes, they start to laugh and cheer and they know it won't be long now, yes, finally, they watch the thread and the thread is shaking and the thread goes snap and, *oh*.

Oh.

Returning to myself, the first thing I hear is a violent, gasping sound but I can't tell where it's coming from. Pink mist clings to the light fixtures and falls from the ceiling, lightly fluttering to the ground with the opaque weight of a wedding veil. As my spatial orientation kicks in and my liminal perception begins to note the boundary between inside and out, I can hear the difference between my own deep sobs and the sudden short breaths coming from Juan. It happens slowly. I come back into my body like a feather falling through the upper atmosphere. My eyes are open but I have no recollection of opening them. Maybe they've been open the whole time and, in fact, as I fall, I still see that other place overlaid on my reality, present behind and inside everything. The pink mist breaks down and gathers like cobwebs around the seams in the walls. I watch it dissipate slowly. The meditation room on the lower level of the beach house solidifies around me as that other place recedes. Once again, I become aware of my surroundings and of my status as a human person, lying on the floor. The DMT is wearing off. I'm already forgetting the contents of the great secret I've been told. Soon, I'll be expected to get up. But I feel no apprehension. I'm going to ride it all the way back down. It'll take as long as it needs to take.

I lift my head to look at Juan. We're alone in the room together. Javi has left.

"Hi."

Juan says, "Hi." He helps me to sit up and looks in my eyes. "Well?"

"Did you play music while I was under?"

Juan giggles, "You heard music, man? That's perfect."

"Was that the source? Do you think I heard the original music?"

Juan tilts his head to listen to my questions more closely, continuing his gentle laugh in the spaces between my sentences.

His face is so wholesome, so entirely kind, that I can't help but join him. As he watches me, Juan's smile takes on a deep tenderness, "Maybe you need to make that answer for yourself. What do you think the experience meant?" His eyes are steady—so many feelings moving through them, so much compassion and empathy.

I reach up and gently touch his cheek, "Life is so beautiful."

He laces his fingers around mine, "Life is beautiful, man."

Juan stands me up, asks me to close my eyes, and guides me toward the door onto the deck overlooking the beach. He turns my body so the sun's on my face.

"Keep your eyes closed," he squeezes my shoulders. "Feel the light."

Sunshine lands in sweet orange slices on my skin. Warmth hums through my body.

"Okay. Now open your eyes."

Fractal solar light splits in a billion rays: the grey sandy beach breaks down into its component colors, runs ten thousand tans and oranges, into prismatic reds and browns and infinite ochre, sizzling up the coast to an ocean swimming with every shade of blue and black and seaweed green. Waves dance under the invisible wind, bobbing and shifting in intricate patterns, so complex that they approach pure chaos. But I'm not high anymore.

"This is what it's like to see. Feel," Juan passes his hand over the beach in a panoramic sweep. "Remember?"

"Were you crying when I was crying?"

Juan takes me by the arm, looks out to the ocean, "My job, man? I get to help people."

He wipes the sun from his eyes and helps me up the stairs.

I've heard that *you can't go home again* but here I am, following the shadow of my plane as it crawls across the desert floor on its way back to New York.

I've heard that the West is the place of dead roads and that one in five miles of interstate must be straight enough to land a plane in an emergency. But the roadway below us is alive with traffic: chrome details flashing off of armored exteriors, passengers inside peacefully unaware that we could swoop down at any moment and commandeer their narrow world for our own. It could happen. Interstates are military roads. I've heard you can see them from space.

I've heard a lot of things, traveling like I have. Every mile of road in America is haunted by history or myth.

I've heard that Route 15 used to be the Old Carolina Road that my great-great-great-grandfather walked on his way home from the Civil War. Having survived Antietam, he starved in Andersonville and stumbled back to Ohio a skeleton. He left markers all along the road for other men in his regiment. But none followed. When their families asked him why he survived and they didn't, he only noted that he was willing to eat bugs, rats—anything—to live and others weren't. I heard that from my own grandfather's lips as cancer hollowed him out in the last week of his time on earth. As I look down at the highway below me, I think maybe this time I'll see one of those markers and finally learn how to survive.

I've heard that Route 66 sleeps underneath Interstate 40 now, briefly raising its head in Chicago and the Grand Canyon, as it slumbers toward the modern Bethlehem of the West. I heard from John Steinbeck that 66 is the path of a people in flight, the mother road, and that it smashed families against their California dreams in a cloud of dust from the 1930s. I heard from Joan Didion that families were still getting crushed along 66 in the California of the '60s, only this time in a cloud of pot smoke and idealism that drifted down from Berkeley and settled into a smog, hanging toxically over Los Angeles. I've seen the grave markers with my own eyes in Oklahoma and New Mexico: *Historic US 66 Route.*

But I believe the road will rise again.

Below our plane, Route 80 cuts straight across the country. Parts of it run absolutely straight for seventy-five miles at a stretch, though roads in North Dakota, Arizona, and Texas stay ruler straight for upward of a hundred miles at a time. There's a county road in Iowa that runs like an arrow for fifty miles through a field of corn. Where it finally curves, the field runs fallow from years of drivers missing the turn. I heard about it, and, still, I missed it. I stranded my bandmates in that field, shivering into the morning, and took photographs of them as they woke up, stumbling bleary-eyed out of the van. Tucker came with me to find civilization. There was none. Instead, we found a pack of dogs, domesticated and discarded, pacing our heels.

No matter how straight and far and fast I run, I can hear those dogs snarling behind me. But I promise myself that I will no longer feed them.

I had heard that The Loneliest Road in America was a stretch of I-50 in western Nevada, just north of oblivion; James Dean took it all the way and became a legend. I had even seen *50* in that famous picture where the road stretched out forever before you, looking like it reached straight into heaven, but then I drove it myself and heaven turned out to be some desolate, snow-capped mountains. Driving it at midnight, we saw white fog drift into our headlights along the surface of the pavement. It looked like dry ice from a horror movie and moved in unexpected ways—first rushing, then reversing, finally parting like a low, white sea. It was so opaque, so solid looking that you swore you could feel it through the gas pedal. When we stopped to fill the tank in Carson City, there was blood splattered along the wheel wells. A gas station attendant spit, rubbed the blood around with a rag, "Rodents. All white. Great big packs of them, migrating home."

The loneliest road is always the one that leads home.

My therapist says I have tendency to get ahead of myself.

She says, "Slow down. Rewind. Take a step back. Now breathe."

My therapist's name is Dr. Shiva-the-Destroyer.

"Shiva the Destroyer?" I repeated into the phone the morning I got back from Mexico.

"*Doctor* Shiva-the-Destroyer," she corrected me. "But you can call me *Shiv*."

I wanted to know, was that first name *Shiva*, last name *The Destroyer*?

"It's all last name," she brought her mouth close to the phone to emphasize the point. "It's hyphenated." She added, as a kind of afterthought, "I mean, my first name is *Mary*, if you can believe it."

"Should I just call you *Mary*?"

"Oh okay," she pulled away from the mouthpiece, affecting the accent of a 1920s gangster, "whatever makes *you* comfortable, dummy."

But I'm getting ahead of myself again.

I have a therapist now. A psychedelic therapist.

That first morning, immediately after landing at LaGuardia, I went straight to my old apartment to try and talk to Liza. She was all I could think about. An electricity filled my limbs at the sound of her name. I repeated it over and over in a whisper, just to charge myself up. *Liza, Liza, Liza*. I needed to make things right. It felt preordained. The sky was shockingly clear. Every light turned green on the way to our apartment. Signs were all around me: I needed to do this now.

Right as I turned the key in our front door, my phone rang. I pulled it out of my pocket. The caller ID said *Urgent Services Inc. New Mexico*. Normally, I'd kick this kind of thing to voicemail, let my automated message discourage further contact. But that morning I had the urge to face every crisis head on. I answered.

A voice said, "Don't do it."

"What?"

The woman on the phone yawned, "Whatever you're about to do. Don't do it."

"Who is this?"

"Your therapist, dummy. Who else calls you up and tells you what to do?"

I told her I already had a therapist and she sounded nothing like him.

"*Psychedelic* therapist," she corrected me. "You had to sign up for six months of post-ibogaine therapeutic management—minimum—in order to even be accepted into the Crossroads program." Intense gum-chewing sounds came from the receiver for several seconds, then abruptly stopped. "You forgot, right?"

I remember looking down at my key, jammed into the lock in our front door. My hand seemed foreign. *Disconnected*, I remember thinking, even though I could see the long span of my arm stretch back to my shoulder without interruption. It just felt so far away from me, whereas Liza was closer than the breath in my lungs.

"Can I call you back? I'm at my apartment. I'm going to try to save my relationship."

"Yup," Dr. Shiva-the-Destroyer blew a bubble with her gum. It popped. "Had a feeling you were about to do something reckless. Is he/she/they expecting you?"

"Liza doesn't know I'm back. It'll be a surprise. A good surprise."

"Stupid," chew, chew, chew. "Ill-advised."

"Can I call you back?"

"Sure. I mean. She's not going to let you in."

Liza agreed with the therapist. She wasn't going to let me in. She wasn't even sure if I'd really gone to Mexico for treatment. Maybe it was just another drug run. She couldn't put it past me. When she peeked through the open security chain crack of our door, I held my hands up in surrender and told her not to worry, saying, "I wouldn't let me in either." It made her laugh. So much tension rushing out of her. A momentary release of tightness in her shoulders.

She had been cooking soup, taking care of herself, when I knocked on the door. She sensed something was different when she saw me but wasn't sure exactly what it was. Neither of us knew what to say but that didn't stop us trying. She told me our little stray cat friend, Lola, seemed to love seafood recently. I stopped in the middle of our conversation, took a deep breath, and started listing the ingredients in her soup, "Coconut, lemongrass, saffron, garlic, red chilies, turmeric, onions, and... cod?" She said it was shallots, not onions, and galangal, not turmeric, but she was floored. She said she figured after years of shoving *that evil shit* up my nose that I'd never be able to smell anything ever again.

That was the first moment she let herself believe. But it was just a moment.

She whispered through the door, "Are you back, for real? For *real*, for real?" I watched a tear land on the door jamb but I couldn't see her face, haloed as she was by the golden morning light coming through the glass at the back of our apartment. I asked her to draw the curtains. I wanted to see her.

For a time, my eyes were sensitive to light. Everything was sensitive after ibogaine. I felt like I'd died and been reborn. Every experience was the first time. Flying into LaGuardia that morning, I sat with my face pressed up against the window, watching our plane come in low on the landing path over Brooklyn. We were gliding above the warning beacons that sit blinking red on the tops of skyscrapers. The compact reality of eleven million people living on top of one another began to sink in. Waves of desire crashed in on me from all sides.

The Brooklyn Clocktower appeared. Fifth Avenue materialized at its feet, widening perspective as it stretched back toward us. Following the line of the street to my old apartment building on Carroll—there since 1897 according to the engraving on the eaves—I could just make out the corner bedroom on the fourth floor, the fresh paint on the windowsill of my old room.

It wasn't just the city undergoing a sudden renewal. Trees moved differently in the breeze. Sunlight slanted at impossible angles. New physics emerged. New feelings. A whole new world with new people in it.

When Liza drew the curtains, I felt I was seeing her for the first time, in a dizzy, newborn light. Tears had been washing her cheeks, leaving dew on her skin. Her eyes were deep and innocent. I had the urge to protect her but the only thing she needed protection from was me. I placed my hand against the metal door. "This is a boundary, right? It's here to keep you safe?"

"Some boundary," she grit her teeth, passed her hand through the small space left open by the chain. I stepped back to let her breathe. She smiled apologetically.

When she moved away from the door, the sunlight fell through the opening, landing on my face. She noticed that the blue had come back into my eyes, said it was almost scary, asked me if I joined a cult down in Mexico.

"You've got *Jesus-eyes*, like those religious fanatics," she told me, a desperate edge in her voice. "It's all too much."

She closed the door in my face.

Her voice came through muffled, "Just give me a minute, okay?"

I stepped out into the hall from our vestibule and waited for my vision to adjust. It occurred to me that she might not have been alone in the apartment. That unbearably handsome Mr. Five-O'clock Shadow who gave her his number at the park might've been in there with her, walking around in his boxers, testing spoonfuls of broth, neatly checking his scruff to make sure he's still a *Men's Health* model. I turned away from the door but I couldn't feel any jealousy constricting my chest. A flash of movement pierced the darkness, a pair of sparrows taking flight just beyond the building's front door. But there was something else too. A silhouette. Someone was leaning against the glass, peering in, hands cupped around his eyes. I was wearing black, so I stood completely still and held my breath, trying to merge with the dark of the hallway.

My man. Could he see me? When his phone rang, he turned away to answer it.

"Nah," he held the phone out in front of his chest and shouted into it, "phone's not ringing. Fuck knows if he's here or not."

I pulled my phone out of my pocket. It was dead. I slid down the wall and curled up in a ball on the ground. My man's voice penetrated the glass door and reached me, undiminished, moving through my black clothes to find its target beneath my skin.

"Sniff out who he's been getting it from. Deal with them. This dude is mine."

When my man turned back toward the glass, he coughed into his fist before smiling at his reflection, "Him? Go without? For ten days? He'd rather be dead."

Then he licked his thumb, carefully smoothed down his heavy brows, and pulled back his lips, showing both rows of teeth in a predatory snarl. I slid my baseball cap down over my eyes, feeling myself become prey. Just as my man turned away, the hallway began to lengthen. His voice got sucked down a long tube. The world outside went black and white. I put my head between my knees and tried to remain conscious.

Liza says she found me like that: passed out in the hallway. By the time she got me to my feet, something in her must've softened toward me. She brought me inside and sat me at the table. There was no handsome stranger in his boxers, no hastily shed clothes strewn across the carpet. Only the faint outline of Lola's soft kitty ears shown in the glass doors at the back of the apartment.

She asked, "When's the last time you slept?"

Hands on the table, I remember watching all the lines in my palms slithering over one another, "You mean science time? Measured on dials and calendars?"

"We'll come back to that," Liza breathed in my ear, sliding a bowl of soup in front of me. "For now, get some of this into you."

Liza says I ate that soup with total concentration, from the first spoonful until the last slurp, straight from the upended bowl. She was standing there in her torn leggings and one of my beat-up Thursday T-shirts, nail polish chipped and cuticles chewed, when I caught her making her worried little kissy motions.

"You okay, sweets?"

Wood panels creaked in the floor beneath her feet. "What do you think *Mr. Cute*—" She stopped with a wince, the pet name turning bitter in her mouth. Her shoulders slumped forward, spilling a few stray hairs into her eyes. "What do you think, Geoff?"

"Thought you might have a guy in here if I'm being honest."

Soup dripped to the floor from the end of her spoon. She pointed at the door, "Bad dog."

"Wasn't being bad!"

"Do not sit."

"Maybe I am a bad dog. But I swear I wasn't starting shit."

"Do not stay."

"I only thought you had a guy over here as like *self-care*."

Liza cocked her hip, stood there, gently tapping the wooden spoon against the palm of her hand. "You really have no idea what that phrase means do you?" She was making her little air-kisses again.

"It takes something out of me, seeing you like this," I told her. "Takes it out, rearranges it, and puts it back inside. You see what I mean?"

Liza sat down beside me, peered into my eyes, and shook her head. "What?"

I steepled my hands on the place mat, resting my chin on the knuckles. "I don't even know. I've missed you. I'm trying to stop being such a nightmare to be around but I don't know how. Mostly I'm sorry. Guess you've heard that before."

"What guarantee do I get that this time is any different?"

"I can't promise it will be. I don't trust me either. I'm a liar. I'm a sneak. A junkie. I only know that I'd rather die trying to change than go on failing you."

We sat looking at each other for a while.

She revisited her earlier question, "When's the last time you got some sleep?"

"I'm not sure I believe in sleep anymore."

"How about lying down?" Liza asked me, gently placing her spoon on the table. "Do you think you might be able to believe in that for a little bit?" She stood up slowly, touching my elbow with her fingertips as she rose. Something about the heat of her attention stopped me in my tracks. I remember thinking that I might explode. I wanted to explode. I wanted to feel the solid matter of my body sublimate and disperse into the air so that she would breathe me in and I could be with her forever.

I was getting ahead of myself again.

She led me into the bedroom, where she peeled back the duvet and guided me down into the thick, feathery mattress in a single, unbroken movement without ever taking her eyes off mine. After pulling the covers to my chin, I gazed up at her, feeling the small, gravitational pull of her body.

She yawned.

I asked her, "Do you believe in lying down for a bit?"

She sat on the furthest edge of the bed, "I might."

I told her about the trip down to Mexico and the people that I met. She stretched out her limbs, slowly relaxing her posture until her cheek was resting against the pillow. Still her eyes held mine. I told her about Duane and Kate and John. I told her about the sleeping giant, Faruk, and the disappearing Ms. Thompson. How she left behind her *Queen Bitch* sweatshirt and how Kate took it as a reminder to stay clean. I told her about Javi and Juan and the Doctor at the clinic. How in tune they were with all our needs. How they'd taken ibogaine in order to qualify for the position at Crossroads. I even told her about my ibogaine trip. How it took place on a path shaped like a giant record. The entire time that I was speaking, Liza kept her eyes on mine. The pull was intensifying between us. I felt her soft gravity promising to untangle me from the molecules of my body. Every so often, I would pause to collect my thoughts and when I began speaking again, Liza would scoot a little bit closer. Each time she got closer, she would interject, "Shhh, you don't need to speak so loudly. I'm right here."

After an hour or so, we were face to face, our noses almost touching. She reached her hands down under the covers and touched my bare skin just above the waist of my pants.

"Shhhh," she whispered, "that's enough."

We slept like that, facing one another, Liza's minty breath warming my lips. Throughout that day and into the stillest part of the night, we barely moved. Two bodies at perfect rest. Then, I heard a shifting somewhere in the next room. My eyes opened but I couldn't sit up for all the adrenaline flooding my system. Was I hearing things? Had I somehow caught Liza's sleep paralysis? I fastened my eyes on the doorway, expecting to see an immaterial man gathering his shadows. But there was no man. And there were no shadows. The moon was full and close, filling our apartment with a cold blue light. I heard the glass doors at the back of our apartment open, hinges creaking. I heard a hissing noise, *shhhhh, shhhhhh.*

Liza was still fast asleep. When I slid out from under the covers, she chewed on the air and turned over, gathering the pillow against her cheek. My feet touched the floor without a sound. Hands flat against the frame, I pressed my ear to the door, certain I could hear winter moving unimpeded through our apartment. The doorknob was cold. My breath visible. *My man* and some of his goons were on the other side of the wall. They were here to teach me a lesson. They would wake Liza, show her how powerless I really was. I looked around for a weapon, though I knew there were none.

I turned the handle. The door opened smoothly. There was nothing. No sound. No one in the apartment. I stepped across the threshold into our living room. My feet were freezing. I looked around. It was so bright. The French doors were thrown wide, wind streaming in. In the courtyard, about ten paces away, three raccoons stood on their hind legs, staring at me. A minute passed, then another. I took a slow step forward, careful not to make any sudden moves. When I was able to get the glass doors shut, all three raccoons dropped to their front paws. They didn't leave the yard. Instead, they paced a circuit: a perfect circle, about five feet in diameter, each raccoon behind the last. The perfectly round face of the moon watched over everything.

Next to the glass doors, my record collection sat, lined up in rows by the turntable. I pulled out one of my band's old LPs and held it up to the glass, completely blocking the circle of the moon. A pinhole of light came through the record's center, landing in the middle of my forehead. For a moment, I saw myself from outside my body. I was recreating an ancient hieroglyphic, taking part in an unbroken ritual, dating back from before my ancestors had names.

The record held the moon's charge. I placed it on the platter, flipped the switch, and stood there, watching it spin. A ribbon of light fluttered over the record's black silk. I turned on a lamp and the reflection of my face appeared in the glass doors. My own body looked at me like a scared animal, afraid of what I might do next. "Sorry for the things I've done to hurt you," I placed an open hand on my own cheek, feeling a sudden tenderness. "You've gotten me out of a lot of bad situations and managed to stay alive when I was trying to kill us both. I promise, from now on, I'm gonna be on your side. I love you." A dense bank of clouds drifted in front of the moon and its lunar force seemed to diminish.

I switched off the lamp but left the record silently spinning and went back into the bedroom, where I slipped under the covers. Liza's breath fluttered. She pulled up the covers, mumbling, "*Mr. Cuteface*, you're a *bad dog.*" The record continued turning on its platter in the next room, a small, black spiral in the dark. My eyelids were getting heavy. The record expanded as it spun, becoming a black hole. Our bed detached from the floor and began drifting toward it. My eyes closed. In the space above our bed, letters were forming. I saw the text message my father sent me, before I left for Mexico, on the nature of Hawking radiation: *...when a very short-lived pair of virtual particles winks into existence in the vacuum, if the pair is on the knife edge of the event horizon, one particle should disappear into the black hole and the other should radiate away.*

Liza and I were a pair of particles drifting in the vacuum. We had blinked into existence at the knife edge of a black hole. According to my father, one of us should have disappeared into it, the other should have radiated away. I had disappeared into the black hole. But Liza stayed right here, waiting for me to come back.

When I woke up, Liza was already at the table, writing in her morning journal. I stretched my shoulders and neck, stepping out of the bedroom. Liza pursed her lips when she saw me, pointing the eraser on her pencil to my phone, which sat buzzing in the charger, "He's been at it all morning." There were thirty missed calls and a string of angry messages from my old drug dealer.

|My man.

|Yo, I got that fire

|Specials 2 for 1

|You there, G?

|Where you been?

|Who you been getting it from? I'll have a talk with them.

|This is my neighborhood. You think you can go around me?

|BE A MAN. ANSWER YOUR PHONE.

|Ok, g... I know where you work. I'll stop by.

|I KNOW WHERE YOU LIVE.

|some people only understand consequences.

|Disappointed to see it go this way.

|But this is my territory

|Be seeing you, G

The morning shivered with the possibility of violence. I wrapped a robe around my shoulders. Liza came up behind me. I felt her warm, delicate hands slide into the fold of my robe. "We should call the cops," she told me, fingers flitting along the white and shadow of my ribs. My whole body tensed, *no*. She wanted to know why I was protecting him. But what she took for misplaced affection was pure, unadulterated fear.

In my years as an addict, I'd spent enough time with my dealer to learn a bit about how the game was played in North Brooklyn. I'd dropped cash at the straight businesses where money got washed. I'd met up with a dozen or so of the guys below my guy. I'd seen the James Bond style mods to their cars and I'd heard them talking about which of their cops were doing well and which were dead-ending their careers, who deserved a bonus and who needed a slap. I'd seen enough.

Liza kissed my shoulder and went to shower, leaving me staring down at my phone as I leaned against the cold glass edge of the morning. There was no choice but to meet this thing head on, though I didn't yet know what to say. While typing the first word, the phone came alive in my hand. My mother was calling.

"I'm a bit preoccupied, Ma."

"Oh," she sounded disappointed, "anything important?"

"My continued health and mobility may depend on it."

"Wonderful—" she began before the line flooded with static.

My father picked up the cordless phone in the other room and shouted, "Hello, my boy!"

"Hey Pops. I heard the folks at LIGO are picking up some noise from deep space."

"Indeed. It looks like Einstein will be proven right yet again. *Gravitational waves.*"

"It's so nice to hear you speaking in complete sentences," my mother sighed, in relief. "I was afraid that crazy drug might fry your brain. I mean, how do you feel today?"

"Not terrible. Which is an improvement, I guess."

"I'll say!" My dad yelled through the extension.

"We're so proud," Mom said. "Is there anything we can do to help you get back on your feet?"

"Well, since you asked, would you mind having a word with the drug dealer who's going to murder me and Liza in our bed as we sleep?"

There was a silence so long that it stretched up through the atmosphere, into the vacuum of space, before bouncing off a satellite and reaching the speaker in my cell phone.

The line crackled, "Geoff? I think we got disconnected. Jack, can you hear him?"

"No, Ma, I'm here. But you gave me an idea. I'll call you later."

I reopened the text message screen, began typing a reply to my dealer.

|I'm sorry. I'm not sure who this is, there is no name saved. Geoff is in the hospital. He had an overdose. We don't

know when he will be recovered or if he'll ever be back in
New York. He lost his job and his girlfriend kicked him out.

I hit send and stared at the phone, waiting.

|Who's this

I bit the thumbnail on my left hand. Then typed,

|This is his mother.

Three dots danced in the space for a reply.

|I'm sorry, ma'am. I didn't mean to be rude.
...
|Sorry to hear about your son.
...
|He going to be ok?

I answered truthfully,

|We don't know yet.

Three dots. Then nothing. I took a deep breath, kept typing,

|Does my son owe you any money?

The reply came quickly,

|Don't worry about nothing like that.

I hesitated, held my breath, and wrote,

|Ok, good. This number will be turned off. We're erasing
the phone. All the numbers. All the messages. No one will

>be contacted. No police. Just please don't try and contact my son.
>
>...
>
>...
>
>|Ok.
>
>...
>
>|Good luck. Your son is a good guy.

Later on, I went to AT&T to get a new number. They performed a factory reset on my phone. But first, I showed Liza the exchange. She climbed her bare feet up on mine, threw her arms around me, and held on tightly. My chin came to rest on top of her head. We began a slow, slow dance, though there was no music. As we turned through our small degrees, I saw that what my dealer had told me in the aisles of C-Town was true: I had walked across an invisible line, into *his* neighborhood, *his* world, full of cash and violence and unpredictable behavior. But, after seeing how he addressed the person he took to be my mother, I understood how easy it was for him to cross the invisible line and come into mine.

Liza began to hum a soft melody against my chest and I felt it tingling in my lungs. As we turned through our slow steps, I had the strange sensation that I could see through the walls and into everything. Different worlds were making themselves visible all around me; the surrounding neighborhoods began to glow softly, rubbing up against one another and overlapping. I could see a spiritual current running from the Russian Orthodox Church on North 11th to the Mosque a block away, lighting up all the different street corners, the competing territories of graffiti writers, their tags glowing in red and black paint. I watched steam coming off the khao soi cooking at our favorite Thai place two blocks away and black pepper being sprinkled into a cup of white borscht down the street at Pyza. People were spitting into the gutters, tipping hats, holding doors open for one another in the fresh fish market shared by so many different cuisines and cultures, all of them cooking in the hot fires of our current American temperature. I knew it wasn't just my imagination, some 3D model I'd constructed to represent the disparate quality of life in these different neighborhoods, all of it decided by the hidden hand of the free market that sorted us into our separate storage containers and shipped us across class lines. No. It felt like the opening of a door. I could see into and behind everything. There were different worlds. All overlaid upon one another, layer by delicate layer, ready to rip as tissue paper.

Ibogaine had helped me to navigate the layers and levels of my own interior world, but now that I was sober, I could still feel them shifting inside me. Every day, the radio anchors and newspaper headlines warned us that the only way to ameliorate danger was to put up walls between these different worlds, to stay isolated inside ourselves, our thoughts and feelings shut up in their own hidden rooms. But I'd already spent long enough isolating myself, long enough compartmentalizing my feelings. I knew where that road led.

My therapist says I'm doing it again. She's right. I have a tendency to get ahead of myself, to try and figure out what it all means. She says, "Slow down. Rewind." She wants me to put some space between myself and the world. So I stop getting stuck in the moment. So I don't get ahead of myself. She brings her mouth close to the receiver and talks to me like an old-timey gangster, "Just the facts, dummy."

"*What's facts got to do, got do with it?*" I sang into the receiver on our second call.

"I adore Tina Turner," Dr. Shiva-the-Destroyer gushed. "So don't ever do that again." Other than her utter and complete aversion to my singing voice, we got along fine. She was taking me through my ibogaine experience, step-by-step.

"You already downloaded the file. I'll help you unzip, decompress, and process the raw information. I just need a few details from you. First off, tell me about the shape of the world inside your head."

I leaned back in my chair. Sunlight dappled the glass doors to our apartment. Time was passing. I watched the wind in the bare branches. "Everything was circular. Circular ruins. Circular cities. Records spinning. Orbits and ellipses. Hurricanes. Tree Rings."

"No shit?" My therapist drawled, stretching the *i* in *shit* until it was a Zen character, containing all of existence. "You're a Turtle."

My therapist said there were different kinds of world paradigms that people saw inside themselves when they took ibogaine. Which one you saw was dependent upon what type of person you were, what type of life you'd lived. The holographic shape of the hallucinations were indicative of which world paradigm you subscribed to. This, apparently, could be immensely useful in determining an individualized therapeutic approach for each patient. In Dr. Shiva-the-Destroyer's work, the most common types of people she encountered were called *Buckshots*: their memories came out all scattershot—blurry, nonlinear—hard to parse.

"You ever try to read a plate of spaghetti, dummy?"

Easy Riders. Star Gazers. Commandos. Each type had their own paradigm, their own psychic architecture, and their own unique approach to the narrative of their lives. Each came with specific challenges, requiring a specialized approach to treatment. Commandos, for instance, required discipline to get sober. Twelve-step programs were seldom enough. My therapist would recommend that they take up a martial art, a new language, a strict dietary regimen.

I bet her a dollar that Duane and John were Commandos.

"Keep it. Duane's a *Super Mario Brother*. He's my favorite. Professionally speaking."

Super Mario Brothers saw the world as a video game, blocky and pixelated but still conforming to an archetypal hero's journey, right out of Joseph Campbell. Super Mario Brothers were always trying to get to the next level. Always trying to earn an extra life. To win the game. My therapist said that this could be so overt that Super Mario Brothers often began their ibogaine trip at a monolithic start screen.

"A real Call to Adventure," she said. "Love that shit."

Dr. Shiv's chewing slowed. She let out a small, contented sigh and told me that my type was a lonely type. Only children, single mothers, orphans. These were the people that commonly ended up conforming to the Turtle paradigm. Also anyone with jobs that isolated them from their peer group: soccer goalies, undercover cops, federal judges. Lead singers.

"You were a lonely kid," chew, chew, chew. "But you were well behaved, right?"

"My mom says she could sit me in front of a white wall and I would stare at it for hours."

"And voilà," chew, chew.

Dr. Shiva-the-Destroyer says that I pull the entire world inside my head, the way turtles pull their limbs inside their shells. For protection. She tells me to stand up, look around. She says liminal perception is a radial line, the end of which forms a circumference. Everything within the bounds of the circle is my world. When you're the center of the universe, she tells me, the world is always going to appear to rotate around you. Control. It's all a matter of who's in charge.

"So tell me, when you were a well-behaved, nice little kid, did you ever have one of those circular mazes with the metal ball trapped inside?" She paused for effect, blew a bubble, let it pop. "What am I saying? Sure you did. Now, remember what happened when you got the silver ball to the center of the maze? That's right, it fell through the hole. So what, right? Freedom, hallelujah! Except, no. Not at all. And thus," chew, chew, chew, "we come to the problem of infinite regress. Or as I prefer to call it, the theory of Turtles All the Way Down."

We discussed the universal mytheme of The Great Turtle that carries the world. I pictured myself as an ancient stone reptile, moss clinging to my shell, all of civilization swaying on my back as I took a slow, labored step.

"But if The Great Turtle carries the world, what carries the turtle?" Dr. Shiv asked, pausing to consider her own question. "Another Turtle, of course, greater than the last. And so on, all the way down." I saw my own prehistoric stone visage amplified through all of eternity, getting larger and older the further down it went, an infinite ego carrying a speck of dust called Earth.

Wind ruffled the treetops outside my window. A pair of cardinals landed on the table top. The redder bird pulled a snail from its shell and fed it to the darker bird. Beak to beak, they kissed the food back and forth, tearing the small creature apart. The sun intensified, warming my hand where it rested on the sill. It was so bright that my senses felt washed out: I heard cicadas, tasted citrus.

"But in your case, dummy," she whispered into the receiver, "you come to the center of the maze and instead of finding yourself, you fall through the hole, and what do you think you find there? That's right. Another iteration of the world, another circular maze fit perfectly inside the shell of the last one. And so on and so forth, ad infinitum, ad nauseam, amen."

I closed my eyes. Dark clouds spiraled around my childhood home. Highway lines radiated out from our lawn. Records spun, universes turned. I felt myself sinking down through the innermost rings of that giant oak tree, falling into the next maze, the next world, the next ruins. Spiraling clouds, tree rings. Another hole. Another fall.

"Infinite regress," Dr. Shiv whispered. "Or, in your case, the infinite hole where the self should be."

A sensation of simultaneous expansion and collapse overtook me: I could see a series of doors opening outward on one side, each larger than the last, and inward on the other, so that my mind raced for an exit that only ever got further away while the hole beneath me continued to deepen.

I pressed my fingertips against my eyelids, "I don't think I want to be a Turtle."

"Turtles never do."

Liza insisted on taking me out to eat at my favorite restaurant. I was tired but our friend Danny owned the place and I was looking forward to seeing him. Plus, I knew the food would be spicy and flavorful. On the ride there, my mouth began to water. My stomach wouldn't stop grumbling. Liza was teasing me about it. Then her stomach growled back.

"They're talking," I told her, "conspiring against us."

"They're planning our dinner," she said, gripping the soft curve of her stomach, "conspiring *for* us."

Upon our arrival, the hostess told us that of course they were expecting us. Servers darted between tables, sending me playful happy birthday greetings, though my birthday was still a few weeks away. I couldn't figure out what all the excitement was about. A vibrant, reckless energy sizzled in the electrical fixtures. Bubbles rose in the fish tank's neon waters. Plates of food steamed on overcrowded tables: potato chips and stringy jerky made from mushrooms populated towering mounds of fried rice. Bowls of molten tofu fluoresced a dangerous shade of red. Candied cherries clung to deeply glazed beef ribs, which reflected mint green light from tarnished fixtures overhead. People were spilling their drinks on one another. Something loud and rhythmic was rapidly blowing out the restaurant's sound system. By the time we reached the balcony, overlooking the back dining area, my nervous system had reached the point of total shutdown. I looked over the railing but there was no depth, no Visual Cliff to throw myself off of. I sensed only a soft and welcoming form of brain damage settling in my frontal lobe. I got the feeling this was the part where I'd be allowed to lie down and go back to sleep.

"Surprise!" A crowd yelled from below.

For a second, I doubted the reality of my surroundings. Maybe I wasn't in a restaurant. In fact, maybe I wasn't anywhere at all. Maybe it *was* my birthday. Isn't that what death is? A kind of birthday party that you don't see coming?

I blocked the scene with my forearm, "Why is this happening?"

"Your friends love you," Liza pointed out Steve and Tucker. She pointed to Tom, who was laughing by the bar with his wife and newborn son, Tuck, named after our drummer. "My friends too," Liza added. "They all love you, see?" She waved at Lisa and Paul and Brendan and Lauren. And Julie and Don and Jesse. And my parents. A few people I had worked with over the years were there too. Liza put her hand on my elbow, whispering, "We didn't think you'd want everyone to know your business, so Danny and I told the staff it was a birthday party. After that, it kind of took on a life of its own."

On the stairs, my steps were tentative. Even my limbs were unsure of their basic capacity for negotiating life. As I passed through the room, each of my friends yelled happy birthday in turn. It had become a kind of running joke among them so I put on one of the cheap party hats lying on the bar and tried my best to shake out a little dance while they cheered me on.

At one point, after I started to relax, Tucker leaned in close, smiling slowly. It was an evocative motion. It reminded me of a Bill Viola installation I had seen in LA, where the artist had filmed people laughing and crying and sneezing at a thousand frames per second so that when they were slowed down, it would expose the fine mechanics of even the simplest gestures. I was noticing the way the muscles smoothed Tucker's skin in waves—creasing some areas around his eyes while releasing the tension in his forehead—when his lips parted slightly and he said, "Hey, Big Man, you've got a giant fucking spider on your shirt."

By the end of his sentence, my sense of time and motion had been restored and now it lurched into a rapid, cartoonish fast forward. Before I could take a breath, the spider crossed the distance from my shirt's hem to the center of my chest. A muscular arm, covered in coarse black hairs, cut through the air, its open hand striking me off axis. The spider ricocheted off the brick wall and fell to the floor, skittering off to a dark corner. I corkscrewed off the same wall, bounced against the bar, and ended up right back where I started. By then, Steve had retracted his arm and held his fist over his mouth in shock. He had really belted me. Tucker doubled over and held on to the bar for support. His laughter was so severe that it made no sound.

All the light in the room dimmed to a fiery, red flicker. The kitchen sent out a cake with a ring of candles on it. My band members sang. My father slipped me a card in a sparkly, red envelope.

Over the singing, I had to shout to be heard, "Liza says it's not really my birthday."

My father knit his brow, "Of course it's not."

Overhead, various shades of red and white began to turn in incandescent spirals through the ceiling of the room. Strips of paper fluttered, cut into perfect fractal patterns, strung in geometric configurations. I felt my consciousness extending out from my body and rising into the center of the light. I felt reality breaking down, the DMT surging in my pineal gland. My entire being flooded with the love that animates the sun, powers the stars.

Danny ducked under a row of paper garlands and whispered, "It's an art installation. A reimagined chandelier. Doesn't the room seem to radiate out from it?"

I turned to face him in the faltering light, "My therapist told me, *Liminal perception is a radial line. Everything within the bounds of the circle is my world.* But it's more than that. We are everything we love. Don't you see what that means? We must love everything."

"Wow, man," Danny adjusted his glasses. "They really did a number on you."

I excused myself.

Down a long corridor, plastic flowers hung from the ceiling above mirrored walls. Thin spotlights scattered the dark. Angelo Badalamenti's opening theme for *Twin Peaks* played on a loop from recessed speakers. Customers at Danny's restaurant got to experience the temporary reprieve of floating through a peaceful void whenever they needed a break from bright lights and spicy food. When I reached the bathroom, I tore through the red paper envelope of my father's card.

> My boy-
>
> I've been reading more about black holes and the separation of particles... Remember I asked, 'What about the mass that was ADDED by the partner that disappeared into the black hole?' Well, according to a book I've got now, that particle is always a 'negative energy' particle, which as far as I can see, must mean it has the ability to cancel the mass and gravity of something in the black hole. I've been a dilettante and nothing has gotten done! Well, I renewed my library card anyway...
>
> Love, your Dad

The card went back in its envelope and into my pocket. I stood at the sink, splashing water on my face. In the mirror above the bathroom sink, a moth circled a light bulb, making little figure eights in the air with its body. In marker, on the wall beneath the bulb, someone had written, *Is this Paradise?*

The door opened behind me. I heard footsteps approaching but I couldn't look away from the moth. Every so often it got too close, and it turned one of its legs to spark against the glowing glass before skittering off to start the loop again.

Tom stood behind me, gazing up at the light, "What do you think it sees in there?"

Everything. It sees everything.

When I turned around, Tom cupped his hand under my chin, "Are you crying?"

"You've always been honest with me, Tom."

Tom took a step closer, "I think we've always been pretty honest with each other."

I could feel the heat of his body. I knew he was real.

"Am I a negative energy particle?"

Tom pulled me into the folds in his jacket. The coarse fibers of his wool sweater rubbed my face, absorbing my tears and giving off a faint agricultural odor. I could feel his right hand grasping his left wrist in the center of my back. Every muscle in his body tightened, squeezing me until it hurt. He pulled me closer, cinching the circle. He was straining himself, fortifying his grip. I couldn't move. I couldn't do anything at all. I was safe.

"Negative Energy Particle," he repeated. "That's a great band name."

In the morning, Liza was up early for a stroll in the park. After a high-calorie night of food and drink, she wanted to walk it off. For me, it was hard enough getting out of bed after a night of club soda. How does anyone face the day without a bag of heroin? It felt like being asked to run a marathon with two broken legs. But I couldn't say no to that smile. She was wearing a knit hat with a giant tassel that made her look like a child. So I put my boots on.

In the bracing cold, dog walkers had strapped jackets and rubber booties on all the pups. Liza was worried about the late season cold front, the harsh frost on delicate young branches. She took us on a circuit of all her favorite trees. We examined the buds of their leaves. Each one contained a miniature world. All of springtime holding its breath inside. She showed me how to identify them: oaks with their long asparagus-like stems and maples with little red brussels spouts at their tips. Liza pet their trunks and spoke to them in a low voice, "Be patient, friends. Spring is almost here. We could all use a fresh start."

Leftover winter stood in dirty piles around the baseball diamond. It must've been too cold for the little dogs; only Malamutes and Samoyeds and St. Bernards were out. Mountain dogs as far as the eye could see. Just ahead of us, a bunch of them were getting agitated. One of the Huskies must've felt the call of its true nature because it broke away and darted over to the nearest snowy mound, pulling a whole pack along with it. They could've been quite a team, if only the walker had brought a sled. Instead, he ended up ass out on the ground, caught in a tangle of thin red ropes, cycling through variations on the phrase, *dirty rat fuckers.*

On the other end of one of the leashes was an absolutely majestic Golden Retriever. If he were my dog, I would've named him Apollo. His fur caught the sun just right. He looked up at me and smiled widely before lifting his leg and peeing on the walker's boots. Poor guy. But the majestic Golden maintained eye contact with me the whole time. He was so proud.

Liza said, "I think you've found a kindred spirit."

I couldn't tell what she was trying to say. Had I been behaving like that dog, in a deeper sense? Had I been proud? Then I caught a look at the walker's face. It was Mr. Five-O'clock Shadow. He was not happy. His metallic aviator glasses advertised a lifestyle in which it was possible to interact with the world from behind a sturdy barrier. But when I looked into those shiny lenses, I didn't see a world of chaos kept safely at bay. I saw a movie screen and all Mr. Five-O'clock's fears were projected out on it. He kept getting tangled up in other people's expectations. The hair, the clothes, the grooming. Masculinity seemed like a pretty dangerous thing to have to protect. There was always a bigger dog waiting for you to slip. And here he was. After the fall. All things considered, I thought he still looked pretty handsome. Maybe I had been a little unfair.

"Should I give him a hand?"

"Very sweet of you, *Mr. Cuteface*," Liza ran her fingers up the scruff at the back of my neck and lazily scratched me behind the ear. "But sometimes we all need a quiet moment for ourselves, to stand peacefully to one side and watch a *Men's Health* model get pissed on. That's my definition of *self-care*."

A few weeks later, I saw my old drug dealer's little brother in a 12-step meeting. He sat in the front row, chewing sunflower seeds. When the round-robin reached him, he swallowed his mouthful, shells and all, before introducing himself.

"I have alcoholism in my family. Addiction? Forget about it. Like you wouldn't believe. Slinging dope with my brother too. For a while, I moved to Pennsylvania. Thought I could get away from it all. Turns out they got drugs there too."

Some of the other guys laughed, nodded their heads up and down, *I hear that, brother.* It was an old story, moving to another state to try and outrun addiction. In the program, they called that the geographical cure.

"Jobs I was working. Needed that shit more than ever. Had me sweeping sunlight off the roof. Can't do that sober. But I came back. Family, right? Yeah, my brother too. It's hard. Not gonna lie. Got to keep conscious at all times that the drugs in his pocket want to kill me. He ain't gonna stop them neither. Only I can."

Maybe he was right. With all of these worlds, all layered on top of each other, maybe the key to crossing between them is to be forever aware of the danger all around us. I thought about that for the rest of the meeting while the group shared their stories.

Before the "moment of silence for the still sick and suffering outside these rooms," the dealer's brother pointed his finger at me, cocked his thumb, and mouthed the word, *bang*. He tilted his head, *Remember me?* Of course I did. Before he got clean, he was the driver. He would check the rearview, watch me read the cartoon logo on the new batch of dope. He'd count the money.

The group said the serenity prayer and the meeting was over. I crossed the room and shook his hand.

"How you doing?"

"Struggling with the guilt. You know? Why should I get to live after selling that shit?" He took another slug of sunflower seeds and popped them in his mouth.

"You for real?" I picked up his chair and stacked it with the others by the wall. "Or is this some kind of test to see if I'm a snitch?"

"It ain't like that," he put his hand over his mouth to stop the sunflower seeds falling out.

"'Cause I'm not a fucking narc."

"Nah, man. I'm here honest. Believe me. The hell I contributed to? That shit ain't okay. What I put into the world. Into your world? You shouldn't even give me the time of day."

He chewed the seeds harder, closed his eyes, and slapped himself hard across the face.

"You're serious…"

He slapped himself again and stopped chewing but didn't say anything more. He stood there, with his eyes closed, cheeks full of sunflower seeds. I felt a loosening in my chest, a sensation of tenderness toward the kid.

"I was going to kill myself."

He looked down at his sneakers and swallowed hard.

"I was going to kill myself before I started doing heroin. It was like a 'last days, all bets are off' thing. Every day that you and your brother got me high was another day off the ledge. But it couldn't last. Now I have to learn how to live with myself. So do you. But don't take on any guilt for my shit. Get sober. Live. Help another person do the same. That's all this program is about. Keep loving your brother, man. Don't let anyone tell you that you can't. Counselors, sponsors, whoever—fuck 'em."

"Hey, new guy," an old timer shouted to the dealer's little brother, "don't listen to Geoff, over here. He's got about five minutes sober. We give him long odds on getting another five."

The kid shook his head, "That's cold."

"It's okay," I told him. "Fuck that guy too."

My therapist says, "If you bring forth what is within you, what you bring forth will save you. If you do not bring forth what is within you, what you do not bring forth will destroy you."

She says, "Slow down. Rewind. Work with what you've got."

She says I need to offer other addicts what I have inside of me: chaos, confusion, self-loathing. "There are going to be a lot of people out there who can relate. They just need someone to say it out loud first. That's *experience*. That's all recovery is: experience, strength, and hope."

She says we're going to work on the strength and hope part. She says it takes time. She says, "That's the thing about this work. You have to give it to get it. Take it from me."

"Sweets," Liza called out, "kitty's back at the take-out window. Still hungry. Do you have her leftovers?"

"I'll get her a fresh can," I yelled from the kitchen. "Salmon Florentine with Garden Vegetables in a Delicate Cream Sauce. It's a new one. I want to see how she likes it."

I rushed to the glass and did a bow before unlocking the doors. The kitty took several steps back and watched me cautiously from underneath a beach chair.

"Here we are, Miss Lola, only the finest cuisine from Tuscany. *Buon Appetito!*"

Lola approached the bowl and took two mouthfuls of food before turning away and angrily slapping her tail against the pavement. She swiveled her head and fixed Liza with a look of contempt.

"Our little food critic kitty. So picky," Liza sighed and turned to scoop some bird seed from a massive, five-pound bag. She had started feeding the birds a few weeks after I got home from Mexico. We'd seen sparrows, mourning doves, cardinals, blue jays, and catbirds.

Liza tossed the seed out the door and the birds began to dive from their telephone wires.

I placed my hand against the glass, "I feed the cat. You feed the birds. Together, we're creating the perfect opportunity for interspecies bloodshed. I'm afraid it's an untenable situation."

Liza looped her hand through the crook of my arm and rested her head on my shoulder, "We've gotten through worse."

I was cooling down after an especially hard workout in the locker room of my gym, drying my hair, when I saw a pair of shadows move along the floor, crawling up my legs, before swallowing all the light in the room.

When I looked up, there he was: *my man*. He had with him one of his guys: a six-foot-seven, 350-pound bruiser, who he called *Subtle*. When I was still using, I had asked my man if *Subtle* was a rapper or wrestler. I'd figured he must have had some outlandish profession that needed a mononym. He'd said, "Nah, G. He's just the subtle threat of violence that I bring with me everywhere I go."

Subtle stopped short, "Oh shit, would you look at this."

"Hey, man," I said, "I didn't realize this was your gym."

They were standing in front of the only light in the room, so I couldn't see their faces, when my man said, "No doubt, G. You good?"

"I'm okay. Still struggling. You know, but sober."

My man said, "Yeah, lil' bro told me. Warned me to stay away from you and shit."

Subtle laughed.

My man put a hand up and Subtle stopped. My man continued, "Said you were mad cool to him on his first day back in New York."

I didn't know what to say, so I just said, "Cool."

Now they both laughed.

"Just remember, G, if one day you're not feeling so *cool*, you know where to find me. This is *my neighborhood*. And you know I got that heat." My man slapped Subtle on the chest and they turned to walk out. The light came back into the room, all at once, and I saw that my man was wearing a *Goofy the Dog* T-shirt from Disney World. I had spent an excruciating week in withdrawal the year before when he took his daughter to Florida for vacation.

I stopped them, "Hey, man. Should I find another gym?"

"Nah, G, this is your neighborhood now too."

Subtle cracked his knuckles, "Just remember to support your local business."

I heard them laughing all the way up the stairs and out the door into the street. The sound carried down the avenue, stopping on the empty corner that marked the end of their territory.

I closed my eyes and visualized leaving the gym. I would follow the sound of their laughter. Where they had stopped at the corner, I would continue down the avenue, through streetlights and stop signs, past bars and clubs. I wouldn't stop. Not for anything. I'd take the Pulaski Bridge, over Newtown Creek, leaving Brooklyn and entering Queens. Through the screech of rush hour traffic, into the park's green hush, my heart would keep pace with the pounding on the blacktop. I'd run. Through the machinery of night, into morning's cold coffee. I'd glide forward on a warm pocket of air, tapping into the ancient, heavenly connection that runs through everything. Faint music getting louder. Starry dynamos turning. Doom, cracking. Bells, ringing.

    I'd go chasing these echoes until I'm years ahead of myself. No slowing down. No taking a breath. The sound will carry me on, finally stopping at the invisible line, separating this world from the next.

Acknowledgments

Thank you to my agent, Monika Woods at Triangle House, for your unflagging enthusiasm and dedication to this book. I don't know where I'd be without your close reading, guidance, and friendship. Thank you to Chelsea Hodson, for starting Rose Books and giving writers like myself a different kind of place for their work. And to my dear friend and the first reader of this book, Wendy Salinger, at the 92nd St. Y, who taught me to see through "the tissue paper separating memoir from fiction."

Thanks to all the early readers of *Someone Who Isn't Me*: Hermione Hoby, Matthew Dickman, David Gordon Green, Norman Brannon, John Chao, Nate Bergman, and Gerard Way. Your notes were helpful, your encouragement was invaluable. To all the writers who've given me a kind word, especially Colum McCann, Darcie Wilder, Amy Rose Spiegel, Hilary Leichter, Elisa Gabbert, Alexandra Kleeman, Kelly Link, Michael Seidlinger, Leslie Jamison, Brandon Stusoy, Brad Philips, Laura van den Berg, Sasha Fletcher, Alexandra Tanner, Bryan Woods, Zac Lipez, Dan Ozzi and it meant more than you could have possibly imagined. Special thanks to Daisy Alioto for providing me with a lengthy and thoughtful nonfiction reading list when asked about writers who deal with the concepts of interior and exterior space in ways both concrete and poetic.

To all the friends that will see their names borrowed for characters in this book; to all the friends that don't see their names in this book but recognize themselves in the characters, thank you. To my early mentor and friend, Tim Gilles, (who would've celebrated the Pitch Doctor character by *administering a god-like beating on my head*) you are missed.

Thank you to Dr. Martin Polanco and everyone at the Crossroads Ibogaine Clinic, for being infinitely more careful and compassionate than any of the fictional characters in this book. You truly gave me a chance to get my life back and I'm forever in your debt. Thank you to MAPS and all the people working to further psychedelic treatments around the world. Thank you to Bill Wilson and all his friends for giving me a design for living without heroin.

To everyone that I have played music with over the years, especially the members of Thursday, No Devotion, United Nations, Ink & Dagger, Turning Point, NARX, and all the musicians who've trusted me as a steward of their dreams, especially My Chemical Romance, Touché Amoré, Wax Idols, Murder by Death, NOTHING, Sick Feeling, The Hotelier, rickyeatacid, (we were)Black Clouds, the Blackout Pact, Creepoid and John Tsung, thank you. Vonnegut was right about music. It is the very best thing.

To the stewards of my career: Tim Borror at STM and Paul Clegg, thanks for having my back. Tom Keeley, Steve Pedulla, Tucker Rule, Stuart Richardson, Lee Gaze, Norman Brannon, Tim Payne, Lukas Previn, Andrew Everding, Don Devore, Shaun Durkin, Hether Fortune, Jonah Bayer, you have all saved my life several times over. I love you, you are family. To Miguel Algarin, thank you for being the best teacher I ever had. Rest in Peace and Power.

To my parents — My mother, Patricia Rickly, whose love of the English Language casts a long shadow on my consciousness. My father, Jack Rickly, whose idea of a bed time story was *Schrödinger's Cat* or *The Pole in the Barn Paradox*. I love you both.

To my one and only, Liza de Guia, thank you for everything. You didn't just share a one bedroom apartment with me for the five years it took to write this book, you were a crucial sounding board for everything inside it. You lived through the worst of it all and believed in me when I had given up on myself. I can't even begin to describe the strength, intelligence, kindness, creativity, and poise that you put into the world. If I could, I would have made this whole book about you and sold a million copies.

About the Author

Geoff Rickly is a musician and record producer living in Brooklyn, New York. He is best known as the lead singer of Thursday, No Devotion, and United Nations, and as the producer of My Chemical Romance's debut album. This is his first book.

Rose Books

001   *Someone Who Isn't Me* by Geoff Rickly

002   *The Holy Day* by Christopher Norris

www.rosebooks.co